"HE WAS COMING AFTER ME, WASN'T HE?"

Mike hated the quiet fear that laced her statement. "Honey, we don't know that—"

"Yes," she interrupted him. "We do. It could be coincidence that a man tied so heavily to organized crime would suddenly show up in a town recently targeted by mob activity. It's just a bit too coincidental that he would also attack a woman who may have been a confidante of a man murdered for what he knew."

"Well, be that as it may, the fact is, Del Evans didn't succeed in getting to you. You have to hold on to that."

"But—"

"Hold on to it, honey." Mike hugged her closer.

Time passed and the shadows inside the room deepened.

At length she said, "They're going to send others."

Mike silently echoed Julie's hushed certainty and felt a hot lump of anger pool in his stomach. It burned like acid. "I'm not going to let anyone get to you."

Also by Tracey Tillis
DEADLY MASQUERADE

TRACEY TILLIS

Night WATCH

A Dell Book

Published by
Dell Publishing
a division of
Bantam Doubleday Dell Publishing Group, Inc.
1540 Broadway
New York, New York 10036

ISBN: 0-440-22053-X

Printed in the United States of America

Published simultaneously in Canada

June 1995

10 9 8 7 6 5 4 3 2

Sis, Toot says, this one's for you.

Prologue

He was a dead man and he knew it.

Phillip Blakemore raised his cigarette to his mouth, took a meditative drag, then lowered it. The movement was steady, measured, like the Lake Michigan waters slapping smoothly against the side of his anchored yacht. Like the moist August night air that lifted and fell gently around him.

For a while as he stood against the railing, his thoughts drifted with the night until they coalesced into one.

Would the hit be tonight? When it came, would it happen before he got the chance to make peace with his boy?

The irony struck him and a bitter smile touched his mouth. If it did, he supposed it would complete some cosmic circle of justice. A fleeting smile, bereft of humor yet rife with irony, twisted his lips.

Conscience was a funny thing; he'd buried it years ago and made himself a prince. He'd never anticipated how the prolonged necessity of betraying the thing most precious to him would reawaken it all these years later and slowly erode his kingdom to dust.

Michael. His quest for atonement now was essential, for Michael. He didn't care anymore that exposing his sins, that revealing the past he'd refused to let reclaim him long ago, would cost him his life.

He wanted peace of mind. He wanted to bridge the twenty-five years of silence he had used to distance his son, to, in effect, play dead. The irony was that now that he had made his move, it was the son who refused to reciprocate. It was the son who insisted on treating the father as if he were, in fact, truly dead.

Well, Blakemore thought, he probably was. He stood here prepared to deal his last hand. Would his son respond to this third letter? Would he find it in his heart to look beyond his ill will to make this requested meet?

Again Blakemore lifted his cigarette, pulled another drag—then he hesitated. Was that a noise behind him?

He turned his head and listened. The glowing red tip of his cigarette hovered in the air. Even as he turned more fully to peer into the shadows, his heartbeat accelerated.

Angling his arm, he flicked his cigarette over the railing and took one step when an empty beer can rolled out of the shadows. It came to rest nearly at his feet.

He breathed. It had fallen off the deck chair where he'd propped it.

Blakemore ran an unsteady hand through his graying hair and leaned against the railing again. He was literally jumping at shadows. But *Jesus Christ*, his old habits were so dulled, his old life so far removed that he hadn't even thought to arm himself.

Presently another sound registered, and his relief was palpable. A car door slammed in the distance back toward the marina parking lot. A glance at the illuminated face of his watch told him that the arrival coincided with the instructions he'd left on Michael's answering machine.

His son had come. God, he had really come! A rush of anticipation swept over Blakemore, but it was almost immediately overshadowed by a cold clutch of fear. He glanced toward the sky, his attitude that of an unwitting supplicant. . . .

———

The killer in the shadows had never viewed a more perfect target. In the split second it took Phillip Blakemore to sense him, the assassin had his garrote wrapped around the old man's throat.

———

Michael Blakemore made his way along the private dock mooring his father's yacht. He was just boarding when he saw the scuffle. His duffel hit the deck and he launched himself at the assassin, unable to help the struggling old man who sagged heavily at their feet.

Mike was within striking distance when the killer exchanged his garrote for a knife. It surprised Mike but it didn't stop him; he'd been trained to deal with such contingencies on the streets of Chicago.

He dodged the attacker's lunge, throwing him off-balance with an elbow to the ribs. The man grunted and regained his faltering balance. His backhand swipe at Mike's face was vicious.

Sheer instinct got Mike's arm up in time to deflect the knife, but his palm took the brunt of the attack. His breath hissed from him as the cut, painless upon impact, seared a moment later like liquid fire.

Breathing hard with pain and exertion, Mike sidestepped the fallen old man at his feet and moved backward, ducking and weaving away from the relentless advance of the killer. The man was breathing heavily too, but he was smiling.

It was the smile that enraged Mike enough to pull his concentration from his wounded hand. With a feral growl he reversed his retreat and rushed his attacker. He allowed a smile of his own when the killer, taken off guard, faltered long enough to allow Mike to tackle him.

They went down, and the fight turned deadly. The knife, jarred from the killer's hand, skittered to rest inches from his reach. Both men gave and received blows equally as punishing, equally as vicious. And then the killer gained a sudden advantage and twisted to his right, grabbing for the knife.

Mike and his opponent made it to their feet together, and Mike braced for another onslaught when suddenly the killer toppled facedown. Confused, Mike looked down and saw the hand of the injured man they'd both forgotten wrapped around the killer's ankle.

Mike moved over to his motionless adversary. He reached down to turn him over. The hilt of the knife protruding from his chest told Mike he was never going to move again.

Moving around the dead body, Mike knelt down to his father.

"Michael!" the man gasped.

A barrage of conflicting emotions tore at Mike, but he pushed them all ruthlessly aside. He needed to know how badly his father was hurt.

"Don't talk. I'll call for help."

"No!" Phillip Blakemore's face contorted, then both of his hands reached convulsively for his chest. "No . . . time!"

The old man's pallor, alarming even in the moonlight, told Mike what was happening. He bent to his father's mouth to catch his halting words.

"Use my death as a starting point, son . . ."

"For what?" Mike demanded. "A starting point for *what*?"

"The evil can be stopped, but there is danger. Police can't know. You . . . your mother . . . danger. Beware . . . Julie Connor. Find her."

"Why did you contact *me*? Who was trying to kill you?"

Phillip Blakemore used his last surge of strength to raise himself slightly. "Your—mother . . . protect—!"

Mike leaned in closer, but it was no use. His father's body went limp as his life's breath surged from his slackened lips.

"Damn you, old man, don't you die on me now!" Mike gave his father a slight shake, but it was no use. Gently he lowered his body to the deck and sat back on his heels.

Angry confusion, a dim memory of love, a dull sense of loss, all of it pumped through Mike's body as hard as the adrenaline. He'd finally found the courage to seek out the tardy explanations for a lifetime of alienation. But he'd reached out too late.

His father had been murdered. *Why?* Why was his mother in danger? How did this all relate to Julie Connor—whoever the hell *she* was?

Mike was desperately trying to make sense of it all when he became aware of something else: gasoline. The smell of it was heavy on the air.

Pushed as much by instinct as by a half-formed thought, he looked apologetically down at his father, then he moved. Phillip Blakemore was dead. His father's assassin was useless. The fumes were overpowering, and Mike knew that if he lingered he'd be dead too.

Even so, he narrowly escaped. He sprinted across the deck, grabbing his duffel on the way. He leaped from the yacht, gained the dock, and ran, barely outdistancing the explosion and flying bits of debris that burned and seared around him. He pounded against the planking that emptied onto the sprawling deserted lot of the marina when suddenly a second blast produced a flashing illumination that pulled his attention to the night sky.

At the side of his car he paused for breath, drawing long, clean draughts of the warm summer air deep inside his lungs. The hand he lifted to wipe the sweat from his brow left a wet stickiness on his skin. He pulled a handkerchief from his duffel bag and used it to wrap his injured hand.

Why had his father been murdered?

He climbed into his car and gunned it out of the lot. Each blow he'd received from the dead killer's fists was starting to throb, and his hand was aching, but the faint wail of emergency sirens in the near distance spurred him on. A desperate idea was taking form now, and he knew he had to move.

He couldn't be seen by anyone who might recognize him later and in so doing place him near the vicinity of the destruction behind him.

"Beware . . . Julie Connor. Find her."

Mike was a half mile away from the lake when he saw the shining beam of an emergency vehicle punch through the darkness opposite him. He slowed to a sedate speed and held it until the vehicle passed.

When no others approached, he picked up his pace. He had to get back to Chicago. He had to have time to absorb, to think, to reason like the cop that he was.

Like the cop he hadn't been for his father.

Michael, I need to see you. I've never asked you for anything, but I'm begging you for this one favor. Please, son, meet me. . . .

Sure as hell, the events tonight made it clear the notes his father had sent to him over the last three weeks, all brief yet identical in tone, had been calls for help.

The miles wore on, and Mike's rational mind reminded him that he'd had more than enough reason to act the wronged son, to ignore his father as he had. But his gut rebuked him for what he knew was the stronger truth: His anger as an abandoned son had interfered with what should have been his reaction as a cop.

He should have acknowledged his father's pleas for what they were and seriously heeded them sooner. If he had, he might have been able to save his father's life.

Instead, he had his father's murder on his hands, a possible threat to his mother, and a single clue: Julie Connor.

He'd get back to Illinois tonight. He'd gather his thoughts and construct a plan of action to find some answers for tonight's violence.

———

An hour later Mike entered the outskirts of Chicago, his course of action clearing. He was going to find out why his father had died, and to do it he was going to have to work solo.

He had no jurisdiction in Indiana, but that was where answers to the mystery he had been pulled into tonight had to lie. Neither did he have any real chance of being allowed to be productive in someone else's investigation since the victim had been family. He might be allowed a token assist at best.

No, his most viable option was to set up his own investigation. He'd configure it to afford him accessibility to his quarry while allowing him to retain some anonymity.

Because despite all of the questions yet to be answered, his objective was clear.

He was going back to Indiana.

He was going back to find Julie Connor.

Part One

Chapter

ONE

One P.M.

"Are you absolutely certain, Dave?" Julianna Connor swiveled her chair away from her computer terminal, readjusted her grip on the phone receiver, and waited with vague frustration for what she knew Dave Mitchell would say.

"I'm sure, Julie. We can't render a verdict yet." The fire chief took a breath. "Aside from having the confirmation from his housekeeper that Phillip Blakemore was on that yacht when it blew up, we don't have much. And that includes most of the remains of Phillip Blakemore.

"What we do have is a joint investigation involving not only us but the police department and the Coast Guard, which means this thing is going to drag on for at least a month before we know anything substantive, hon. Sorry."

So was Julie. "Have you recovered anything at all that could suggest arson?"

"Like I said, it's too early." Mitchell paused. "You know something that should cause us to look for arson?"

"No, Dave, I don't," Julie answered carefully. "It's just a hazard of my trade, my being prone to look for shadows where there aren't any. It was no secret around here that Phillip was an excellent sailor. The possibility of pilot error just seems so bizarre, I guess."

Julie's frustration with Dave's findings was as undiminished as it had been at the start of their conversation ten minutes ago. But she'd pushed as hard as she could and knew it was time to back off for now, or at least to tread lightly. Dave suddenly cleared his throat, alerting Julie that he wasn't through talking.

"Listen, Julie, as hard as it is to accept, the fact remains that pilot error is probably going to be behind the explanation for this tragedy. Careless accidents kill people all the time. Yes, Phillip Blakemore was an experienced sailor, and no, you wouldn't think he could be someone who would screw up so badly. But a second fact of life is that people make mistakes. Sometimes fatal."

And, Julie thought silently, a third fact was that most people here wouldn't have reason to assume that a scenario darker than that of an accident could be a possibility in this low-key town.

She hesitated, wanting to glean something more from Dave's remarks, something that might give her some insight into what was making her uneasy. The problem was, she couldn't articulate her unease to herself, let alone to her friend.

"Okay, Dave, thanks. Like I said, just doing my job."

"I know, kid. It's a hell of a thing. Phillip was my friend too."

"Yeah."

Mitchell let the thought settle, then said, "Doro-

thy says to come over for supper. She's got this
new—''

''Recipe she's dying to try out, I know.'' Julie's
reply was filled with the warm good humor of long-
standing friendship. ''Soon, I promise.''

Her smile didn't last after she hung up, and her
initial musings returned. The fire had been so intense, the devastation of the yacht so complete that
they hadn't, as Dave said, been able to recover much
of Blakemore's body. And she knew what little
wreckage they had been able to sift from the explosion most probably would support a no-fault incident.

Yeah, sure, she chided herself a moment later. She
could have bought it were it not for the unexpected
phone call and subsequent meeting she'd had with
Blakemore's business associate, Pete Henry, the day
before the tragedy.

Henry had told her Blakemore had information
about the recent influx of drug trafficking into town.

It was, Julie knew, activity anyone who read the
paper knew she'd included in a series of investigative
articles she'd been writing over the last two months.
What they didn't know was that many of those articles had been facilitated by the help of an anonymous news source adamant about maintaining his
anonymity.

His tips had directed her to the scenes of some of
the more sensational drug- and gang-related crimes
that had transpired in and around town. And even if
after a while his persistence in refusing to tell her
who he was had begun to make her uneasy, she had
gradually learned to dampen her unease beneath the
blanket of professional accolades and community respect her exposés earned her.

On a deeper level, however, Julie's discomfort with her silent ally persisted. That was why she had been particularly interested when Henry further explained that the information Blakemore had was information he was willing to share only with her. In turn she needed to give Blakemore her assurance, via Henry, that she'd keep his involvement in the matter strictly confidential.

Henry had called her at the paper, asking her to meet him at a popular downtown restaurant for lunch. Catching her eye at the table she'd grabbed for them, he'd seated himself across from her and offered a leisurely hello.

"This is your show," Julie said, glancing at their approaching waitress, then back over at Henry.

"Phillip told me to meet you."

"Told you?" Julie placed her order and waited for Henry to do the same. "Do you always do what you're told?"

"No." He smiled slightly. "Phillip told me you could be prickly. He also said you were good and that for what he had he needed somebody good."

Julie leaned back in her chair, letting the dim murmur of the restaurant patrons wash over her. Her gaze was frankly skeptical.

"Seems to me you're taking an awful lot of what Phillip Blakemore told you on faith. Is he that persuasive, or are you that loyal?"

"Let's just say my *loyalty* to Phillip runs deep. I was a kid going nowhere when he took an interest and mentored me to where I am today. If all these years later Phillip finally asks me to do him a favor, I'm not going to balk."

He smiled and lit a cigarette while the waitress approached with refills of water. "Maybe one day your cynicism will ease enough for you to appreciate the simplicity of this, Ms. Connor. I owe him."

Julie watched him while he looked out over the other diners and smoked. She wasn't affronted at what he called her cynicism. But she was willing to concede that maybe in this case it was precipitous.

"All right, Mr. Henry. Continue."

"Thank you, Ms. Connor," he said with exaggerated politeness.

Julie merely took another sip of her water and waited.

"Phillip said you're the media contact he wants to trust with this. He was impressed with you when you worked with him on that story last year about his philanthropic activities."

"That's flattering. I was impressed with him too. But I was only doing my job. Since then I've seen him here, he's seen me there. It's hardly made us bosom buddies."

"Nevertheless, Ms. Connor, it's Phillip's wish that you believe this. He says he knows something that could be pertinent to your news investigation into the vice infiltrating this town."

Julie observed him while he paused to unhurriedly light another cigarette, then he continued.

"He's given me no details about what he knows. But he did give me a carefully shaded suggestion not to probe, which I obliged."

"Considerate of you."

"He told me he has good reason to believe a major operation with links to organized crime is trying to gain a toehold in the community."

Julie nodded, willing him to say more. He didn't.

"That's all?" Her question was level. "Why isn't Blakemore talking to the police?"

"I have no more to tell you," Henry said with maddening calm as he slid his chair back. "When you're ready, Phillip will talk."

He reached again inside his breast pocket, withdrew a square of paper, and pushed it across the table to Julie. Then he got up, glancing at his watch. "His home number will do when you decide to make contact. And when you do—"

"Yes?" Julie said, noting with thinning patience the number written on the paper. The cloak-and-dagger routine was wearing on her nerves.

"Just give your first name, Julianna. It's the signal of your acceptance he'll be waiting for."

Signal? For God's sake, she'd thought as he strode away from the table and out of the restaurant.

And two days later Phillip Blakemore was dead.

Her desk phone beeped, jarring her from her introspection. She reached to grab it. "Connor, here."

"You still going to Blakemore's memorial service today?"

"Yes." She glanced at the thin silver watch encircling her wrist. "In fact," she told her editor, "I'd better be taking off right now. You need something before I go?"

"Just an answer to one question," Hank Finley said. "Is there something about this Blakemore thing you'd like to tell me?"

Julie paused in pulling her purse from the back of her desk drawer and silently swore. Her boss's acuity, normally as well appreciated by her as by anyone on the news staff, was an intrusion right now on her restless thoughts. "Hank," she prevaricated, "when have I ever held out on you?"

"Don't be cute, Connor, just answer my question. You were pretty distracted in the editorial meeting this morning when we started batting around ideas for the Blakemore coverage."

Julie's gaze lifted briefly to the framed Associated Press news award she'd mounted just last week on the wall of her cubicle. Had Henry suddenly decided to show his face, having been her nameless informant all along? If so, what had been his motives in seeking her out instead of the police? Most disturbingly of all, what had Phillip known that had caused him to die?

"My sources haven't told me anything they haven't told anybody else," she finally said to Hank. She wanted more answers from Henry before she invited her editor's confidence.

"Uh-huh."

"Look, I guess it's just hitting me how tragic it is that such a good man's life has been so abruptly snuffed out. He'll be missed. You know all he's done for this town."

Finley said nothing. Julie sighed with impatience. She wasn't in the mood to be pressed.

"I don't have anything, Hank," she said flatly. "You'll have my story by deadline for the morning edition." She replaced the receiver.

And I'll have the chance to see Pete Henry again to get something more definitive from him about what's really going on, she promised herself.

As she got up from her desk, she reached inside her purse and unzipped the inner compartment where she kept her car keys. She felt the square of paper with Blakemore's private number on it. It made her conversation with Henry vivid again and that, in turn, stoked her unease.

ONE THIRTY P.M.

The blow snapped Pete Henry's head back against the wooden rungs of the chair. His bound hands clenched behind him and tears spurted from his bruised eyes. His accuser calmly asked the question again.

"What did Blakemore tell her?"

"I don't know!" Henry's lip split with the next backhand blow. "God! Please *stop* . . ."

"What did Blakemore tell her?" The accuser's voice was unruffled, inexorable.

"I don't . . ." Henry was barely conscious.

"We tapped his line, Pete. We heard him tell you about his plans to be out of the office last Friday so that he could prepare to go sailing that weekend. We put a trace on you afterward and followed you to your cozy little meeting with the investigative reporter.

"You're Blakemore's right-hand man. We're betting you were his mouthpiece too. Tell me we weren't wrong."

Henry peered up at the man above him through dull, throbbing eyes, saying nothing. What was the use? He braced himself for the next blow as the accuser's hand was raised—then he relaxed fractionally when another voice from the shadows across the room stayed that blow.

Henry vaguely registered the voice of the watcher in the shadows or what it said to summon his accuser. He was just grateful for the respite from the physical punishment.

Time passed and Henry dropped his head forward. He felt strangely disembodied from the pain of his throbbing face, from the nauseating metallic taste of the blood filling his mouth, from the nightmare of the millionth, endless hour of this brutal interrogation. The voices of his accuser and the mystery man in the shadows seemed to come from behind him, before him, all around him. Maybe he was dying.

Without warning a rough hand grabbed his hair, and Henry moaned involuntarily as his head was yanked back. He wouldn't have had the energy to open his eyes even if they hadn't been nearly swollen shut.

"You're a stubborn bastard, aren't you, Pete?"

The flat monotone voice registered as soft puffs of air against Henry's ear. He didn't even attempt to answer. What was the use?

"Still nothing to say? No matter. I've decided to let you rest awhile, think about what it is you have at stake." The hand holding his hair abruptly relaxed. The rough, stroking fingers Henry felt against his cheek shook him as the brutality of the torture had ceased to hours ago. He shuddered and flinched from the accuser's soft touch.

The watcher in the shadows chuckled.

"Sleep for a while, Pete," the accuser whispered. "We have all night to talk."

TWO P.M.

"She's just now leaving," the man observing Julie's slim, darkly clad figure said.

He noted with interest how she stood apart for a moment, scanning the crowd as if searching for someone. As he leaned forward slightly to get a clearer look at her through his windshield, she seemed to give up and turned to blend in with the rest of the mourners. "The service just broke up. Should I take her?"

"No, not yet. Watch her. She may lead us to something significant before the day is through."

"First Henry, now her. She hasn't led us anywhere in a week. All she's been doing is asking questions about Blakemore."

"Correction, Evans. About Phillip Blakemore's personal connections. If she knows enough to do that, she may know something more that could be dangerous for us."

"Then why shouldn't I just grab her now?"

"Because she might save us some tedious footwork."

"Well"—Evans hesitated—"you're the boss. I still think it's just a waste of time."

"Like you said," came the cool response, "I'm the boss, which means you don't have to think. Just do what you're told."

Evans said nothing into the cellular phone while he watched Julie climb into her low-slung, sporty little car. When she put it into gear, he did likewise, knowing that to anyone who might be looking he was just another mourner in the crowd.

"You got that, Evans?" the imperative voice demanded.

"Yeah," Evans murmured, his mind slowly tracking down another path. He smiled slowly, thoughtfully. "It might not be too bad an idea at that. Julie Connor is way easy on the eye. You didn't tell me that."

"You just keep your mind on the assignment, you damned freak," came the disgusted response.

"Hey, man, don't worry about that. Right now my mind ain't on nothing else. I'll give her some rope." And when she comes to the end of it, he vowed, he'd have her.

He pulled out of the lot a few paces behind her and followed her back to the paper.

ONE A.M.

Julie reached to unlock her car door when a muscular arm manacled her from behind. The cold, impersonal blade of a knife lodged at the base of her throat.

"Please!" she gasped.

"Do what I say and maybe I'll let you live."

The arm tightened brutally, squeezing the air from her lungs. Julie thought she heard the whisper of a laugh, and her eyes slid closed.

The warm, hazy, moonlit night seemed to darken more around her. The dull ebb and rush of water along the Michigan lakeshore, ever constant, sounded stark and empty.

After she'd finished putting in the overtime at work, she'd driven to her aunt's beach house and lingered just long enough to make sure Peg had taken her medication. Fewer than five minutes had passed since she'd walked down to the beach to let the calm night relax her before she left. Now her impulsiveness had trapped her in some random act of violence as she desperately tried to assess her options in a situation her gut told her was grim at best. The closest house sat nearly a mile down the beach, and it had been vacant for months.

There was no one to hear her if she screamed or died.

"Take my money," she told her attacker in a controlled voice. "It's all in my purse." She felt him move behind her and guessed he'd shifted to glance at the purse that had fallen to the ground. "It's all I have to give you."

"Pick it up," came the guttural reply.

Julie's heart thudded at the uncompromising aggression in the man's voice. His arm loosened, but the knife's proximity didn't lessen.

Cautiously Julie dipped her knees and groped along the sandy grass for her purse. The brightness of the moon helped her locate it. She was starting to stand when it was wrenched from her. It unnerved her greatly that her attacker chose to operate from behind her.

Again the knife was at her throat, and her assailant turned the purse upside down, spilling its contents to the ground. When everything lay scattered at their feet, Julie's wrist was reclaimed in a painful grip and she was propelled forward to her knees. Her assailant followed her down, then sent her sprawling on her face with a hard shove.

His heavy knee pinned her while he riffled through the contents of her purse. Julie risked turning her head.

His large, muscular hand was gloved, but the pale skin above the edge of the glove seemed unnaturally illuminated in the moonlight. Julie was mesmerized, unable to look away as it sought and located her billfold.

She saw him flip open the leather flap one-handed and extract the forty dollars tucked within.

"Very good," she heard him say. His right knee flexed, and she sensed he had shoved the cash inside his pants pocket. She also sensed him hesitate. Her heart started to pound.

"So what happens now?"

When he spoke his voice was close to Julie's ear, and she felt him shift his weight to straddle her. "Now the fun starts."

"Oh, God," Julie gasped involuntarily as the knife thudded lightly to the sand beside her head. She started to fight.

Her attacker was a big man, but Julie was driven by terror and rage. The intensity of her resistance must have taken him by surprise because for a split second she threw him off-balance, dislodging his weight.

She scrambled from under him and started crawling awkwardly away. Split seconds were all she had, and her attacker blocked her way to the side path leading back to her car; she'd have a better chance trying for the house.

Julie made it to her knees. But her attacker was quicker.

She was tackled once again and hit the sand. This time she was flipped over and finally came face-to-face with her assailant. Just before he came down upon her, Julie tried to claw at his face. The next moment she cried out in pain as his leather-bound hands intercepted her fragile wrists in a bone-crushing grip. His face was unmasked, distorted with anger.

Through her terror, Julie registered the fact that his features were not those of a monster. They were regular, even nondescript. His pale hair clung sweatily to his neck, and the expulsion of breath through his bared teeth was queerly soundless.

When he started to rub his lower body against hers, Julie bucked against him in desperation. This time he wouldn't be moved. He only grunted, and she knew from the hard pressure against the soft juncture of her thighs that further struggles against him would be worse than useless.

Nothing, not anger, not pleading, not providence, was going to save her. But she hadn't forgotten the knife. It lay less than a foot away; freed of his weight, she could reach it with a lunge.

He would do this vile thing to her now, but the inevitable moment would come when he was vulnerable. She would be ready. The thought narrowed her amber eyes and her fingers curved inward against his cruel grip. "Get it over with, damn you!" she spat out.

She took satisfaction at the way her lack of defeat again seemed to disconcert him. For stark moments they watched each other like gladiators poised to join in battle. Then he shook himself a little and deftly adjusted his grip until both Julie's wrists were caught in his hard one-handed grasp. He slid his other hand between their bodies and started pulling at the snap of his jeans.

"Just like the rest, aren't you," he muttered. "Pretending you don't want it when you do." Again the soundless expulsion. "That'll only make it hotter."

"Wrong, you son of a bitch," came the whisper-soft reply from above them.

Chapter

TWO

Her assailant's head was jerked viciously back and his weight was yanked from her body. Julie got a glimpse of light-colored running shoes and long, bare, hard-muscled legs before everything around her dissolved into a shadowy blur of speed and motion.

She managed to crawl back until she was out of the way of the struggle going on before her.

In what seemed like seconds, her assailant was kneeling in the sand, a snub-nosed pistol jammed to his temple by the lightly panting stranger who gripped it. Everything had happened so fast that Julie was still trying to take it all in when the man with the gun spoke to her.

"You just gonna stand there, or are you gonna get me some help?" He punctuated the question with a calm nod toward the house. Only after the man kneeling in the sand jerked against the fist in his hair and received a blow from the butt of the gun did Julie snap out of her paralysis.

She knelt and groped along the sand until she located her keys. Her hands were so unsteady she had to make two tries for them before she held on and ran for the house. Inside, she snapped on the living room light and hurried to the phone to call the police.

She relayed the necessary information with as much calm as she could manage, then she hung up and stood numb, her hand resting on the receiver. In the space of—she glanced at her watch—ten minutes, she'd been accosted, assaulted, then miraculously rescued. Delayed reaction set in, and again she began trembling. "This can't be happening," she whispered.

"Julie?"

She turned at the sound of Peg's groggy voice.

Peg shuffled in from the darkened hallway, took one look at her niece's face, and made a visible effort to shake off her drowsiness. "What's happened?"

"Oh, Auntie," Julie whispered, not realizing she had reverted to the old childhood diminutive in her distress. She still couldn't move, not until her aunt made her slow, deliberate way toward her and took Julie in her arms. Julie hugged her strongly, but only for a moment. She'd let in the fear later. Right now there was a man outside, a very brave one, who needed her strength.

"Peg, I don't have time to explain now. Just trust me when I tell you everything is all right." She hated the fear that entered the gentle old woman's eyes, but she didn't have time to allay it.

"You're scaring me, honey."

Julie leaned back to stroke the loose strands of hair along her aunt's temple into the long gray braid at her back. She swallowed, then walked over to the panel of light switches beside the front door. When she flipped the middle one up, bold, beautiful light

spilled onto the porch and out onto the sandy backyard just beyond it. She hoped it would give her
rescuer some comfort.

"There's been some trouble outside," Julie said.
She turned to face Peg. "But it's under control now.
I called the police and they're coming."

"What happened to your blouse?"

Julie registered her aunt's horrified tone and
glanced down at herself. The upper buttons of her
cotton shirt were gone. The fabric gaped where her
assailant had ripped it so that the ecru lace at the top
of her bra and the beginnings of delicate cleavage
peeked through. Until this moment she hadn't even
realized the damage had been done. She pushed the
panic down again.

"Tell me what's happened to you now, Julie!"

"I'm not hurt." She hesitated, gauging. "A man
tried but he didn't succeed."

"Oh, dear God." Peg's thin hand went to her
throat. Tears welled in her eyes. "Were you——?"

Julie was spared by the faint wail of sirens approaching from the distance. "A man came along
and helped me. Now, I want you to stay here and
send the police out to us down on the beach. I have
to go back outside for a minute to help him."

As Julie stepped out onto the porch and then into
the yard, she looked back once to see her aunt sil-
houetted in the doorway.

From the sounds of it, several squad cars arrived
at the front of the house. No doubt the exclusivity of
their destination accounted for the show of force,
Julie speculated; as she made her way to her rescuer's side, she watched at least a half dozen officers
jog down the bluff behind her.

Her rescuer was holding his own. Neither the gun nor her attacker appeared to have moved.

"Are you all right?" she whispered at his shoulder, her eyes on the man who had tried to hurt her.

"You ask me that," the man returned in a husky voice. "By all rights that's my line, don't you think?"

Julie wasn't expecting the irony in the softly spoken words nor the measure of comfort they lent her shaky nerves. Two of the officers were nearly upon them, and as they approached, the man relaxed enough to turn his head toward Julie. He was still waiting for her response. Julie took advantage of the moonlight to study his profile.

He had strong, brown, chiseled features that looked aggressive in the darkness, but in a way that was wholly comforting. Wavy black hair hugged his well-shaped head and grew slightly long at his neck. His jaw was darkened by either a slight beard or heavy stubble; Julie couldn't be sure. Everything about his appearance, from the determination in his features to his long, sinewy, hard-bodied grace, bespoke strength.

In that moment Julie was suddenly certain few others would have diffused a crisis situation as capably as he had. Again she thanked the higher power who had sent this man to her.

One of the officers hauled the kneeling man to his feet, cuffed him, and led him away while reading him his rights. His partner turned to Julie. "You Julie Connor?"

Julie sensed more than saw her rescuer's sharpened attention. "Yes, Officer. This man saved my life."

She watched the officer take stock of the man at her side. She noted the way the officer's eyes went to the waistband of the man's denim shorts where he had shoved his pistol. "You got a permit for that thing, I suppose," she heard him say.

"The lady's alive," came the laconic response. "You gonna tell me it would matter a whole hell of a lot if I didn't?"

The officer didn't like that one bit, Julie saw.

"I've got a permit," the stranger said more conciliatorily.

"You got an attitude too, buddy."

"Hey, you people just carted away the bad guy," Julie interrupted him. "I told you, this man saved my life!"

The officer cleared his throat and shifted under her censure. "This is the fourth assault in a year in this area. That's four more than we've had since I been around. You'll understand that we're a little tense." He looked at them both in turn.

Julie took a calming breath. "Sorry."

He nodded, his gaze encompassing the man at Julie's side. "Yeah, me too. Could we go inside maybe to get some details down?"

Julie glanced worriedly behind her. She didn't want Peg more upset than she was already.

Then again, maybe quick and dirty was the best way to get the explanation out of the way. Julie knew the sooner her aunt heard the particulars, the sooner she could relax. It was just that she hated to give Peg one more reason to worry about her when she'd already done enough worrying for a lifetime.

She stepped away from the man at her side and was mildly surprised at the loss of security she felt.

"Let's go," she said, stooping to gather the spilled contents of her purse.

Julie led the way to the house, and Peg gave the

three of them a worried look as she stepped away from the door to let them in. When the screen door shut behind them, she walked over to Julie. Julie bent slightly to drop a soft kiss on Peg's lined brow. "Can we make this brief, Officer?" she said, watching the old woman. "My aunt isn't well."

"I'll try." He pulled a notebook from his pocket and waited for Julie and Peg to settle themselves onto the sofa. Nodding to Julie, he said, "Whenever you're ready."

Suddenly unsure, Julie looked down at the polished oak floor and tried to organize her thoughts. Her adrenaline was still running high, and now that she had nowhere to focus it other than on recounting what had happened, she started to tighten up again. An impulse she couldn't explain made her look up, needing to connect, if only visually, with the one who had gotten her through this ordeal.

He was standing beside the door, arms folded across his broad chest, watching her. Despite the innocuousness of his appearance, the faded well-worn shorts, the sleeveless cotton T-shirt that accompanied them, the battered running shoes, and his relaxed posture, he reminded Julie of a sentry standing guard. And despite the slight lifting of one corner of his mouth, which she supposed was a smile meant to reassure her, she sensed a tenseness about him.

Though his steady dark gaze linked with hers, reassuring her, giving her strength, she had the unshakable impression he was restless, eager to get away. That he stayed warmed her and restored the courage that had momentarily failed her.

Julie talked until her story was done, and then she fell silent. For a moment no one spoke. The sound of the night was underscored only by the dull ebb and rush of Lake Michigan. The officer turned to the tall, silent man by the door. "Your name?"

Only then did the man's gaze leave Julie. He seemed slightly startled. And irritated, she thought.

"The name's Mike Quinn," he said tersely.

The officer waited for more. When it didn't come, he looked annoyed, but he let it go. Julie was intrigued.

"Does your account agree with the lady's?"

"Yes."

Again he allowed only what was necessary, Julie noted.

The officer's pencil moved across his notebook. "How did you happen to be in the vicinity when Miss Connor was being attacked?"

"I was jogging."

The officer gave Mike a skeptical look. "After midnight? With a gun?"

"Fortunate for her, wouldn't you say?"

"You live around here, Quinn?"

"Just down the beach."

Julie caught her breath. He had to be talking about the Morrison place. She was out at the lakeshore every week. How could he have been inhabiting it without her hearing about it?

As if sensing her thoughts, Mike's eyes shifted to hers. "I just moved in this morning."

"You originally from around here?" the officer asked.

Mike's attention returned to him. "Yes."

"Where?" This time the officer pushed.

Mike pushed back. "Look, the point is, Miss Connor was being assaulted. I was lucky enough to happen upon the situation before it got tragic.

"Now, we're all tired here," he continued. "Miss

Connor and her aunt look like they're going to drop. Are we through?''

The officer snapped his book closed. "For a hero, you sure seem to enjoy being difficult."

"I'm just tired, like I said." And Mike suddenly realized it was true.

It had been a bitch of a day, which was why he had been running off his frustration when he'd heard sounds of a struggle and traced them to the woman —Julie Connor.

"All right," the officer was saying. "I guess I've got all I need for now." He turned to Julie. "Will you be okay?"

"Fine."

Mike sighed, hearing the brittleness in her tone, trying not to be touched by her vulnerability or beauty.

He'd expected to have a bit of time to get acclimated before making his move to locate the mysterious Ms. Connor. Being thrown into her acquaintance in such a dramatic way was the last thing he expected would happen to him his first week back in Indiana. Indeed, finding out that the house his friend was letting him occupy shared the beach with her relative went beyond coincidence.

It was disconcerting. Most thoroughly disconcerting was this inexplicable urge he was feeling to get personally involved with his quarry when doing so would be the worst thing he could do.

Vaguely he registered how Julie was trying to reassure her aunt that she wasn't hurt. He wondered what could be buried in the past of one so young to demand such tough self-reliance.

But his greater concern was over what he was going to do about this compulsion to help her when he knew he should turn right around and disappear back into the night. Impatient with himself, Mike pushed away from the wall and turned to leave.

"Quinn, I—thank you."

The catch in her voice and the hurried way she offered the words held him where he stood. He didn't even realize he'd dropped his hand from the door and was as startled as anyone to hear himself say, "Come on, I'll take you home."

His words settled into a void of watchful silence. Then that void was filled by the ringing of the phone. Everyone's attention turned to Peg, who picked it up. She listened, then held the receiver out to the officer.

While hushed words were exchanged, Mike's attention moved back to Julie. She was watching him, and the gratitude he saw in her gaze frustrated him even while it warmed him. *Dammit*, he thought with a quiet sigh.

"I see," the officer was saying. He gave everyone in the room an encompassing glance, letting his eyes linger first on Julie, then on Mike. "Yeah. Well, sometimes it can happen like that. Don't question it, just accept it. Yeah. Talk to you later." He hung up.

"Well, hero, looks like you might have caught him."

"Who?" Julie asked.

"The Lake Shore Rapist."

"Oh, my God," Peg gasped softly.

"He's just a suspect, but since he is, I'd be mighty grateful, Miss Connor, if you and Mr. Quinn here could come on down to the station now and give us a more formal statement."

"Well, I guess so. All right," Julie said. She got up and took her keys from the coffee table.

"I'll drive," Mike said.

"Listen, you've done enough."

Mike was caught by the defensiveness behind the rudeness. He ignored the curious way the others were watching them and said, "I'm aware of the fact that you can handle it from here, but the point is, you don't have to." He pressed his advantage when the lines of tension marring her soft brow eased marginally. "You don't have to fight me too, Julie."

He watched her struggle with her indecision. Presently she walked across the room to her aunt, and until she spoke, Mike, like the others, had no idea what she would do.

Patting Peg's hand once more, Julie murmured, "I'll be right back." When she returned from her aunt's bedroom she had donned a white, summer-weight sweater. She scooped up her oversized purse, then looked directly into Mike's eyes. "Let's go."

Mike took the keys she handed him and stepped to the side of the doorway, holding the screen door open for Julie to pass. She brushed by him, trailing some delicate scent. Turning from the softness of it, he followed her and let the officer bring up the rear.

——

For about a mile the ride was silent. As another mile wore on, a perverse curl of impatience with Quinn's noncommunicativeness prompted Julie to half turn in her seat to study him.

The passing streetlights occasionally silvered his dark hair. Regular beats of white brightness alternated with moonlight to cast dappled shadows on his strongly sinewed hands. They gripped the wheel lightly yet capably.

"Who are you?" she asked without preamble.

Mike spared a glance her way. "I told you back at the house."

"No. You stated what was expedient to satisfy the cop." She noted with satisfaction that he was slower to look away this time.

His reply was quiet. "Then let's just leave it at that."

"If you really meant that, you wouldn't be here now, would you?"

"Don't read something into this situation that doesn't exist, sweetheart."

Julie watched him for a space of moments, but he only punctuated his comment with an enigmatic look. Involuntarily she shivered because she clearly discerned his message through the darkness. He'd meant what he said about leaving it. But again his attempt to shut her down only evoked an opposite effect.

There was a mystery about him. She was certain of it, and that certainty added another dimension to this strange encounter. The events of this night would run their course, but knowing that did little to lessen Julie's odd reluctance to let the mysterious Mr. Quinn fade out of her life as precipitously as he'd entered it.

Chapter

THREE

They pulled into the lot of the station and Mike killed the engine. Juggling Julie's keys, he opened his door and smiled wryly as Julie opened hers before he could even try to assist her.

Julie caught the smile and silently dared him to comment. Mike just handed over her keys with exaggerated politeness, then took her arm.

They were ushered through to the sheriff, who greeted them with a tired nod and cursory smile. "We'll make it short and sweet," he said by way of greeting. "Just bear with me."

Julie and Mike did for the next hour. Mike found himself using the time to study Julie, to puzzle the contradiction she presented.

It hadn't been easy for him to conceal his surprise when he'd found out she was the one linked to his father's murder. He hadn't been surprised by her strength; his father's dying, frightened words had planted in Mike's mind an embryo image of the she-wolf he had imagined Julie Connor would be.

What did surprise him was her softness. In fact, it had more than surprised him. He wondered which element, hard or soft, more honestly embodied the real woman.

Back in Chicago, as he had debated about how best to deduce who she was and track her down, he had quickly determined that she was probably someone tapped into a significant information, possibly community, network. Not quite sure of how to interpret his father's garbled words about the police, Mike had naturally wondered if she was a cop.

It would make sense. His father had obviously been in deep trouble, and he had told Mike to seek out this Julie Connor.

Though he'd come up empty, Mike hadn't been discouraged, because his next logical choice had been the media. A reporter would have the knowledge and the means to get things done on behalf of a man in trouble—or to use that knowledge against him if the motivation were less than honorable or even deadly.

It hadn't taken him long to find out that she was a reporter with a Michigan City daily newspaper. And afterward it had been easy to collect samples of Ms. Connor's work, through which he had discerned not only her obvious talent but also her incisive brain.

Most of her stories weren't pretty. Deception, occasional corruption, and violence were recurring themes for her unflinching forays into the community breakdowns around her. For Mike, her stories created the persona of a woman outraged by what she reported but resigned to the fact that as long as people were fallible, crime wasn't going to go away.

Leaning back, he sighed and mused on how that woman was the same one who had stood before him a short while ago, shaken and uncertain of how to cope when the very violence she so zealously wrote about personally touched her.

Julie was an intriguing dichotomy, and Mike leaned back to study her again. Her calm, composed responses to Sheriff Wilkins kept getting juxtaposed in his memory with her desperate struggles against the bastard who had attacked her.

Logic told him some of that calm was probably shock. He'd seen that kind of shock numb sexual-assault victims before. Still, his gut told him some inner resource that was uniquely Julie's was helping her keep her composure. And again he wondered at her courage.

Then he reminded himself again that he shouldn't care. This whole night might have shot his bid for anonymity to hell.

She was a delicate thing. With those exotic brown eyes of hers framed by long, sooty lashes, the creamy chocolate of her skin, the fall of ebony hair, and the slim jeans and oversize white cotton sweater that emphasized her slender frame, she looked as sleek and soft as a kitten. But he'd seen her claws and instantly felt a tug of admiration and something more he simply couldn't afford to feel.

He couldn't let anything distract him from his purpose here. That included witchy-eyed damsels in distress.

Wilkins finished, and Mike ushered Julie to the door. The sheriff stopped them at the threshold.

"Miss Connor, will you be all right?"

Julie looked at the officer's red-rimmed eyes, the tired lines of his face, his jaw, scratchy with a graying stubble that seemed to enhance his fatigue. She'd been relieved by the courtesy he'd shown her and his deft handling of her questioning. Now she was touched by his solicitousness when he was so obviously dog tired.

"I'll be fine," she answered. She watched Wilkins assess her escort. He apparently reached the decision she was in good hands when, after a moment, he dismissed them both with a nod. Julie couldn't help glancing at Quinn. She thought she caught a fleeting smile and waited for his comment. When it didn't come, she preceded him out the door.

They'd gotten halfway down the corridor when Julie hesitated and stopped. She turned thoughtfully to Quinn.

"What?" he asked softly.

"Could we maybe—go somewhere, get some coffee? Something?"

No, he thought instinctively. But then he stayed that impulse because it was the inner man responding. The cop recognized the fact that she was offering him the perfect opportunity to prolong his study of her.

He glanced down at her, then at his watch. When he raised his eyes back to hers, he saw she was wary too. Whether it was of him or herself, he couldn't tell. All he knew was that her hesitation urged him to meet her challenge.

"Where to?" he asked.

Julie hadn't quite expected him to take her up on her request. Now that he had, she wasn't sure how she felt about his acquiescence. She wanted his company, or rather, she told herself, she wanted to postpone being alone.

But even as she walked beside him out into the balmy August night, his silently conveyed warning to her earlier, to keep her distance, came clearly to mind.

Was she being a fool in not letting him go? she wondered.

She took the wheel this time. A small gesture maybe, but her insides were still shakier than she liked to admit, and taking the small initiative helped.

They pulled into an all-night diner, and Mike noted the customers were as comfortably low-key as their surroundings. He also noted the way the otherwise taciturn cook behind the grill greeted Julie with easy familiarity as did a couple of guys hanging around a pinball machine near the back of the room. He didn't miss the way their eyes summed him up, shifted to Julie and then back to him.

Mike heard Julie murmur a mild hello before she seated herself across from him in a booth. The pinball resumed, but an ingrained instinct had Mike sensing the men's continued interest.

He waited for Julie to catch his eye, then he gave a slight nod away from the table. "You need to call them off or something?"

Julie glanced away from the booth. She caught a couple of mildly curious looks and smiled. "They're harmless."

Mike watched her a moment longer, then shrugged. "If you say so."

The unspoken "why" behind his observation almost coaxed from Julie the fact that she and her coworkers frequented the place. But a sixth sense or maybe a professional instinct had her keeping the explanation to herself.

Mike ordered two coffees, and when the waitress arrived with them, Julie used the distraction to give herself a mental shake. She had to be sharper. This man struck her as someone who was used to having the upper hand.

"Considering the fact that you've saved my life, not to mention potentially this community a whole lot more grief, why are you trying so damned hard to fade back into the woodwork?"

Mike smiled. Frontal attack. Now why wasn't he surprised? Actually he was only surprised it had taken her this long. He debated what to give her in place of the truth.

"Let's make a deal," he said. "The coffee's hot, the atmosphere is low-key, and we're both appreciating the company. Let's keep it simple."

"Why?" Julie demanded, certain that somehow it wasn't simple.

Mike's eyes narrowed. That she was beautiful was obvious. That she had guts she'd demonstrated earlier. Now she was peering beneath the surface of him with a penetration that went beyond mere curiosity. She was quizzing the complexity beneath his exterior, and that evidenced one more thing. She was smart.

In fact the lady was a lethal combination. He signaled for two more coffees and said nothing.

"Oh, so you're going to play it strong and silent. Hmm," Julie murmured. She studied him over the rim of her cup. Again a little warning bell urged her toward caution. After all, what would she gain from interrogating him? Probably little that would go beyond satisfying her habitual reflex to probe.

Setting down her cup, Julie made the decision to pull back the gauntlet. She didn't need to be inviting dangerous complications into her life, and despite his silence this man, she guessed, spelled danger with a capital *D*.

His attention appeared focused on her. Yet no one but a trained observer would notice everything around him the way he was doing, which Julie knew because she was a trained observer herself.

"At least let me thank you again for saving my life," she said.

Mike frowned and dropped his gaze to the table. "You don't have to thank me. It's just fortunate I was around to help."

More equivocation, Julie thought.

"You're taking over the old Morrison place," she said. "Why?"

"It's a beautiful area here. I was looking for a place, and I know the Morrisons' son. Since their deaths, he's been looking for a buyer, and he agreed to let me sort of test-lease their place for a while at a prime rate. Easy decision."

Glib evasion, Julie guessed. "You're from around here, you said."

"I lived west of here for a while." His eyes held hers. "There's really nothing mysterious about it, Julie, or about me. Now let me ask you something."

Julie leaned against the back of the banquette. "Go ahead."

"Why were you driving back to town so late?"

Immediately Julie stiffened. "You're asking me why I was foolish enough to make myself a target in an area known to be a hunting ground for a rapist?"

Mike saw his mistake and regretted his clumsiness. "I wasn't blaming you, Julie. I was just curious about why you chose not to stay the night with your aunt. It was pretty obvious you two are close."

Julie watched him for a moment, then forced herself to relax. There were times she regretted the hasty way she made assumptions about people, like the hasty one she had just made about Quinn. He'd already proved he meant her no harm, hadn't he?

"Tonight was part of a routine," she explained evenly. "Peg has rheumatoid arthritis. Once a week I come down to check on her, to make sure she has her medication, that she doesn't need anything. We're the only family each other's got." She took a last sip of coffee, then absently brushed a dark tendril of hair from her brow.

"Tonight was unusual. She'd had a hard day and the pain was bad, so I sat with her until her medicine kicked in. Normally she doesn't like to feel coddled, you see, and I try to respect that."

She looked up at him, not realizing, he was sure, the fierce protectiveness she projected. For a split second something stirred inside him, and he wondered what man in her life was lucky enough to generate that same depth of emotion. No one as vibrant as she was could possibly be alone.

He glanced out into the room to give the disturbing thought time to dissipate. It helped when she didn't seem to notice his distraction. Still, he didn't turn back to her until he'd made damned sure his speculations and the restlessness they aroused were tightly under control.

He usually wasn't nearly this reticent when he interrogated a subject. But his reaction to this subject wasn't usual, and he just wasn't inclined to ask her anything that would invite reciprocal questions.

Or maybe his common sense, which seemed to be deserting him, was just telling him it was time to wrap this up. It was enough to know that despite her allure, Julie was still potentially dangerous as an undefined player in his father's murder. And it was also enough to know that he would do whatever it took to keep her within his sights until he could make that definition.

He reached inside his pocket and pulled out enough money to cover their bill.

"Quinn, let me tell you something."

His eyes glanced off hers and his nod was brief as he signaled the waitress for the last time. When the bill was paid and he couldn't avoid looking into her beautiful eyes any longer, he settled back against his seat and waited for whatever she was going to say.

She hesitated, and it brought him to an alertness her earlier inquisitiveness hadn't.

"I realize you can't get away from here fast enough," she began. "No," she insisted when he started to interrupt, "I know it's true."

Her uncertainty made him feel like a heel. But dammit, how could he refute her assumption without inviting a proximity he couldn't afford? Her slender fingers were fiddling restlessly with a plastic menu beside the napkin holder. Her hair had fallen over one slender shoulder to curtain the fine line of her face from his view. All in all, she was a study of uncertainty and vulnerability.

And the image struck him all the more forcefully because he knew it was the last image she wanted to project.

"I just want to say before we leave that . . . if there's anything I can ever do for you, anything, it's done."

She looked at him fully, and the depth of her sincerity shook him. But since he was years of experience beyond betraying what he was feeling, he said with deceptive ease, "Thanks. Maybe I'll take you up on that sometime."

Julie lowered her eyes, and Mike could sense her embarrassment as clearly as if she had voiced it. Abruptly she gathered her purse and stood to leave.

Mike got up, and she started toward the door without waiting for him. He watched her dig a quarter from the jumbled depths of her purse and push it into a pay phone beside the door. She started punching in numbers.

As he reached her side she murmured a soft goodbye into the phone, hung up, and turned to him.

"You needn't see me home. I'll get my car tomorrow," she told him. "A friend of mine is coming to pick me up, and afterward you can feel free to consider your duty discharged." Without another word she turned and walked out.

They were standing in the warm night air a little away from the lights of the diner when Mike took her arm. Julie didn't even turn her head but started to pull away when he urged her to wait.

"I'll probably damn myself for this in the morning," he murmured, more than a little startled to hear himself ignore the little voice that was warning him to stop before he made a big mistake. "I can't walk away like this," he intoned.

Julie went still.

"I should, but I can't."

Julie turned to face him, waiting to hear whatever it was he had to say.

Mike's words were slow yet filled with reluctant urgency. "If—circumstances—were different, I . . ." He stepped even closer to her until his warm breath ghosted over her face. And when his eyes traced each of her features, he thought he detected a delicate shiver even in the moonlight.

He reached out, clasped her hands, and joined them at their sides. A tangle of protectiveness and undefined need burgeoned inside him. He rested his forehead gently against hers and rapidly lost the strength to question the strangeness of what he was feeling. Then he felt the gentle squeeze of her hands and with dawning intuition realized he wasn't being affected alone.

"You feel it too, don't you?" he whispered. He wasn't even sure his words were audible until he felt the pressure of her fingers tighten against his. When Julie shifted before him, he raised his head a little and looked down at her. His breath grew slightly uneven as an exhilaration that should have unnerved him slowly suffused him.

The uncertainty he saw beneath her delicate lashes touched him until nothing seemed as important as enfolding her within the safety of his arms.

"Quinn," he heard her whisper once. Then he stayed even that gentle emission by raising one hand to touch the softness of her lips. He doubted she even realized the small needy sound she made before she laid her head against his shoulder in a heart-stopping gesture of trust.

Julie couldn't have moved if her life depended on it. And all at once she realized she didn't want to move because this man was giving her exactly what her life did depend on at this incredible moment.

He was offering her gentleness, affection, his warmth, all of which erased an emptiness she had determined to ignore. She should let him go, she thought. But she couldn't. Not yet. Because now she knew despite what he said, despite whether she ever saw him again, he had in the end been no more indifferent to her than she to him.

The pressure of his embrace remained light, non-threatening, and Julie couldn't suppress an involuntary tremor. The vulnerability caused Mike to rest his chin against her hair.

After what seemed to both timeless moments later, he raised a hand and touched the back of his fingers to Julie's soft cheek. He took a faint trace of moisture away with the touch and went very still as Julie raised her head to regard him with fathomless, shimmering eyes.

She observed how the planes of his face remained stark. Yet the delicacy of his gesture belied his stern expression. Julie's heart trembled at the poignancy of his touch. Then before she could prepare herself for it, his hands resolutely pushed her away. At the same time they both became aware of a car approaching the lot.

"Quinn, no. Don't . . ." Her words trailed into nothing at the slow negative shake of his head.

"Go home, Julie. Go on," he added with a nod toward the car when she hesitated.

What could she say? How could she argue with him the wisdom of aborting this attraction she had already told herself it was folly to pursue?

Because the conflicts of the question confused her, she dropped her eyes, trying in her heart to seek an answer before Quinn was gone. But when she looked up, he was gone. Ignoring the two short taps of her friend Meg's car horn, Julie took a step forward, searching all around in the darkness.

It was no use.

The man who had materialized out of the night like an avenging angel to save her life had slipped just as mysteriously back into its shadows.

Chapter
FOUR

"Come on, Pete, we're gonna get a little fresh air."

Pete Henry fought his way up from the depths of an exhausted sleep, trying to make sense of the rough words that preceded the rough hands fumbling at the rope at his wrists.

He hadn't managed more than a rusty croak when the hands hauled him off his chair. The inflicted pains and aches that had lain dormant for the handful of hours he'd been allowed to sleep came roaring back to life. Henry's knees buckled, and the impatient yank at his arm forced a moan from him.

His eyes were still swollen, but that didn't stop his accuser from wrapping a musty-smelling cloth around his head as a blindfold. In a strange sort of way Henry was glad for the blind. Maybe it meant his torturer wasn't going to kill him after all, since he was bothering to keep their destination secret.

Henry was hustled out of the room, down a flight of narrow stairs, and outside. He'd taken fewer than half a dozen steps when pavement gave way to grass. A half dozen more and his ankles were damp. From that dewy moisture and the volume of birdsong he guessed it must be early morning.

He was shoved inside a car. The only detail he could make out was of vinyl beneath him. The give of it seemed strange. He heard the door beside him slam and thought he was alone until something hard pressed into his side. When he heard the unmistakable click of a gun being cocked, his heart sank. And then he didn't have time to think because the front door slammed, the car was thrown into gear, and they were off.

"You comfortable, Pete?"

Henry flinched at the easy tone of the question tossed from the front of the car.

"Because if you are, maybe you'd like to try again to remember how much Connor knows, courtesy of your dead friend."

A dull sense of resignation enveloped Henry. At least, he thought, he could try to do something for the girl.

"She doesn't know any more than I do," he said.

"Well, that's too bad for you."

The tone was still easy. They drove on and Henry was lulled by the soft hum of the motor, the gentle motion of the car. Surrounding traffic sounds seemed nonexistent in the air-conditioned confines, and, incredibly, he felt himself drifting off to sleep again.

"Kill him."

Henry barely roused. The pressure at his side increased. An oddly muffled spit was the last thing Pete Henry ever heard.

"Mama, don't!" Julie twisted away from the shadowy dream woman's cruel grip and raised a childish hand to block a slap. She cried harder as the woman leaned in to her, screaming. Julie's pain was sharp, her fear dull and somehow familiar.

She was still trying to pull away from the woman and the hateful words being spewed at her when those words were obscured by a pounding on the front-room door behind them.

Julie felt the vise on her wrist loosening when the second spate of knocking, as insistent as the first, pushed the woman further into the shadows. Gradually she drifted up toward consciousness and realized the knocking was no longer part of her dream.

Fully awake, she lay still for a moment trying to catch her breath. When her heartbeat started to slow, she wiped a thin trail of moisture from her cheek, snatched her robe off the foot of the bed, and padded sleepily through her living room to the front door.

A glance through the peephole had her throwing off the last vestiges of her nightmare. Smiling slightly, she threw back the dead bolt.

"Don't think I'm not glad to see you, Meg," she said in a sleep-husky voice, "but, like I said last night, I'm okay."

"Yeah, blah, blah, blah. Since my assumption is that you have enough sense to stay home from work today, I thought I'd check up on you on my way in."

Julie stepped aside. Her friend breezed past her and headed straight to the overstuffed sofa, where she unceremoniously plopped down.

"Got any coffee? I'll fix it." Meg O'Brien pushed herself right back up and walked into Julie's tiny galley kitchen.

Julie smiled, watching her. When she didn't have sleep in her eyes, she shared a similar energy. It was useless to get in her friend's way, so she just perched on the sofa and waited.

"And you can take that smile off your face, Connor. I know you consider yourself something of a wonder girl, but last night would have strung anyone out. So"—Meg turned from the freshly loaded coffeemaker, her tone and attitude very serious—"tell me how you are. Really."

Julie thought of her dream and the violence last night, then shoved both thoughts aside. "A little shaky but basically all right." She rested her head against the back of the sofa and closed her eyes. "I was very lucky." She felt Meg's weight depress the cushion but kept her eyes closed.

"You were pretty quiet last night."

Julie opened her eyes and turned her head against the backrest. "Like I said, I was very lucky."

"Uh-huh." Meg observed the way Julie's gaze slid from hers. "And of course no small part of that luck had to do with the opportune arrival of your own personal guardian angel, yes?"

Thoughts of Quinn and the way they had parted stirred all sorts of conflicting emotions inside Julie. Gratitude, certainly. But also an odd low-grade regret. The combination was novel. She couldn't remember ever having felt it with another man.

Maybe that was why she preferred to hug all of her impressions about Mike Quinn close to herself for a while. She smiled at Meg. "I guess it just goes to show that heroes really do exist."

Meg smiled back, wondering what those slightly red eyes and introspective shadows crossing her friend's face really meant. "Yeah, just goes."

"Come on," Julie said, slapping the cushion beside her. "Since you have me up and your shift doesn't start for another hour, I'll throw some eggs together to go with your coffee."

The two women worked together companionably until they had produced not only eggs but crisp buttered toast and several strips of grilled bacon. When they took their seats at the breakfast bar, Julie looked at Meg. She could tell Meg wanted to continue talking seriously and felt herself tensing.

"Why didn't you tell me you'd caught the Lake Shore Rapist?" Meg said.

Julie looked calmly up from her coffee. "Because no one knows for sure the guy who attacked me is that rapist." She took a sip. "And at any rate, if we're being strictly accurate about this, I didn't catch him."

"That's not Pete Wilkins's story." Meg leaned back in her chair and waited. She hadn't gotten much from Julie last night aside from the bare facts of the assault. But then, she hadn't even tried pushing since the only thing Julie had needed was someone to be with her. And even at that, Julie had sent her home in the wee hours.

But she'd wanted answers then, and she wanted them now. And since it looked as though Julie wasn't going to give more, Meg had taken it upon herself to be enterprising this morning.

Julie set down her mug and said, "This isn't Joe Q. Public, O'Brien, it's me, the press. I know what Sheriff Wilkins told you, and that was a damned lame attempt to get me to tell you something he hadn't.

"Now, we both know that you know about Mike Quinn and his part in this—including the fact that he chose to disappear, without fanfare, back into the hazy though presumably law-abiding anonymity he came from."

She ignored the twinge that truth evoked. He didn't want to see her again. She'd accept it. Never let it be said Julianna Connor foisted herself on someone who didn't want her.

Meg's eyes narrowed. "And you're telling me you're just going to leave it at that?"

Julie grabbed her plate and got up to carry it to the counter. "Why shouldn't I?" She reached for the dishwashing detergent and started to fill the stainless-steel sink.

Meg didn't say a word. She just gathered her own breakfast dishes and stacked them beside Julie's. When her friend kept ignoring her, Meg leaned her derriere against the counter, crossed her arms, and studied her silk-encased legs.

"Now who's being lame, Connor? What happened between you two?"

Julie's hands hesitated infinitesimally. She didn't want to field these particular questions. They unsettled her because they were questions she still hadn't answers for.

"Just leave it alone. Please, Meg. He saved my life, he may have done this community a big favor, and he wants to be left alone. That's the end of it."

Julie's quiet candor sobered Meg. She was so used to thinking of Julie as her support that there were times she actually forgot she was twelve years older than her friend. Only occasionally was that awareness prompted by a look, a word, a silence Julie unwittingly let slip through her breezy manner. Now was one of those times.

Meg was startled to hear, let alone see, the degree

of vulnerability Julie was revealing. Oh, she understood there were layers to Julie even she hadn't been allowed to glimpse. But their six-year friendship had included its share of confidences, late-night laments over life and loves, and professional bolsterings when good-old-boy politics stirred up headaches for them in the newsroom.

They both had confided much of their personal histories to each other, perhaps because each in her own way was a survivor. They understood each other in ways others who had lived their lives relatively unscathed couldn't understand.

Still, Meg knew there was a part of Julie that demanded solitude, that needed isolation. That was why she was surprised now. The attack, or maybe something in its aftermath, had apparently touched Julie's shell.

But because Meg knew her friend would never acknowledge that to herself, let alone to her, she backed off. She'd always respected Julie's wishes. The wish for privacy that she was expressing now wouldn't be treated any differently.

"Well," Meg said, "I'll trust you know what you're doing." She moved toward the door. "But if you ever decide you want to talk, you know you don't have to ask."

"Yeah, Meg, I know." Julie's expression cleared and she offered a smile. "Thanks. But I guess I didn't have to tell you that either."

"Right, kiddo. Oh, and by the way, my ulterior motive for coming over was to tell you that Wilkins says the bad news is they're still trying to determine whether or not that creep is our rapist.

"The better news is there are indications the creep could have information about other nefarious

things that have been going on around here of late.''
With a wink, Meg turned and let herself out of the
apartment.

———

Later that afternoon, just as Julie was about to
leave to run an errand, her phone rang. She back-
tracked to get it.

"I thought you'd be interested to know. They just
found Phillip Blakemore's law partner dead.''

Julie absorbed her editor's news and leaned into
the telephone stand beside her. "When? Where?''

"About an hour ago. Some Michigan tourists
were taking a hike through the woods. The husband
noticed something that didn't look quite like a bag of
trash along one of those little Podunk county roads.
It had been halfway dug up and gotten at by some
animal. One of the cops who showed up to check it
out by some fluke knew Phillip Blakemore. He was
able to peg the body as Pete Henry's.''

"How did he die?'' With a sinking feeling Julie
realized the method didn't really matter; the simple
fact that·Henry had been murdered no doubt explained why he hadn't been at Blakemore's memorial service.

"Shot. But I also got some inside word from the
coroner that the condition of the body indicated
Henry had suffered a fair amount of physical abuse
prior to his murder.''

"Oh, my God.'' Julie's voice was hushed.

"I have to bring it up again, Julie. Do you think
this is connected to the Blakemore death? No, let me
rephrase that. Do you have reason to believe Pete

Henry's murder could be linked to Phillip Blakemore's death?''

"No, Hank." Julie thought of her news stories, of
the crime that had fueled them, of what Pete Henry
had implied about Phillip Blakemore's knowledge of
it all. A link? Maybe. But she didn't have anything
verifiable to substantiate any maybes and knew she'd
told Hank Finley the truth.

"All right," Hank said after a bit. "If it were anybody but you, Connor, I wouldn't trust that."

"Thanks, Hank." But she accepted his thanks
with a pang. Her conversation with Henry rushed to
mind. Deep down she feared she might not have
told Hank the truth after all.

"So, when are you coming in? You don't have to
rush, you know. You've got some time coming."

"A couple of days," Julie answered absently. Her
long-overdue vacation was the last thing on her
mind. Having a little time alone to think was. "I'll
see you then."

"If you insist. Take it easy, kid."

After Hank hung up, Julie walked over to the sofa
and pulled her feet under her. She gazed absently
out her living room window and saw without really
seeing two children racing their bikes along the walk
in front of her complex.

What was she going to do? She should go to the
police, but with what? Hunches? Unexplained infer-
ences from dead men? Half-formed speculations of
her own?

Restlessly she pushed herself up from the sofa and
walked over to the front table where she'd dropped
her purse. She pulled Blakemore's number from it
and carried it with her across the room, where she

studied it before sitting down and dropping it in her lap.

Why had he chosen to trust her with his secrets rather than the police? He had to know she wasn't equipped to deal with whatever had gotten him killed, because with Pete Henry's death she no longer had any doubts whatsoever that Phillip Blakemore had been murdered.

Abruptly Julie raised her head and gazed unseeingly across the room. If the people who had engineered Pete Henry's death had done it to silence him, what was to say they hadn't known that he had reached out to her? In fact, couldn't there be every likelihood that they might believe she knew more than she did?

She got up to pace the floor. What had Hank said, that Henry had obviously been worked over before he'd died? If that was so, it stood to reason that odds were Blakemore's killers might have gotten their hands on Henry too only to find out that he was, in fact, as clueless as she.

"Oh, God," she murmured. She walked over to the phone and punched in a number.

"Sheriff's Department," a brisk voice answered.

"I need to speak to Sheriff Wilkins."

"Hold on, please—"

Julie listened to some papers rustling and to the woman on the other end of the line answer a question called to her from the distance.

"Sorry 'bout that. The sheriff's out at the moment. Can I take a message?"

"Yes—" Julie thought, then she hesitated. What message? What was she prepared to say? "That's all right. When will he be back in?"

"It could be late. He's gone down to Indianapolis

on business that'll probably keep him out of the office for the rest of the day. Do you need immediate assistance?''

Dammit. ''No. I'll try him later.'' She hung up. No sooner had the receiver hit its cradle than the phone rang again. Julie jumped a little and picked it up.

''Hello?''

It was the hospital.

———

Two hours later Julie walked out into the hot August sun across the hospital parking lot. She'd seen her aunt admitted and talked with her doctor. The three of them had agreed that Peg would stay to have the hip replacement she'd been postponing for far too long now.

Julie loved the old woman more than she had ever loved her father or her mother, Peggy's little sister. But more and more she felt guilty about the emotional responsibility Peggy still felt for her.

Julie knew it was foolish, but increasingly she couldn't help feeling she was the reason Peggy seemed more and more inclined to neglect her health in a stubborn effort to be strong for her niece. The fall that she'd taken at the mall this afternoon, when she should never have gone out alone, was a perfect example of that. It bothered Julie, but at the same time she loved her aunt even more for it. For as long as she lived, she'd never forget that it had been Peg who had given her her first taste of unconditional love.

Julie negotiated the late-afternoon traffic by reflex, her mind on what she would need to do to close up her apartment before she took up temporary residence in Peg's beach house. She'd assured Peg she'd sit the house for the duration of her convalescence. She'd already called Hank from the hospital to tell him she'd be staying at the beach in case he needed to get in touch before she came back to work.

Now that she thought of it, however, she could put her downtime to good use.

Swinging right off Franklin Street, she drove east until she reached her newspaper offices. She had some old files on Blakemore in her desk drawer. Maybe another look through them would jog her memory about something she had forgotten.

She was hailed by a couple of other reporters who were working late as she made her way through the maze of the newsroom to her own cubicle. She dropped her purse on her chair, and as she did she noticed that three messages had come in while she'd been out.

The first two were returned calls from sources connected to feature stories Hank told her he'd already reassigned, but the third message caused her to pause. The caller's name was absent but the number on the slip was one Julie knew all too well, and the date was this morning's.

Julie felt chilled. She picked up the phone and dialed. Three rings later it was answered.

"Yes?" a terse voice said.

"Julie Connor." She heard an audible sigh then a chuckle.

"Well, well, well. I didn't think I'd get lucky enough to hear from you for a while. I heard about the assault."

"What do you want?" Julie's voice was calm though her heart was pounding. She'd thought, maybe even hoped, that these calls had died with Blakemore.

"Same as always, sweetheart. I got some information. You interested?"

Again Julie heard his chuckle and the certainty behind it. She wanted to hang up. But as usual her instinct cautioned her that it was more important to listen.

"Go ahead."

"There's a kid named Charlie Martinez . . ."

Julie listened and took down the information on the yellow notepad she always kept beside her phone. "Why hasn't Charlie gone to the police if he's being forced to mule for these people?"

"Oldest reason in the world, baby. Blackmail, pure and simple. He and his family are here illegally. Should anything untimely befall any of his business associates, Charlie and his family get their Latin asses shipped right back across the water where they came from. That is, if they don't end up dead."

Julie kept jotting until she had not only the bare bones of Charlie's story but also a slum address where she could find him.

"Why does he want to talk to me?"

" 'Cause he's still young enough to be stupid. He figures that he screwed up, but that spelling out how through a story of yours might help some other dumb kid."

Julie dropped her pencil. "You're disgusting. You know this stuff and a hell of a lot more, and still you keep it from the authorities, who could possibly be in a position to help Charlie and other children like him. Why do you do it? What do you get out of it?"

"The satisfaction of being a Good Samaritan in my own way. After all, why do I need to go to the police when I got my very own little ace reporter to be my mouthpiece?

"I would suggest the real question isn't why I do it, baby," he continued. "The better question is, why do you?"

"Go to hell."

Julie hung up and sank into her chair. Her head fell forward, and she slowly ran her fingers through her hair.

He was slime. He knew these things before they happened, while they could still be stopped. And yet he let them happen anyway for only God knew why.

She hadn't asked to be his confidante, but since he'd chosen her, she retaliated the only way she knew how: with the power of her words, with the force of her indignation, with her determination to use her news stories to throw a spotlight on the futility of crime and corruption.

The violence of her childhood couldn't stand for nothing. With the help of Peggy's nurturing she'd long ago determined she wouldn't let it; hanging on to that determination was the only way she had survived. And if continued survival demanded she protect and cultivate her unwanted ally, then so be it. She'd keep finding a way to live with it.

Besides, he'd be of little benefit to the police. It was her experience that lowlifes like him nearly always chose smug silence over spilling what they knew to the authorities.

Glancing down, she saw that the drawer she had started to open a few minutes ago stood ajar enough to reveal the alphabetical divider labeled *B*. A slight smile relaxed her mouth; she took it as an omen and a reminder of why she was here.

Reaching over, she pulled the drawer out a bit

farther until she located the file she was looking for: BLAKEMORE.

She removed the folder, pushed the drawer back, and picked up her purse. There had to be something in the file beyond the innocuous social acquaintances and business associates she'd already spoken to following his death. She'd use her time off to find it.

And after she found it, she'd take everything she knew to the police, if necessary. Her informant's inference was wrong. She didn't need to horde the glory of her stories as a validation of her professional self-worth.

I never have and I never will, she told herself. Slinging her purse over her shoulder, she walked out of the office.

Chapter

FIVE

Mike cracked open his beer, got comfortable against his sofa, and nestled the phone against his shoulder. "What did you find out, Tom?"

"That your hunch was right on, man. Del Evans has an organized crime history, and it's a nasty one. Drugs, robbery, sexual assault. Want me to go on?"

"No. Where's he been?"

"Well, obviously right here in Chicago. But the trail I'm on indicates he's also been at it in New York, New Jersey, and all along that coast. He might have been active along the West Coast too. I'm waiting for confirmations before I'll know for sure."

"How's he walked?"

"Same damned song and dance, playing kissy kissy with the feds. They reeled in bigger fish by using him then letting him go."

Mike leaned forward to set his beer down on the coffee table. "I'll be in touch."

"Yeah," Tom said with measured patience. "That's all I'm gonna get, friend?"

Mike said nothing. His mind was already playing with possibilities.

If the assault on Julie hadn't been random, and he didn't believe for a moment it had, chances were Evans had been indulging a personal diversion before getting to the main event. Which presented the question. What had that event been? Terrorism? Murder? Both?

Neither answer aligned with his father's implications. But one thing was for sure. Ambiguities Mike hadn't counted on were cropping up.

What had his old man pulled him into?

Mike was reminded that Tom had been waiting for some answer when his friend said, "You just watch yourself, man."

When Tom rang off, Mike propped his feet on the coffee table and sighed.

He was uneasy. Aside from his father's dying words, he knew the primary reason lay with roughly one hundred and ten pounds of what he suspected was concealed dynamite named Julianna Connor.

He'd ruthlessly relegated her to a proper niche last night. So why the hell couldn't he get her face, her scent, her entreating eyes out of his mind? None of it fit the image of the woman he needed to assume, for caution's sake, was the enemy. With a muttered curse, he finished his beer and tossed the can into a corner wastebasket.

Restlessly he pushed himself up and walked to the picture window where he watched the lake roll against the base of the slate-gray skyline. The water's moodiness perfectly reflected his own.

———

A week to the day of the attack, Julie ran methodically, rhythmically along the beach, letting the pure sepia sunrise soothe her. She had been thinking about Mike too.

She'd grown up with the Morrisons' son, Taylor. Though he was a little older than she and lived in Chicago, she'd remained relatively close to him and hadn't hesitated two days ago to call him up.

He'd confirmed the friendship claimed by Quinn. Julie knew she'd been prying, but the curious journalist inside her had needed the satisfaction of hearing Taylor back Quinn's story.

Despite what Quinn wanted, despite what she sensed was right, she just couldn't forget him. His quiet strength drew her in a way she had never been drawn to any other man. But while her reflections about him warmed her, what had preceded Mike's entry into her life turned her cold.

Del Evans was pure bad luck.

Or was he? a treacherous little voice whispered to Julie as the Morrison place came into sight. Worries about Phillip Blakemore and Pete Henry amplified that question with each pounding step she took, and so she didn't realize her solitude had been breached until a hailing voice pulled her out of her introspection.

Julie slowed, continuing to jog in place, and looked out toward the water. She raised her hands to shield her eyes from the rising sun. As the owner of the voice moved into view, the unexpectedness of his appearance slowed her to a stop.

For an instant she had the overwhelming urge to run on. But he was already striding out of the water, and her innate curiosity held her in place. He watched her, a bit warily, she thought, as he walked up to her.

"Morning."

"Good morning, Mike." Her reply was as easy as his greeting. In fact, she was surprised at how calm she sounded. Considering the way they had parted and the impressive sight his lean, water-slicked body had just made as he swam powerfully through the waves, she was downright impressed with her cool.

Mike hesitated, and Julie got the distinct impression that he was undecided about what to say.

"Great sunrise."

Julie's grin was spontaneous; she couldn't help it.

Mike dropped his head, planted both hands on his hips and expelled a softly rueful "Shit." Then he smiled too.

Julie felt some of her tension ease. "Yeah," she said. "It is nice weather we're having. But—?"

He glanced up. "Look, are you all right?"

"Yeah." Julie wondered at the impatience underscoring the inquiry. "Thanks for asking."

"The other night—" he began.

She understood perfectly, of course, what he was referring to and held her silence, forcing him to go on. His face tightened as if he were weighing something. Then his expression cleared.

"Listen, let's go over there for a minute." He gestured toward the column of stone stairs behind them that led up to his place.

"What is it?" she hedged. "I really need to get to work."

"On a Saturday?"

"For a while, yes. I'm playing catch-up today."

He studied her, then he looked out toward the water. He ran a broad hand along the back of his neck. When he looked back around, he said simply, "Please?"

Julie relented, again gripped by a surge of curiosity. She followed him across the sand and after they were seated waited for him to begin.

"I thought you lived in Michigan City proper," he said at length.

Julie's head was resting upon her arms, which she had wrapped around her knees. Mike's question sounded like an accusation. She turned her head to look at him.

"I do. My aunt is in the hospital, so I'm sitting her house while she's gone."

"She seems like a nice lady."

"She's the best. She raised me."

More time passed while Mike watched the water. "Tell me about the town. Did you grow up in it?"

Julie shifted her head so that she too could gaze back out across the beach. "Yeah, I was raised here even though I was born in Chicago. My parents died when I was a kid, and by that time Peggy had moved back home to Indiana from New York. She lost her husband right before I lost my family. I don't really have memories of much of anything before my parents' deaths."

She thought of the dream she'd had the morning of Meg's visit, then shut it out.

"Seems like a pretty low-key little hamlet," Mike prompted.

"It is. Small and quiet. Nothing much disturbs the status quo here."

He tossed her a look.

"Yeah, well, usually." Julie found herself reluctant to qualify her denial, to mention the odd upswing in violence. Maybe it was the small-town girl in her, she mused ruefully, leaping to defend what was comfortable and familiar about her home against an outsider.

"According to the paper, the status quo was disturbed in a pretty big way not too long ago, wasn't it? Wasn't some old guy, a town father or something, killed in a boating accident?"

Julie leaned back on her elbows so that she could look fully at Mike. "Not a town father, exactly. He was a transplant from Chicago. But he was awfully influential around here, and he was awfully well liked too."

"Sorry. I didn't mean to tread on sacred ground."

Julie sighed and relaxed again. "You didn't. It's just—"

"Just?" Mike watched her closely.

"Nothing," she said softly, after a moment.

"Sounds as if the two of you were close."

"Not really," Julie said, thinking uncomfortably of Pete Henry. "Like lots of other folks around here, I kept tabs on him mainly through what he was doing around town. He was big into charitable causes for minorities, disadvantaged youth, the homeless, things like that."

Mike thought of his father's conspicuous absence from his own life. He smiled slightly, feeling more than a twinge of bitterness. Hell, maybe that had been the saving grace of his old man's desertion, a guilty conscience that had kicked him hard enough in the ass to do something with his life that meant a damn to somebody else.

"What attracted you to the beach?"

Julie's question brought Mike out of his reverie. "Like I said, I needed a change of scenery. Actually, I was planning to go on to Michigan to scout out a condo when Taylor's offer intervened."

He thought of how he hadn't been in touch with Taylor for most of the ten years that had passed since they'd graduated from college. He thought of how he had renewed that contact by using his badge and an unspecified emergency as his basis of request to use Taylor's family home.

Taylor had been far from reluctant; in fact he'd seemed to get a vicarious thrill from Mike's request to help him preserve his deep-cover posture by supporting the Quinn alias to anyone who might ask.

"So what do you do, Mike? I mean, if you'll pardon me for commenting, area prices here don't run cheap. You strike me as a laid-back sort of guy."

"I'm on sabbatical." At Julie's questioning look he added, "I write."

Again Julie raised a delicate brow. "Anything I'd recognize?"

"Mike's lips quirked. "Probably not. It's all very academic, more than a little esoteric."

Julie shifted to rest her elbows on her knees.

"What about you? You're a reporter, yes?"

"You've read my stuff," she stated.

"You're damned good."

"Thanks." Julie was pleased and a little surprised at the readiness of his compliment. "I love it. I've been an investigative reporter in this town for almost five years now."

"You must be in a position to keep pretty close tabs on what goes on around here then. Dirty dealings, shady community doings. That's the kind of stuff in your beat, right?"

Julie looked at him. For some reason her uneasy alliance with her informant and the stories he had recently been putting her onto came to mind. It made her defensive. "Is there something that interests you in particular?"

"No." Mike reminded himself to tread carefully if

he wanted to keep her talking. "That title—investigative reporter—just always sounded glamorous to me. I wondered if in your case it was."

Julie's sensors were telling her he was wondering about something much more complex than what he was letting on. He wanted something from this early-morning tête-à-tête. "Well, it can be exciting, all right, but I don't know if glamorous is really the term to describe it. Long hours, indifferent pay, fleeting recognition unless the story's really big."

"Like the Blakemore thing."

Again Julie studied him.

"Like you said, I've read some back issues of your paper. It seemed like a good way to get a feel for the people and happenings around here."

"That sounds like the logic of a pro. Have you moved around a lot, Mike Quinn?"

"No, Julie Connor." He chuckled outright at her suspicion. "As I told you once before, there's nothing mysterious about me. Cross my heart." He did so with a lingering smile and teasing arch of his brows.

Julie sighed softly, willing to let it go for now. But not for a moment was she diverted from her curiosity about his curiosity.

So she smiled. "Something tells me you're full of it." Something also told her he was far from the placid literary academic he would have her believe.

No academics she knew jogged with guns, wielded them with a degree of comfort that seemed to be second nature, and fought like dervishes.

She wondered what the real purpose behind Mike Quinn's interrogation was, because that was what this was. A very skillful interrogation.

"Sun's coming up," Mike observed, levering himself up from his step. "I should let you get on to work."

Julie agreed but, strangely enough, regretted seeing this interlude come to an end. The regret was foolish because in the cold light of day during this second encounter with Mike Quinn she had learned two things.

The first was that she didn't entirely trust him. The second was that despite the mistrust she was still attracted to him. *Dangerous*, she thought, shaking her head as she got up.

"What?"

"Nothing. Look, I know you value your privacy and I value mine. But seeing as how we're going to be each other's closest neighbor for a while, you think we could agree to a friendly standoff?" Julie held out her hand.

Mike looked at it before extending his own. Getting close to her was turning out to be easier than he could have hoped. *Oh, hell, Blakemore,* he thought impatiently. *Admit it. You're glad for the easy access, but you're also liking it for reasons a hell of a lot more basic than that.*

Keeping his attraction to Julianna Connor separate from his suspicion of her was going to require some damned fancy sidestepping. He released her hand and watched her jog away.

"Hey!" he called to her before she'd gotten very far.

She turned and slowly jogged backward, waiting for his question.

"You heard any more about Del Evans?"

"Nothing worth anything," Julie called. "They haven't been able to nail him as the Lake Shore Rapist yet."

Mike nodded. "I'll see you around."

"Later," Julie called back.

Mike walked up the steps, then on an impulse turned back to watch her retreating figure. Clever she-wolf or damsel in distress?

He walked inside to get dressed.

———

The next evening Julie made her way across the beach to his house.

He didn't seem to be readily on hand to notice her approach, and she was glad. It allowed her to brace again for the intensity of him and what she guessed was going to be his resistance to her own attempt at interrogation.

She'd debated whether or not to do this late into the previous night and, again, this morning. Eventually curiosity had won over prudence. Quite simply, he was up to something, and the reporter in her overrode the caution of the woman.

So here she was, crashing his privacy to probe, disguised as the dispenser of a little neighborly housewarming.

She juggled her casserole dish to a more comfortable position against her hip and climbed the stone stairs.

As she got closer to his front door, she could see him standing behind his picture window. One arm was propped against the frame and his forehead rested against the back of his hand. Pale blue jeans and a faded gray sweatshirt fit his rangy body familiarly enough to let her know both were old friends.

Just before Julie came into his line of vision, she

took in his tense face, his withdrawn expression. Wondering at the cause, she rang his bell.

Mike was slightly startled to see the woman who was dominating his thoughts standing on his front porch.

"Tell me I'm bothering you or interrupting something and I'll leave," she said.

Mike stood aside to let her enter. She stepped into the foyer, took a thorough yet noninvasive look around, then turned to face him.

Her look was questioning, as if she wasn't sure if she was going to be going or staying. He guessed that was up to him.

"I'm not doing anything, really." Immediately he thought maybe he shouldn't have sounded so inviting, that maybe he should have lied and given her a mental nudge toward the door. But the fact was, she'd caught him feeling more than a little melancholy.

Standing there in some summer confection of floaty white cotton and lace, she looked as irresistible as the proverbial forbidden fruit she was. And whatever she had under wraps at her side smelled awfully damned good.

He pushed the door behind him shut.

Julie was surprised by the nerves that suddenly gripped her. But more than that she was impatient because they were as uncharacteristic to her as the slight intimidation she felt beneath Quinn's unblinking gaze. She moved decisively past him, not waiting for him to lead the way inside.

Mike smiled a little, admiring her conscious decision to throw off the passiveness and take the bull by the horns. This was the Julie he knew and was fascinated by, the dangerous seducer of his common sense and rational thought.

"Here, I'll take that," he said, reaching for her dish as he led her to the living room.

The phone rang from somewhere to their right, and Mike glanced at her, slowing a bit. He nodded straight ahead. "Make yourself comfortable in there. I'll store this in the kitchen and be with you in a minute."

For Julie the call couldn't have been more convenient. It presented her with an opportunity to take a look around, to gather some insight into the enigma she'd come to investigate.

What would he do when he finished his call? she wondered. Field her questions with that same tough, polished deflection he'd demonstrated so effectively already? Eat her food, thank her for her company, and then decisively, yet oh so smoothly, push her right back out the front door?

She smiled ruefully, fingering a piece of bric-a-brac that rested on the mantel of a huge fireplace dominating one wall. That scenario wasn't at all hard to imagine.

Julie glanced toward the kitchen. Apparently his call was going to take longer than a minute. Choosing a point of origin and glancing at her watch to gauge the time, she made her way across the room to a large, plushly cushioned wicker fan chair near the sofa. Actually, it seemed there was hardly anything to be learned about this house's new inhabitant as of yet; the walls, floor, and shelves were still pretty bare.

But, she reasoned, no doubt the contents of the boxes she saw scattered here and there might be able to change that.

Julie dropped her purse to the floor. As she did, her eye fell on one small box that rested at the side of the chair.

Later she couldn't pinpoint what had compelled her to start with that particular box instead of something bigger that looked likely to yield more. Maybe it was the Cubs baseball cap that lay haphazardly on top. Chicago. Was that what his definition of "around here" constituted?

When he'd said "west," she'd been thinking more along the lines of Gary, Indiana, maybe. Never once considering she was seriously invading personal belongings that, after all, were laid out in plain sight, Julie leaned down a little to take a closer look at what was at her feet.

Beneath the cap rested a plain white ceramic coffee mug. Turning it, she saw lettering along the bottom. It was a logo for the Chicago Police Department. Was he a *cop*? Not even caring if she was snooping at this point, Julie started to dig further into the box. She encountered a motley assortment of housewares and magazines before her hands encountered the next interesting thing.

It was a small, black, leather-bound journal with the departmental initials embossed in the lower-right-hand corner. Julie opened it and started to flip through. She didn't have to go very far to get a jolt that was entirely unexpected.

Under the *B* section was an address, and in parentheses beside it two boldly scrawled words: PHILLIP BLAKEMORE.

"Put it down, Julie."

She jumped at Mike's softly issued command and the journal slipped from her fingers. Turning to face him, she instantly chose the offensive.

"You lied to me. What's a Chicago cop doing in Indiana asking questions about Phillip Blakemore?"

Mike said nothing, watching her as he made his way over to his sofa and settled himself into it. He bent one knee across the other.

"You're surely not going to try to deny it?" In the face of his silence Julie abruptly realized she was standing directly in the glare of a floor lamp that predominantly illuminated her side of the darkening room. She felt uncomfortably like a suspect trapped in the spotlight, and she moved out of the lamp's glow to take the fan chair, reminding herself that it wasn't she, in this situation, who was being duplicitous.

"No," Mike said at length. "I'd be a fool to deny it, wouldn't I?"

"Then perhaps you'd like to explain it." Julie leaned back at her own ease and waited, feeling somehow betrayed.

Beneath his relaxed facade Mike had been doing some fast thinking. He'd been careless, and she'd been clever enough not only to come looking for two and two at his house, but to find it and put it together with a speed that had, for the time being, pushed his back to the wall. His options were limited, but there was one.

"I'm here in conjunction with a federal investigation," he said, elaborating on the lie he had planted with Taylor. He saw her eyes widen and he breathed marginally, still angling as he talked, trying to buy himself time by mingling truth with fiction.

"The federal authorities are looking into some drug trafficking that has been traced to East Chicago and other areas straddling the Illinois–Indiana border."

"Then why are you here in, as you put it, this quiet little hamlet of Michigan City?"

"I can't tell you anything else unless you're willing to give me a promise, Julie. You've got to understand that anything else I say, were it to be discovered, could compromise more than this investigation, which is very deep cover. It could compromise lives, including your own, since, with what I'm telling you, you've become involved.

"So I'll give you a choice. You can walk out of here, forgetting that you ever saw what was in that box. Or you can give me your promise of confidentiality, and I'll go on."

Julie was subdued by what Mike was telling her and impressed enough to hesitate. Her life didn't need complications. But, then, could she really walk away from this, even knowing as little as she knew? As Mike had pointed out, she was already involved. And besides, if the man opposite her hadn't considered her a worthy confidante, he never would have said as much as he already had.

With full certainty, she knew he would have elected to keep his secrets and let her walk away.

"You have my promise," she said simply.

Again Mike applauded her moxie, regretting that he was forced to deal with this woman in only half-truths. "Okay, then. Here it is, straight."

What he gave her was a story of how Chicago vice detectives had been communicating with Northern Indiana authorities in relation to racketeering action in Indiana that bore signatures of a Chicago-based drug cartel. The specific link between the Illinois and Indiana authorities had come through a tip that had been lodged with the Chicago authorities.

That tip had involved the names of Chicago players and, unexpectedly, a prominent Michigan City, Indiana, attorney named Phillip Blakemore.

"The connection wasn't defined," Mike said. "But authorities back home decided this Blakemore needed checking out. An arrangement was being made with the Indiana people to do it when Blakemore so inconveniently turned up dead.

"Knowing the nature of the cartel we were dealing with, my department immediately got suspicious. In light of our suspicion and our familiarity with the organization, we were requested by the feds to send one of our own vice detectives to work undercover along with a federal officer here in Michigan City to investigate the Blakemore link. That includes his killing."

"You're certain it was a killing, then, and not an accident?"

Memories of blood and violence and fire flashed across Mike's mind. "Yes," he said starkly.

"And what about the local authorities? How deeply have they been pulled into this?"

"That's where it gets tricky," Mike told her, thinking of his father's caution against the police. What he was about to say next might not be that far off base. "Someone had to leak the information about Blakemore's possible involvement with this thing. The only possibility we have points to law enforcement."

"So what you're saying is the line of thinking among you and your superiors is that someone here in the department may have sold Phillip Blakemore out." Julie had seen much during her career, but this tale Mike was weaving of murder and police corruption was particularly unsettling.

"Yes." Again Mike's tone was stark.

Lying had become a routine part of his job description, a tool necessary for his survival on the streets. He was employing it now because the professional in him realized that this case was just another variation of the job.

It was for survival's sake, he reminded himself, that he was ignoring his gut hunch that in Julie's case the smarter move might be to reveal more truth.

"Now you know," he concluded. "My profile needs to stay low, and my resources here are proportionately limited. Yours, on the other hand, are vast. You have a knowledge not only of Blakemore, but of this town and its people that would cost me valuable time to learn."

He sat forward, rested his elbows on his thighs, and propped his fists beneath his chin. "On the other hand, you could use what I've told you to add yet another scoop to your collection."

At her wary look he smiled slightly, but it was without humor. "That's right, your propensity for beating the competition to some of the juicier episodes of local mayhem didn't escape my notice when I was reading all those articles and doing my homework.

"So the upshot, Julie Connor, is this," he said. "You have it entirely within your power to play the reporter and coldcock me, or you can help me. Which is it going to be?"

Damn him. The professional lure was there, and it was undeniably strong. But so was the moral obligation on her part. What had she done to impress upon him an opinion of her that was so poor? Did he really think she could believe she had a choice when lives, as he had said, were at stake?

She sat forward, allowing her face to rest fully

within the lamp's glow. His gaze was locked on hers, his noncommittal eyes dark and, she fancied, almost glittering.

Her ambition could have shaped her answer in several ways. In the end, her conscience only allowed her one.

"What can I do?"

Part Two

Chapter

SIX

"I've already done some preliminary work." Julie stepped back to let Mike walk past her into her foyer. She watched him do a quick assessment of the living room beyond, last seen on a moonlit night when nerves had been thin and tensions had been high.

The cheery sunlight splashing across the white-washed walls and gleaming hardwood floors set a much different tone today, and Julie was charged, ready to take advantage of it.

She thought that Mike was of much the same mood, gauging by his terse nod and the look of determination that narrowed his dark eyes. She recalled the last night that they had been together.

The same unsmiling look had tautened his features in the wake of her promise to keep his confidentiality. And afterward his mood hadn't lightened as they'd eaten her casserole and she'd revealed to him everything about her encounter with Pete Henry, including her own forebodings in the wake of his and Blakemore's deaths.

"Make yourself at home," she invited him now,

gesturing through to the dining area. "I've already put together some files that might help."

She stepped back, allowing Mike to precede her over to the dining room table where she had spread out about a dozen manila folders, all neatly categorized and labeled according to news issues and surnames.

They were, Mike listened as she explained, the files of sources she'd used over the years who had particularly interesting inroads into racketeering-related subjects she had written about. All of the sources were low profile and relatively invisible to those who conducted their daily lives around them.

Mike was impressed. He'd seen files of fellow detectives that were less comprehensive.

"What about this one?" he asked her awhile later, leafing through the folder of one Jimmy Sales, a convicted drug dealer. According to the clips inside his file, Jimmy had been paroled a month ago from the state prison.

Julie pursed her lips, nodding. "He was always a good one for keeping his ear to the ground."

She didn't see the way Mike's eyes caressed the top of her head or the way his gaze tracked the bare nape of her neck.

Mike registered her answer but at the moment was more fascinated by the way the dark strands of her hair brushed the clean line of her face before falling to one delicate shoulder, where she had controlled them loosely with a gold clip. He cleared his throat and looked away from her when she lifted her eyes to his.

"Is he worth getting to know?" Mike gestured at Jimmy's grainy black-and-white photo.

"Maybe." Julie shrugged. "He was a minor player

before he went in, but he did turn out to have some interesting connections. Could be he knows somebody who was plugged into the secret side of Phillip Blakemore."

"Can you set up a meeting?"

Julie thought about it. "Give me a couple of days and I'll see what I can do. Who else?"

Mike shuffled through five more files. "What about him?"

"Roy Bronson. He's a strange one," Julie said slowly. "A small businessman who dabbles in this and that. He put me onto a source who had some knowledge about a loan-sharking operation that was busted up a couple of years ago. Presently he owns a small tavern in town."

The subtle tension that stiffened her shoulders as she leaned over Bronson's file spoke to Mike as clearly as the hesitation underlying her words. "Why strange?"

"Well, to put it simply, I can't figure out if he's just a well-informed good guy or an exceptionally crafty bad one. These others here are pretty plain to read, as clear as the photos on these pages. But Bronson, I don't know.

"For as long as I can remember, I've heard whispers about his being in the know about some pretty unsavory things that have gone down here over the years, including extortion and prostitution. In fact, that's what prompted me to use him as a source in the first place."

She pushed his folder back over with the rest. "Still, he never seems to be in trouble with the law, and I'll confess, I never really spent the time to dig deeper into the enigma of Mr. Bronson, beyond what I needed from him to help get my story." She looked at him closely. "What made you single him out?"

In truth, Mike couldn't say beyond the faint mental bell that had sounded in the back of his mind as he'd scanned through Bronson's file.

"Maybe it's something similar to what you've just said. The very innocuousness of the stuff printed here strikes me as curious. If Bronson is as well connected yet as low-key as you say, it follows that the nature of his connections probably bears some checking out."

"Something in line with, if you lie down with dogs—"

"—you wake up with fleas, yeah," Mike murmured, impressed again with Julie's shrewdness.

Closing Bronson's file, he looked up at her. "Why do you do this?" he asked abruptly. He hadn't intended to ask her until he'd actually said the words.

She looked puzzled.

"Investigative reporting," he elaborated.

"The pace suits me."

"How?" She'd said that calmly enough but something had flickered behind her eyes.

"The speed of it, the grit. I don't know, the *realness* of it, I guess. The consequences of it make an immediate difference to people. The repercussions of my stories pierce beyond a theoretical level, and I guess that appeals to me."

And what else? Mike wondered, studying her shuttered expression.

"Why are you a cop?" Julie asked.

The smoothly turned table caught Mike off guard a bit. Not the fact that she'd asked the question; he recognized a diversionary tactic when he heard it. What stopped him for a moment was how to frame what his answer would be. He'd never stopped to analyze the why of it before.

"Maybe for reasons similar to yours," he said slowly, thinking it through as he spoke. "I like the speed too." *The adrenaline*, he mentally amended. "And the satisfaction of helping people who can't fight for themselves hit back at the bad guys. Beyond that?" He shrugged. "All I know is that for me being a cop is a good fit. When I get home at night, I sleep."

Alone? The thought popped into Julie's head apropos of nothing. She dropped her eyes from the broody intensity of his and hastily pushed back her chair. "Let's take a break." She smoothed her hands down the sides of her jeans. "I've put together some sandwiches, if you're hungry. No, stay," she said as he started to rise. "I won't be a minute."

Mike let her go into the kitchen and wondered at that flare of awareness he'd glimpsed before she'd gotten skittish and run.

Damn, she was beautiful. And damn, she was still getting to him, no matter how hard he lectured himself about staying immune.

Yes, he'd decided to coax her to help, and indications so far were that the decision was a good one. That decision to trust her had been a strategic one based solely on his need for knowledge and what he had gambled on as being her ability to supply it.

Her subsequent revelation about Pete Henry and his father's supposed knowledge of organized crime explained her involvement with his father, if she were to be believed. The problem was, he wasn't quite ready to believe her yet because he was having a damnable time separating his attraction for her from his dispassionate ability to judge her sincerity.

He pushed his chair back a little and sighed, telling himself that all in all he was comfortable with the choice he had made.

What he wasn't comfortable with was this ache that continued to gnaw at his insides every time he thought about her, every time he pondered the possible angles to her motives and, even more disturbingly, the whys for her unerring determination to submerge her obvious softness beneath a calculated overlay of toughness.

Lust he could handle. He'd been comfortably controlling that drive for years. Desire, however, was something else.

To his irritation he was finding there was nothing predictable or easy to handle about desire. It sneaked up on you like a thief, and once it found you, it clung to you just as doggedly.

Impatient with the direction of his thoughts and his inability to curb them, Mike got up to pace. What was the matter with him? Was it just this proximity to a beautiful woman and the decided seductiveness of their surroundings that made him lower his guard?

He paused, leaning a hip against the table. But since whatever it was appeared to be affecting Julie too, maybe he'd be doing them both a favor to walk right into that kitchen and eradicate it once and for all.

Julie sensed his presence even though she hadn't heard a sound. She stilled in the process of peeling an apple she intended to add to the bowl of fruit she was preparing. The fine hairs on the back of her nape stirred as the whispered sound of his soft-soled shoes advanced slowly across the parquet floor.

Her knife clattered to the counter. She couldn't move.

When his broad, calloused hands settled upon her bare shoulders, her breathing suspended, then escaped in a sighing rush. She was crazy to let this happen, but when she felt the entire tough length of him press gently against her back, ensconcing her between his warm virility and the cool steel of the kitchen sink, she was damned if she could resist.

When Mike felt the gentle sigh of her submission, the clarity of his intentions blurred. A reluctant groan escaped him, and he raised one hand to push the swath of hair shielding her neck aside. His open mouth took its place, and the warm, moist caress of his lips and tongue drew a sound from Julie that was as needy as his own.

Swiftly urgency overcame them and the momentum changed. Mike turned her in his arms, and she came willingly. Her mouth reached for his even as his dropped to take hers. The contact was electric.

Mike pressed against her even more closely, savoring the warm eagerness of her response, loving the fragile feel of her. The soft crush of her delicate breasts against his chest; the thin cotton shirt covering them, no more substantial than the summer-weight cotton of his own, was driving him crazy. Abruptly he eased the contact with her body enough to give himself tactile access to her.

His hands gently cupped her breasts, and his thumbs found her sensitized crests and caressed until Julie shivered and gripped his shoulders for support.

Jesus, this was getting out of hand, Mike thought, feeling dazed. He kissed her again. But even as he did he was compelled to break the contact a second time and gaze down to see the effect his ministrations were having on Julie's body. The sight of her peaked nipples made him feverish. He groaned again.

He pressed his hips into hers, making her explicitly aware of his increasing desire. Her breath caught audibly, and for a space of moments she accommodated him. And then, just as Mike felt his senses overload, it registered that Julie was pulling back, that she was pushing him away.

When he could think, his first response was bewilderment. When the haze cleared a little more, his second was irritation. But when he held Julie away from him, searching for the reason why she had stopped what they both so obviously wanted, he saw her expression. It wiped away his frustration and brought back his common sense in a rush.

She looked shaken, as if someone had knocked the wind out of her.

"Mike, listen—"

"Julie—"

They both spoke over each other and stopped, each waiting for the other to resume.

"I'm sorry, Mike," Julie began. Shaking her head, she let go of him and pushed away awkwardly, as if she had temporarily lost coordination of her arms and legs. "I don't want this. I'm not a tease, and I'm sorry, but I don't . . . want this."

She looked desperate. She looked shattered. Now that the heat was cooling, Mike was feeling much the same.

He ran an unsteady hand around the back of his neck and turned away from her, giving himself some distance. He couldn't face her; he was having trouble facing himself.

What the *hell* had happened? For the first time in his life he was a stranger to himself. He had never lost control like that. While he'd come in here thinking to douse a simple case of lust, he'd ignited something that had singed them both.

He finally turned to her, trying to give her an answer and an explanation of his part in what had happened. "I didn't want that either." At her incredulous look he had to smile.

"All right, maybe I did. What I mean to say is, I didn't come in here looking for—I didn't expect—oh, hell." He tried again. "I'm sorry."

It was inadequate, but it was the best he could summon. He'd never been in this situation before. He needed to get away—they both did. They both needed a large reclamation of some equilibrium and a healthy dose of perspective with it.

"Look, I'll leave. Do what you can about setting up a meeting with Jimmy Sales." He tried to think of something more substantial to add and couldn't. "I'll be in touch."

Julie nodded and waited for him to leave. He looked as if he wanted to say something else, and she prayed he wouldn't.

It wasn't until she heard the front door shut behind him that she found the strength to take a much needed breath. She held it in, letting her pulse calm and her heartbeat slow before she released it.

She'd thought the pull was purely physical. She never would have had the courage to allow that first kiss if she hadn't. But she had, and the sensations that had flooded her, pulled her under, and threatened not to let her go had cut to the bone.

She'd sensed from the first that he could have power over her. What had happened not only reinforced that, it mocked her arrogant assumption. She'd been mistaken to fool herself into believing that all he had inspired was a transitory itch. In letting him scratch, her rationalizations had gone up in smoke along with her confidence in her invulnerability.

She didn't even know the man. So why had her emotions been involved in every touch, every kiss, every caress? It was terrifying.

It was too reminiscent of Adam. And yet it wasn't; Adam was dead.

Belatedly she remembered the platter of food she had been preparing before Mike had come to her. The last thing she wanted now was food. She took down some aluminum foil from a cabinet, covered both the platter of sandwiches and the fruit bowl, and set them inside the refrigerator. When that was done, she walked aimlessly back into the dining room.

What could she say to him when she saw him again? And then remembering his own apparent need to get just as far away from her as she wanted to be from him, she knew. She'd follow his lead.

She'd say nothing and treat their interlude as if it had never happened. She valued the simplicity of her life, just as it had been before he'd entered it. Just as she'd vowed to keep it seven years ago when a singular lack of judgment had crushed her innocence forever.

Besides, she had more than enough to worry about with Blakemore's murderer running loose and her newly formed professional collaboration with a cop involved with federal agents. She just needed to keep in mind that Michael Quinn wasn't for her; no man who possessed the ability to get so close so fast was.

They'd verbalized a boundary of sorts before he'd left. All she needed to do now was her damnedest to make sure she didn't cross it. He might have been the first man to seriously compete with the past, but he certainly wouldn't be the last. Nor would the memory of his embrace endure to surpass that of a ghost's.

Chapter

SEVEN

Julie made a couple of calls the next morning and by early that afternoon had the information she needed to make the meet with Jimmy Sales. She'd lectured herself firmly the night before, and so it was with only a little trepidation that she called Mike, following her midmorning visit at the hospital with Peg, and offered to pick him up.

The heat of the day was at its zenith as they drove to the north side of the city. With his canvas deck shoes, tan khaki walking shorts, and tan short-sleeved polo shirt, Mike, Julie observed, had conceded as comfortably as she to the humidity. He seemed to be preoccupied with his thoughts, and well into the drive she glanced once over at him, reluctantly noting the wonderful things the soft beige did for his dark coloring.

He started to turn his head her way, and she turned hers back to the road, only slightly misjudging the time she needed to make a smooth merge into the turn lane. She ignored the irritated honk of the driver who accelerated past her but grew irritated at herself when, from the corner of her eye, she saw Mike's smile.

Julie drove them into the downtown district and resigned herself to slowing with the traffic. It wasn't easy. Summer was annually the height of the season. The tourist crowd, many of whom had filtered in from Illinois and Michigan to enjoy the lake activities of the little backwater town, was thick. Julie and Mike joined them, making their way to the town's prominent shopping mall, a collection of trendy designer-outlet shops atmospherically called the Lighthouse Place.

Jimmy was sitting at one of the benches in the courtyard formed by a square of stores. When he spotted Julie and Mike approaching, he paused slightly in midsip of his soft drink, tipped the can until he'd finished the contents, and casually tossed it into a trash dispenser behind him.

"Hey, Jimmy," Julie greeted him easily. "How's it going?" She watched him give Mike a thoughtful once-over and was amused when Mike, just as thoughtfully, returned the study.

"Well enough, you pretty thing." He looked back at her, smiling widely enough to reveal a gold cap on his right front tooth.

It was new, Julie noted, and just as startling against his milk-white skin as his distinctive mane of carrot-red hair.

"Somehow, I don't think you've brought him along"—he jerked his head at Mike—"to reminisce about the good old days we never had. Is he a reporter too? What gives?"

"Scoot over." Julie sat down, not giving Jimmy time to consider the request. She waited for Mike to follow suit. "He's with me," she said evasively, "and what I'd like to know is this: Is there anything you can tell me about the private side of Phillip Blakemore that I'm not likely to find out in any public record?"

Jimmy stroked his chin, then smiled. "You mean, like what were his downtime habits? His recreational preferences? Stuff like that?"

"Yeah."

"Well, I don't know, Julie."

"Don't worry, I won't let anything you tell me get traced back to you. I couldn't care less how you spend your time on the outside now that you're out on parole. I just want some input to my question, and you know I can be discreet."

"You always did play fair; that's why I've always liked you. So"—Jimmy leaned back and stretched both his skinny arms along the back of the bench— "you know as well as I do what a straight arrow the old man was." One hand idly began toying with Julie's hair.

She tilted her head away, and Jimmy smiled.

"You don't know what you're missing, girl. I always told you that."

Julie continued to regard him in a way that made it clear she was unimpressed. "Just get to the point, Jimmy."

He smiled again and Julie felt Mike shift beside her. She was startled when she felt his hand casually perch on her thigh, but she didn't acknowledge it, concentrating instead on the answer to her question.

"Okay." Jimmy duly noted Mike's territorialism. "Honest truth. As long as I been around, Blakemore's name has never come up as a player in any of this town's action.

"However, I do remember hearing something before I went into the joint this last time. Seems there was some talk about approaching him, you know, seeing if a connection could be made with the establishment." He shrugged. "I went in before I heard more."

"What about now?" Mike leaned forward so that Sales could clearly see him beside Julie. "Since you've been back on the streets, have you heard about any repercussions from Blakemore's death?"

Jimmy shook his head. "No, man, but you sound like there's something there to hear."

"You're in a better position than I am to know that, Sales."

Jimmy spread his hands expansively. "Hey, I'm a pretty smart guy, but even my knowledge is limited. Besides, I ain't looking for an express ride back to prison."

Mike smiled. His next words were quiet and knowing. "What are you looking for, Jimmy?"

Julie's head went from one to the other. She sensed the game was escalating. She leaned back and waited for Jimmy's answer.

"A little help, for starters. You understand, just to ease things." His mouth was smiling but his eyes had gone hard.

Without breaking the punk's gaze, Mike reached inside his pants pocket and pulled out several bills.

"Now, if I were to part with a little of this money, Sales, I wouldn't just be putting it in the wind, would I?"

Jimmy just watched him.

Julie watched Jimmy in return, noticing as she never had before how intently his palely lashed eyes seemed to calculate. In fact she was suddenly vastly uncomfortable with the way his whole demeanor re-minded her of a snake.

"Because if that turned out to be the case, man," Mike continued calmly, "I'd find out. And you can bet your ass I'd be pissed."

"He-e-ey," Jimmy said at length, his smile slowly returning. "I'm just talking about a little fun money. Parting with pocket change never hurt anybody."

Still holding the man's gaze, Mike thumbed off two twenties and reached across Julie to pass them along. "Usually. But as you said earlier, you're a smart guy. I'm betting as a smart guy you know there's a first time for everything."

Jimmy lost his smile again. "Like I said, man, I just got out of trouble. I ain't looking for more. I like this lady, here. That's why I agreed to meet her, that's why I'm telling you what I know about Blake-more. Nothing. And as for the other, I'm out here all by myself. I don't answer to anybody, and that's the way it's going to stay."

Julie turned her head to Mike. She shivered at the threat that lurked like a promise behind his easy smile. When at last he relaxed fractionally and she turned to see Jimmy reach a lanky hand up to wipe away some slight moisture that had gathered on his brow, she released the breath she hadn't known she was holding.

"There's more where that came from, Jimmy, should you feel the need to talk." Mike's tone was abruptly unruffled, as if he were commenting on the weather. "Go play."

Julie was bemused to see the redhead shoot up from the bench. He took two hurried steps away, then paused and turned so that he was doing a lei-surely backpedal.

"You could do better, sweet cheeks," he called to Julie. He tossed Mike a last furtive look before he turned around and hurried away.

Mike took Julie's hand and started to stand. "Come on, I could eat something. Tell me what's good around here and I'll treat."

Julie stayed seated, pulling her hand away. "What the hell was all that about?"

Mike patiently reached down and took her hand again. His grasp was gentle yet firm. "Come with me, 'sweet cheeks,' and I'll be glad to tell you."

Puzzled at what she was only just coming to realize was Mike's thinly suppressed anger, Julie let herself be pulled to her feet. She pointed him to a hot dog stand just a few feet away where they got sandwiches loaded with the works, chips, and soda. A lady with a stroller considered the bench they'd just vacated before deciding against it. As if of one mind, Julie and Mike made a beeline for it.

Julie delicately polished off her food and suffered Mike's silence while he aggressively finished his own. If he thought she lacked the patience to wait him out, he had another think coming. With casual deliberation she looked out across the bustling courtyard and popped the lid on her soft drink.

"What is it with you?" Mike demanded.

Julie took a second long drink and lowered the can. Only then did she turn her body and attention toward Mike. "Can you be a little more precise?"

"Sweetheart, I can be downright incisive." He leaned in closer, all but purring.

"Does it turn you on to associate with a scumbag like Sales, a little punk who would just as soon sell you and his mother out as he would go take a crap?

Or is your ego, your delusion of invulnerability so big that you just don't care?"

"How dare you—"

"I'll tell you how I dare. *Jimmy*, as you so endearingly call him, was all smiling and ready to take your earnest curiosity about Blakemore and your empathy about keeping him shielded from the law and sell it to the highest bidder on the streets."

"The highest—?"

"*Bidder*, sweetheart. Or had you forgotten what got Jimmy-boy sent away to the slammer in the first place? Didn't you see those fresh needle marks on his arm? Didn't you notice the red nose and that persistent little sniffle?

"Didn't it occur to you that the *precise* reason he agreed to this meeting at all was because he figured you might clue him in to some tidbit of curiosity he might find useful to finance his habit? If I hadn't been here to call him on it and push back, you might not have made it through the rest of this week, or even the rest of this day, in one piece."

Julie had never underestimated the risk of cultivating the network of particularly questionable contacts she used. But it hadn't backfired on her yet, and she resented this admonishment Mike was giving her, as if she were some unthinking child.

The fact that his points were valid only abetted her resentment.

"You listen to me, mister." She did some leaning in of her own. "I know exactly what I'm doing, and as for knowing who and what I'm dealing with, you have no idea. You can't. You don't know me or anything about me.

"The 'streets,' as you so dramatically call them, aren't something I, unlike others I bet I can name, became acquainted with solely through the training of a profession. I grew up on them, and I've given my pound of flesh to them.

"It's precisely because I have that I use them now to fight back, to get my job done and in the process throw some light on the booby traps out there just waiting to ensnare the unlucky or unwise or feckless, one of whom you seem to think I am."

Leaving her trash where it was, Julie pushed herself up from the bench and started to stride away. She'd gotten less than a foot from Mike before he caught up with her and grasped her arm.

Julie shook him off. "Since you're so damn smart, I'm sure you can figure out how to get yourself home." She started walking again.

Mike trotted around her until he faced her and blocked her way. This time he caught her by her shoulders. They both ignored the odd look a passing couple gave them.

"Dammit, will you wait!" Mike held on to her while she calmed down enough to listen to him. "I'm sorry."

Again Julie shook him off, but this time she stayed put.

"I—overreacted—" He ran a hand along the back of his neck and pushed a tight breath through his clenched teeth. "It makes me crazy, the risks you take."

What he was implying was starting to break through Julie's haze. "Why?" she asked quietly.

"I don't know why!" he said, realizing that wasn't strictly true. He was frustrated and unreasonably disturbed by the thought of Julie's being in danger. He was also close to shouting. He threw an irritated look around, pulled in a breath, and searched for the

words to neutralize his temporary loss of detachment.

"It's just that I've seen too many do-gooding,
gung ho civilians let their cockiness get them strung
up. I don't like to see innocents get themselves need-
lessly hurt."

Mike's concerned explanation calmed Julie to a
level that had her temper melting into something
that was far less bitter but no less volatile. She didn't
want to be touched. Neither did she want to be reminded of another occasion when she had surren-
dered to her vulnerability in a moonlit parking lot
and been pushed away for her efforts.

She turned away now, and Mike fell into step.

"Your apology is accepted, Mike," she said
calmly. "But I won't be coddled. I don't like it." She
stopped and forced him to face her, though she
knew he couldn't understand. "And I don't need it."
She could see Mike reserve judgment on that score,
but he merely nodded and they walked on.

When they reached Julie's car and settled in for
the drive back to the beach, Mike said, "I'd like you
to do some digging into Roy Bronson's background.
That material in your file provides a good start, but I
have a feeling that if we push, we may find a little
more."

Julie put the car into gear and maneuvered
around a lane of slowed traffic, heading for the state
road turnoff she needed. "What are you thinking
there is to be found?"

"It will probably be on the order of something
befitting the sophistication of the man, unlike our
friend Sales. As an entrepreneur, he's likely to have
access to more extensive avenues of significant busi-

ness transactions and the money that drives them. If that knowledge exists, I want it."

They were less than five minutes away from the lakeshore when Julie said, "About what I said back there—"

Mike looked over at her, waiting a bit uneasily for her to put a cap on a topic he'd hoped they'd closed.

"It's not that I'm unappreciative or ungrateful for your concern. It's just that I've been looking out for myself for so long . . . sometimes I forget the simple niceties of accepting a helping hand." She sighed. "What I'm very clumsily trying to say is, thanks."

She was unused to accepting it? Mike grimaced inwardly. If only she knew how unused he was to giving it, at least with the degree of emotional involvement with which he'd given it to her.

For reasons totally unrelated to why he needed to be here, involved in her life, Mike had the distinct feeling he was sliding into big trouble.

———

"Yes?"

The secretary duly noted the impatience beneath the clipped inquiry and pushed the inlaid-mahogany door to her boss's cavernous study-cum-sanctum farther ajar. Her manner and tone of voice turned respectfully deferential. "I know you asked not to be disturbed, but Mr. Simmons is on line one and insists on speaking with you."

"That's all right, Celia"—the response was brisk —"I'll take it. Make sure the door is closed on your way out."

Celia did.

"What is it, Paul? I've got that acquisition meeting with Berger in"—a glance was tossed at the crystal clock at the corner of the desk—"twenty minutes."

"Yes, I know. You can bet I wouldn't be disturbing you if this weren't important. Del Evans has become a problem."

"How?"

"I used him to put a wrap on the Connor thing as we agreed. Unfortunately, he got careless and decided to have himself a little fun with her before he grabbed her."

"And? I put you in charge of that operation. Is everything in control or isn't it? My time is too valuable to be wasted with trivialities."

"The authorities down there arrested him for rape."

The silver-plated ballpoint pen that had been tapping impatiently against the edge of the desk paused in midtap, then skittered across the desk's ink blotter. "Jesus Christ. Are our lawyers getting him out?"

"I have Andrews working on it. That son of a bitch's imminent release, however, is neither my primary concern nor the reason I called you. While Andrews was lining up his strings to pull, he discovered something interesting. Five years before Evans joined us, he was a sometime informant for the feds."

Heavy seconds ticked by. "Explain."

"I've already had the report compiled. For right now suffice it to say our soldier sang for them almost right up to the point before he joined us. Now that his stupidity has landed him on the tricky side of the law again, I frankly don't think he's a liability we can afford to retain."

"How long has he been in jail? And why wasn't I told things were getting out of control before this?"

"Less than a couple of weeks. And you weren't told because until this little tidbit showed up to skew the plan, things weren't out of control. We would have had Evans released in another week, tops. And as for Henry, I oversaw Evans's handling of him myself. He was expendable. The Connor woman is still within our reach and doesn't show any signs of going anywhere soon."

"I take it damage control for Evans has been initiated?"

Simmons absorbed the impatience and bristled. "Of course. Andrews is working with someone we know on the inside who can shut Del up, in case he's considering going back to his old ways."

"Easy words, Paul. The Connor abduction should have been easy too, shouldn't it?"

There was no graceful comeback that Simmons could make.

"I want it cleaned up within the week. The *week*, Paul. Do we understand each other?"

"Perfectly."

Two phone receivers clicked softly in their cradles.

———

Jail food sucked.

Royce Manners grimaced at the bland liquid in his bowl, then choked down another spoonful of his allotment of slop they called stew. If everything went according to plan, he wouldn't be eating it too much longer. The thought provided some consolation, and he smiled.

Like the model prisoner he was, he cleaned his bowl, finished every drop of his milk, and then neatly stacked his used dishes on the tray sitting beside him on his cot. He even gave his plastic spoon a last thorough lick to get rid of any nasty residue that might be offensive to the eye.

Smiling, he absently smoothed his hand across his full stomach, thinking of what a simple matter it had been to execute the setup that would finish Evans off.

They'd been in the recreation area watching television when Royce had nonchalantly started to peel the wrapper from the candy bar he saved from lunch. He knew Evans's eyes had been on him, knew, thanks to his visitor earlier that day, that the man had an absolute addiction to chocolate. So he'd drawn the process of eating the candy out, making it just tantalizing enough to snag and hold Evans's attention.

"You gonna finish that, man?" Evans had leaned forward, giving Manners a goofy smile.

Royce had paused, as if he hadn't been aware of Evans's interest. "You want it?" He'd held the remainder out, thinking of poison fruit and reflecting on how appropriately designed the method of Evans's destruction had been.

Evans had taken the candy, and Royce had watched him wrap it carefully back up, saving it for an after-lockdown treat. He thought of how unpleasant the lethally laced portion he'd carefully stopped just short of eating, per the wrapper markings he'd been instructed to heed, was going to be.

So now it was just a matter of time, and Royce didn't waste any more of it giving thought to who could have paid off whom to arrange to slip the poisoned candy to him. For that matter, he had questioned neither his own public defender's dismissal nor the mysterious arrival of the fancy rich lawyer dude who had arrived, taking the defender's place, and surprising everyone, including Royce, by behaving like Royce's long-lost friend.

All Royce cared to glean was that the works for this hit had been put into place long before the lawyer ever approached him. And for the reward of carrying it out, the lawyer would see to it the judicial process recognized its mistake in putting Royce Manners in jail and even wave good-bye as he was released.

He inhaled calmly and continued to recline on his back, supporting his bullet head with his blunt, laced fingers. He started to whistle. He even dozed, dreaming sporadically of the thick, juicy porterhouse steak he was going to eat just as fast as he could get his hands on it.

Yeah, he was really going to celebrate big on the day he got released.

Chapter

EIGHT

The phone was on its third ring before Julie really heard it. She felt for the television remote lying on the sofa cushion beside her, picked it up, and hit the mute button. She might as well have turned it off since she really hadn't heard much more of the news telecast beyond the story about Del Evans.

On the fourth ring she got up and walked over to the phone stand.

"Julie, you heard?"

"Yeah." She hadn't been anticipating Mike's concern but she was grateful. She needed it. She shook the phone cord out, dislodging it enough to pull across the room.

Tucking her feet beneath her, she settled down against the sofa. "That's some pedigree he carried, huh?"

Since it wasn't exactly news to Mike, he let the question pass.

"Why do you think he was murdered, Mike?"

Mike didn't like Julie's tone; it sounded too detached. "I'm coming over."

"No, you don't have to do that. I'm okay, really."

"I'll be there in a minute."

Julie waited for him to hang up first. After he had, she replaced the receiver and set the phone on the floor.

Why had Del Evans been poisoned in his cell? Despite the accidental death angle the department of corrections was trying to sell to the media, Julie didn't buy it. She'd spoken to Meg, who had interviewed corrections officials about the death as a regular part of her crime beat.

Officials had told her Evans had suffered an extreme allergic reaction to something he had eaten and, as a result, had died of anaphylactic shock. But media probings of unusual deaths were usually not shut down in so blatant a manner, and Meg had been shut down. Meg had confided to Julie that the abruptness with which she had been handled had frankly planted a notion in her head of foul play.

Which meant that if Meg's hunch was true, anyone who had managed to get to Evans inside a jail had to have done it as a result of some very deliberate planning and maybe even with some outside help.

Which meant one thing to Julie: Del Evans had been murdered, but that murder had more probably been a hit.

She lay on her back and rested one arm across her eyes. Which made Del Evans's motivation for attacking her on the beach the real issue for her, more so than his death.

That attack had to have been specifically motivated too; nothing the police had come up with had exclusively linked him to the area rapes. And so given that lack of conclusiveness, Del Evans's connection with her seemed to become something less than casual.

The heavy knocking on her door caught her attention. She pushed herself up, trying to fight the numb lethargy that had gripped her in the wake of this incident. When she answered her door, the sight of Mike helped make the fight marginally easier.

He edged past her, taking in her tense features as she let him by. Instead of taking a chair, he turned, folding his arms across his chest, observing her. She closed the door and stood looking at him, though she didn't really appear to be seeing him. When she raised her hands to rub her slender arms as if she were chilled, Mike moved.

Her vulnerability nudged aside his reluctance to hold her.

Julie stepped willingly into his embrace, lacking the strength just now to challenge her need to be held. Her arms went around his waist as he pulled her closer, inviting her to lean in to his strength.

Julie absorbed Mike's support for a bit, but when she eventually started to pull away, Mike let her. She surprised herself as well as him when she took his hand and led him to the sofa.

They sat down together, and Mike used his hard body as a supportive bulwark behind hers. He angled his position, making enough room for her to curl back against his chest and into the circle of his arms.

"He was coming after me, wasn't he?"

Mike hated the quiet fear that laced her statement. But he couldn't refute it, so he just tried to comfort. "Honey, we don't know that—"

"Yes," she interrupted him. "We do. That news report put it in perspective. It could be coincidence that a man tied so heavily to organized crime would suddenly show up in a town recently targeted by mob activity. It's just a bit too coincidental that he would also attack a woman who may have been a confidante of a man murdered for what he knew.''

''Well, be that as it may, the fact is, Del Evans didn't succeed in getting to you. You have to hold on to that.''

''But—''

''Hold on to it, honey.'' Mike hugged her closer.

Time passed and the shadows inside the room deepened. Neither really seemed to care enough to move away from the other. Julie sensed some bridge was silently being crossed in their relationship, and while it disquieted her, it also offered her a surprising amount of comfort.

Of what he was feeling, Mike didn't speak. But that he was feeling something similar became apparent to Julie through his continued silence and seeming ease at letting her rest in his arms.

At length she said, ''They're going to send others.''

Mike silently echoed Julie's hushed certainty and felt a hot lump of anger pool in his stomach. It burned like acid. ''I'm not going to let anyone get to you.''

Julie turned her head to look into his eyes. They were dark and fierce, and his determination touched her. He was declaring himself her protector. But as she'd learned once before in another lifetime, all the fierceness of a man's declaration couldn't change the fact that he was just a man.

She raised a hand to his cheek and smiled softly as she pulled away from him. Facing him, she drew both legs up onto the cushion and crossed them Indian style. She needed to talk but not, perhaps, exactly about what Mike expected.

"Why do you care?"

Mike's look turned guarded.

Julie smiled with a touch of melancholy. "You don't trust me. I've sensed that from the first."

She was right and she was wrong. "It's not that I don't trust you, Julie," Mike said. "It's just that I know the pitfalls of getting too close to someone it's my responsibility to protect."

"So what I am to you is a responsibility, a piece of the puzzle you're assembling to solve your case."

Now he'd hurt her. But because he was on shaky ground, he didn't quite know how to make it up.

"It's all right," Julie said, embarrassed that apparently she had miscalculated after all. She unfolded herself. "I understand." She moved away from him to walk over to the wide, unshaded picture window.

Mike knew he should have just let her. But when she kept her back to him and maintained her silence, his resolve wavered. When she leaned her slight weight in to the sill and rubbed her arms, again she looked forlorn, as if the weight of the world had settled upon her slender shoulders.

It was too much. It took a mere space of moments for Mike to reach her.

It took an equal amount of time for Julie to decide to reject the surrender that beckoned. Mike's touch on her arm was rendered no more substantial than a butterfly's kiss as she moved from his outstretched hand and turned to face him. It took a surprising amount of effort, but she made her voice as strong as her resolve.

"I told you once before, Mike, I can take care of myself. I also told you I appreciate your concern.

You don't have to worry that I'll ask you for any more than that."

"Dammit, Julie!"

"I'm out of my league in this mess, I know that. And so as a professional your expertise and protection is welcome. But don't confuse my appreciation as a need for pity."

She could make him feel lower than a worm quicker than anybody else he had ever known. "Why do you do that?" he demanded.

"What?"

"Shield yourself like that. You're not a hard case, but whenever I threaten to get close, you pull a shell of pride and false courage over yourself and dare me to penetrate it."

Maybe it was true. But she wasn't alone, because if she retreated, so did he. She thought of how moments ago he'd backed away from the intimacy he'd obviously been feeling. If he couldn't see that he'd done that, he wasn't ready for her answer.

"Don't try to psychoanalyze me, Mike. It isn't worth the effort. To quote someone else I once heard, there's nothing mysterious about me."

Maybe not. But she was fascinating to him in some way that he couldn't shake loose. The problem was, more and more he was starting to wonder if he really wanted to. And all at once, because the question was novel and confusing, Mike had to know if she was as cool as she appeared, or if she was being bombarded by like emotions.

"So," Julie said brightly—maybe too much so, judging from Mike's sharp look—"let's start thinking about Roy Bronson."

In two strides Mike was at Julie's side. "Screw Roy Bronson," he murmured before his lips took hers in a raw kiss, aching with unanswered questions and unwilling need.

Julie pressed against his shoulders, but in the seconds it took the heat of his lips to melt into hers, her resistance wavered. The force of his passion and the answering flicker of her own contributed, certainly. But to her distress, the certainty grew within her that the resistance she sought was less from Mike than from herself.

"Stop," she whispered, pushing him away.

"Why?" His voice was just as hushed, but he had to know this time because she wanted him too.

"I don't want to be responsible for what happens. Not again."

Though her answer was impassioned, he still had to strain to hear it. It so surprised him that this time when she pushed he let her go.

"Responsible? Julie, what are you talking about?"

She looked at him, distressed to feel tears come to her eyes.

He put his arms around her again. "Talk to me."

This time the embrace was without passion, but it was no less rife with intimacy. The sweetness of it suddenly rendered Julie weary of disavowing everything that was going on inside her.

"Seven years ago there was . . . someone I loved. He died because of me."

Mike stilled. Did she even realize she was comparing their situation to this other, which had involved a man she had loved? He wasn't sure how her words made him feel; he would analyze it later. All he knew now was that she needed to talk, so he held on.

"He thought I was vulnerable too, too ill equipped to cope with a situation we fell into on the

streets we grew up on. My mistake was in letting
him." She took a shuddery breath, the darkness she
had been living with for seven years brought for the
first time into the light. "It's why he's dead."

Though what Julie was saying was muffled against
Mike's shoulder, it was clearly audible. With clear
intuition he murmured, "Is that what you meant
that day about having given your pound of flesh?"

She drew back to look up at him, something in
her eyes unfathomable.

It was, he realized. "Come on, let's sit down."

She didn't protest being led to the sofa and she
didn't protest when he drew her down with him and
settled her again within the circle of his arms.

"Tell me," he said simply.

She couldn't without knowing one thing first.
"Why do you really want to know, Mike?"

*Because against everything I know to be my better
judgment, I care for you.* He knew that was what she
hoped, maybe needed to hear. But something deep
inside him, something that had been rooted in an
emotional vacuum as old as his childhood and
shaped by a lifetime of denial stayed the words in his
heart.

"I don't like to see you hurting." It was partial
truth even if it probably wasn't enough.

Julie turned her head to look at him. Her amber
eyes pierced into the darkness of his own. Mike
knew she was searching. What she found he didn't
know. But apparently it was enough because she
turned away from him, leaned back against his chest,
and began talking once more.

"His name was Adam Torres," she stated quietly.
"We were both eighteen, just out of school and de-
serving of our reputations as holy terrors. Adam was

from a broken home, and I . . ." Julie paused, not really ready after all to reveal quite so much. "My parents were dead," she said simply.

"Anyway," she continued, "neither of us had an easy time growing up. Adam was the youngest in his family, and I only had Aunt Peggy. Adam's mother was too busy blaming her kids for the fact that she had no life because she had to work to support them. Peggy was wonderful for me, but she entered relatively late into my childhood.

"I don't say all of this to suggest the proverbial sob story, I just say it to make you understand why both of us learned very early on to value self-sufficiency. It was probably because each of us recognized a maverick element in the other that we even gravitated toward each other and eventually loved."

She smiled, remembering. "Adam was a wild one. He used to blame it on his Hispanic blood and he'd teasingly accuse me of only wanting to hang out with him because I got a kick out of playing Pancho to his Cisco Kid. But that wasn't it. Adam took risks, and he had a temper, but he also had what most people who knew him didn't see. He had a good heart."

Mike felt Julie shift a little in his arms, trying to get a little more comfortable against him. It was a small gesture, but it pleased him somehow because it delicately underscored that she was here with him now, not with the ghost she was so painstakingly resurrecting.

He made an effort to tamp down his jealousy and, with his silence, urged her on.

"Neither or us had really made any plans about college or anything else substantial in our lives. It was enough in those days to be daring and in love. And then one day the ease of it all changed."

"How?" Mike prompted. For the first time in the recounting she seemed to hesitate.

"Adam got approached by some drug dealers to make a run, to pick up merchandise from Illinois and transport it back to Indiana. He wasn't a user. In fact, despite his other vices he always was adamant about staying away from the stuff. He'd seen it slowly kill his older brother. That had been all the lesson he needed."

"But he didn't walk away from that offer either," Mike guessed.

"No. He didn't walk away. He wanted to do it strictly for the money, he said. He told me it was maybe a two-, three-time deal at most. When it was over, he said, he'd have enough money to take us both out of the state to settle somewhere and make our own start together."

"On drug money?"

Again, Julie tossed him that unfathomable look, then she said with admirable honesty, "I was tempted. But I knew that no matter how easy that money could make things, I wouldn't be able to live with it in the end. And I wouldn't be able to live with the sort of man who could."

Mike studied her, gauging, reassessing the layers, and he came to realize something. No matter how much he'd told himself he admired her strength, he had on a very macho level been underestimating her depth.

From the first, her soft beauty and delicacy had aroused a very male urge to take over and protect. It had also caused him to make easy assumptions about the limitations of her strength.

He was hearing now testimony to what she had railed at him the other day following their encounter with Jimmy Sales. Sobered, he said, "And Adam, did you bring him around to sharing your view?"

"I knew one of the guys who had contacted him. He and Adam and I had been in school together, played together. We'd known him all our lives. And so I took it upon myself to pay him a visit to tell him to lay off Adam. He didn't listen.

"Instead, he knocked me around a little before he decided to let me leave. Just before he did, he told me to go see Adam so that he'd get the message not to send his women in the future to beg favors he wasn't man enough to ask for himself."

"Dammit, Julie." Mike's exclamation was quiet and more of sorrow than admonishment.

He wasn't surprised that her headstrong decision had been to rush in where angels feared to tread. But understanding didn't lessen his black rage for what she had suffered. "Did you go to the police?"

She shook her head. "I was too shocked and hurt and, let's face it, basically scared. Not only for myself but for Adam. I knew his temper, and I knew he wouldn't let it rest, and I knew if he heard about it on the streets before he heard about it from me, he'd try to retaliate before he stopped to think.

"So I did go to him, and I begged him to come with me to the police. He didn't listen. I'd seen him angry before, but never like that. When he saw what had been done to me, something at the core of him turned icy, unreachable . . ."

"And what?"

"And . . . what really hurt me was my realizing that in the wake of that mess, even the attack on me, it wasn't *us* that Adam was thinking about. He was thinking more about salvaging his reputation, aveng-ing his pride. It turned out that his reputation meant more to him than *us*, more than doing the right thing."

"Even so, you still didn't go to the police yourself, did you?"

"No." Julie's voice had dropped again nearly to a whisper. As close to her as he was, Mike still had to strain to hear it.

"He told me he couldn't be a man in his own eyes if he didn't retaliate. He told me if I couldn't understand that, I wasn't really his woman or even half the woman he thought I was.

"Don't worry," Mike heard her say and knew she had sensed his disgust with the guilt trip Adam Torres had laid on her. Her rueful laugh was tinged with bitterness.

"A part of me, even then, knew what he was saying was macho bullshit. But a deeper part of me"—a part long starved for the affirmation of having truly earned someone's love, she acknowledged—"still wanted Adam. So I said nothing, and I let him walk alone into a den of lions. Even as I let him walk, I knew he was going to a certain death I might have prevented."

"Adam caused his own death, Julie."

"Yes, I know that to an extent he did. I knew it then. But I also knew that if I hadn't been so needy, I probably could have saved his life all the same."

Mike digested that and everything else she hadn't said. What she hadn't needed to verbalize. It stunned him and even thrilled him. But he'd had no experience handling the degree of emotion Julie's story embodied, an emotion she was possibly on the brink of offering to him. The potential responsibility of it scared him.

She'd just revealed enough of herself to help him

understand why she was so quick to defend her independence. But she had no way of knowing she'd just defeated her own purpose in doing so. Even now he felt his need to protect her lodge even deeper inside him.

He dropped a light kiss on her shoulder. When she turned her head in surprise, tipping her misty gaze up to him, he transferred the caress to her lips.

The severing of the contact was leisurely and mutual, and when it was done, Julie's reaction was direct in its simplicity.

"I told you once before, Mike, I'm not looking for pity, I never have. The truth is, I could very easily start to care for you."

"I know. Honey, I know," he murmured, her stark honesty compelling him to offer the same. "But there are all sorts of reasons why it's not prudent, let alone wise."

"Yes. You've implied that before, though you won't explain." Julie pushed away from him and put enough distance between them so that she could squarely face him. "And you're not going to now."

No. How could he? And yet he was feeling a revelation of emotion too, and nothing would have pleased him better than to have been able to say more.

But he owed a dead man his silence. He owed his threatened mother the reasoning of his head over his heart. And that reasoning was saying that even though Julie in all likelihood hadn't set out to participate in a murder, she was still in some way presenting a block to its resolution. Maybe even a danger to innocents affected by it.

"Listen to me, Julie, and believe this because I'm being as honest with you as I can. If there are things I seem to hold back from you, it's because there are pieces to this Blakemore murder I need to understand first.

"I've been a cop a lot of years, and something indelible my experience has taught me is to side with discretion when it comes to things I absolutely don't know."

Julie nodded. "So says the cop. But what about the man, Mike? That's who I've been talking to. That's from whom I've got to know. What does the man say about us?"

He owed her candidness. But perhaps even more, he owed it to himself.

"The man cares, Julie. He definitely cares. But beyond that admission he's not certain how far he can take it."

Julie watched him, thinking, pondering, weighing. "Then if that's all I can get, I'm willing to take it for now."

Mike nodded slowly, wondering at the full extent of what had just passed between them. And because he was unsure, as so often was becoming the case with this woman, he bent his head. Perhaps if he avoided looking at her, he could regain some equilibrium from the confusion her clear gaze inspired.

He hadn't even realized he'd lifted his hand in a habitual gesture of agitation to rub the back of his neck until he felt hers catch it. His slightly startled gaze flew to hers, and he swallowed when he saw the soft patience that waited there. He swallowed again when he realized what her touch and that gentle look meant.

As he had done for her earlier, she held on.

Chapter
NINE

Julie became aware of the morning light first. It bathed her closed eyelids in a pale warm glow. She lay against her pillows and let it wash over her for a deliciously relaxed moment, letting that uniquely still quality that was very early morning engulf her.

The freshness of it, the possibilities inherent in the day, magnified the good feelings still coursing through her from last night. She understood that what she and Mike had discovered about each other was still very sketchy. She had no illusions about that. But the fact that they had revealed themselves at all, given the intensely private people they both were, still amazed her.

And warmed her.

She opened her eyes and got out of bed, refusing for this morning at least to dissect. What she was feeling was too new, and she didn't want to disturb it just yet. Adam had been her first love, yes, and there had been other relationships in the wake of what she had found with him. But this thing with Mike was so strong, so elemental, that she knew with an almost scary certainty it was edging into a category all its own.

At base, she was no more comfortable with it than he. But neither was she willing to use it to make that discomfort a precedent in her life for backing away from what challenged her. For now, she was content to let instinct be her watchword and to let fate guide her where it would.

That was why she wasn't really surprised to see Mike lounging on her stretch of beach down by the edge of the lake when she walked out onto her porch thirty minutes later. No one else was around to share the morning yet. And when he looked over his shoulder, obviously having heard the screen door slap the wood of the doorframe behind her, she knew he too had been waiting.

She steadied her coffee mug in both hands and made her way across the yard and down to the beach toward him.

He watched her approach, enjoying the short, funky fit of her summer-white cotton shorts, the long brown length of her slender legs extending beneath them, the slouchy seductiveness of the over-size white T-shirt she had tucked in loosely at her waist. When she got close enough, he scooted over in the sand, making plain his desire that she sit close.

Julie nodded at him over the rim of her mug, smiled slightly, and complied.

For a while neither spoke; both were content with each other's silence, with each other's willingness to let the timeless conversation between the morning sun and the wind-kissed water provide the communication for them.

Gradually Julie finished her coffee and set her mug down in the sand. Stretching her legs out before her, she leaned back a little, bracing herself on both hands. She kept her gaze focused out over the water, declining to verbally break this communion with Mike even after she felt his big hand warmly smooth the back of her own.

"Good morning," he said quietly.

Julie smiled. That was simple enough. Prosaic even. But they both knew the greeting held a wealth of meaning that rendered it more than simple.

She looked at him, letting her eyes drift over his handsome features, noting that the shadow along his jaw had somewhere along the way turned into a full-fledged, neatly trimmed beard. It added a dimension of attractive toughness to an already strong face. Feeling a little shiver of pure feminine reaction, she smiled again straight into his eyes.

Mike got the distinct impression she wanted to touch him. And as her light eyes said things to his, things last night's exchanges now made it impossible for him to resist, he felt his heart stumble and realized she already had.

He wanted suddenly all at once to run and to be near her. His solitary reflections deep into last night had brought home with exhausting clarity the habit he'd made of choosing the former. He'd wondered, as he'd spiraled closer to sleep, if with her he dared sample the latter.

"What are you going to do today?" Mike's question was hushed. As he waited for her answer, he shifted his hand, encouraging her to turn her palm up against his. She did, and again the contact went straight to his heart. He knew that wherever she did, wherever she went, he just wanted to be with her.

It was a startling revelation for a man of his self-containment.

"I don't know, I thought I might go here and there, nowhere. You know." Julie's voice was as subdued as his, her attention as preoccupied by what their cautious hearts were saying.

"Then I have a suggestion," Mike ventured.

"What?"

"Let's do it together."

Julie looked up from their joined hands and saw the gentle smile that curved his well-formed lips.

"Hmm, is that a proposition, Mr. Quinn?" she offered teasingly.

Mike's smile chilled fractionally, her address of him reminding him uncomfortably of one of the lies he was by necessity perpetrating with her. But then he remembered that for today, by his own personal decree, that was all part of something he was distancing far from this moment, from this day. His answer was a gently off-center leer.

"You might say that, sweetheart. Are you up to it?"

"I think I can handle it," she said, pushing herself to her feet. She waited for him to do the same before asking casually, "You up to a little exploring?"

He was up to anything if she came along with the deal. But since he wasn't openly ready to go quite that far, he answered with soft congeniality, "Yes."

"Good. You might want to change those sandals for walking shoes." At his amused look she guessed what he probably thought she was suggesting. "No, I'm not planning on walking you all around and across the town. But I do have a destination in mind that's more conducive to sneakers."

"I trust you." Mike laughed, suddenly feeling younger than he'd felt in years. An adventure was pending, and not just of the tourist kind. "I'll meet you at your house in thirty minutes?"

"Deal." Julie watched him walk away, noting how the long, tough muscles in his brown, hair-dusted legs shifted impressively with each powerful stride. Again her heart fluttered, and she laughed aloud for the sheer joy of being young and alive and, if not in love, definitely on the brink of something. Though she'd come close, she suddenly realized with perfect clarity that she'd never quite felt this way before.

Julie drove them west of their stretch of beach, though she didn't really take them far from the vicinity. Mike noted with interest how the long tree-shaded state road she selected, barren on either side except for an abundance of marram grass, finally emptied into greener grounds. They hosted a rambling chaletlike structure.

As Julie headed into the already packed parking lot, Mike caught the adjoining freestanding marquee and saw they had pulled into the visitor and tourist center for the Indiana Dunes National Lakeshore. He didn't know exactly what they were in for, but he appreciated her advice that had caused him to change not only into Top-Siders but also comfortable, well-worn jeans.

They got out of the car, and Mike hung back long enough to take advantage of the view Julie offered. She had changed into jeans herself, and if the shorts did great things for her legs and posterior, the jeans, he thought with a private smile, did something no less than criminal.

Julie looked back over her shoulder to see what was taking him so long. From her puzzled exasperation Mike could tell she was oblivious to the scrutiny, and it pleased him in an entirely male way to have that private little secret from her.

Inside were a gift shop, a mini movie theater, and booths of maps and souvenirs and guide books typical of visitor centers everywhere. But Mike quickly decided that being with Julie made an activity that should have been only pleasantly mundane into something exciting and a little special.

By mutual consent, they became tourists for the day. Julie admitted she hadn't toured the park since she was a child, and Mike was glad that she could share at least a small sense of his first-time impressions.

They saw a fifteen-minute movie that gave the history of the dunes and its wildlife. Then they struck out with a sizable crowd of students and families with fretting children on the next leg of the tour program, a self-guided walking tour.

Ten minutes into the wooded walk, they were ascending a particularly steep incline along a narrow column of stone steps when Julie said, "You aren't bored, are you?"

Mike draped his arm across her shoulders and pulled her close. Their hips bumped companionably as they climbed.

"Not in the least, honey. I'm having a wonderful time."

Julie had been half prepared for him to respond with a degree of sarcasm or maybe polite tolerance. She was relieved when he didn't, happy that she wasn't enjoying this simple pleasure alone.

At some point they deviated from the others and drove a short distance to Mount Baldy, which boasted, according to the film, the reputation of being the largest living dune along the lakeshore.

At its base they paused and looked up at its impressive height, letting the crowd move and chatter around them.

"One thing about this I do remember is that when I was a kid, it used to be the thing to do to race to the top." She slanted him a challenging look. "You interested, Quinn?"

Mike dropped a quick kiss to her mouth. Before Julie knew what he was about, he murmured, "Go!"

He was already half a dozen strides ahead before she recovered and moved. His longer legs and superior conditioning predetermined the outcome, but Julie was amused all the same when he paused just short of the summit to let her regain some face by closing the distance.

When she was within a hairbreadth of him, he reached his hand out to her. Julie wasn't too proud to take it, and as he hauled her close to him, she breathed in deeply, trying to get her breath.

Mike pulled her against him, aligning her back to his front. He wrapped his arms around her trim midriff.

"Look at that," he breathed, resting his chin on her head, enjoying the feel of her pressed snugly against him.

Julie did. With an awesome expanse of Lake Michigan undulating before her, the shifting sands of a majestic windswept dune beneath her feet, and the strong arms of this surprisingly whimsical Mike holding her, Julie knew she had never experienced anything quite as lovely.

She didn't want to fall in love, but she feared that was exactly what was happening.

"Mike," she murmured once, not really looking for a response, just needing to say his name.

All the same, a response was what she got. Mike slowly turned her, taking care to hold her just as close. When she was forced by the position of their bodies to look up, he took advantage of her imbalance to pull her even tighter against him. And at the soft touch of his lips Julie slid her arms around him and she kissed him back just as languidly, letting her senses swim, letting her eyes close.

Mike shifted his head, changing the angle and depth of the kiss, and Julie felt herself melting even further into his embrace. The public venue of their surroundings kept the contact outwardly chaste, yet inside Julie was starting to heat. She could tell by the subtle tension invading Mike's body that she wasn't alone.

When by mutual consent, a simultaneous bid for prudence, they pulled slowly apart, they were startled by the small smattering of applause that greeted their descent back to earth.

Mike took Julie's hand and offered, for the delectation of the surrounding indulgent gazes, a slight, mocking bow. Julie punched him lightly on the shoulder and ducked her head in sudden embarrassment. Scattered laughter erupted again, and Julie pulled at Mike, telling him in a playful murmur, "Come on, mister. Instead of providing the show, why don't we pay for one."

Mike laughed and fell in step beside her, keeping one possessive hand on a gently rounded hip.

In town, they headed toward a cinema and scanned the selections, finally agreeing to sit in on a summer-weight slapstick comedy. By the time they'd waited for a tub of popcorn to be buttered to Mike's satisfaction, collected their sodas, and taken their seats, they were five minutes late. Under other circumstances Julie would have been annoyed, but she found herself pleasantly indulgent of this man and yet another of his unexpected little quirks.

As she reached across his lap to take another handful of the delicious buttery food, she laughed at some inane sightgag on the screen and reflected that there was something decidedly endearing about such a big, strong man who took his junk food so seriously.

By the time they walked out of the movie, it was late afternoon.

Julie said, "Can we make one more stop before we go home?"

"Where are you going to drag me now?" He chuckled, letting her know he really didn't mind at all.

"I have a store I want to hit at the mall. And afterward I've decided to make you dinner since you've been such a good sport all day."

Mike grinned. "Deal." It was amazing, he thought, how many women one could be with over the course of a lifetime and still never really know the quiet joy of genuine companionship until a connection was made with the right one.

Julie was having much the same sorts of thoughts. No doubt that was why her mood turned sentimental when they entered the record shop she sought. On impulse she picked up a cassette disk filled with a particularly bluesy selection of old Billie Holiday classics, then made her usual rounds through the alternative music bins. While she browsed, she noted with interest that Mike wandered over to an area stocked with classic rhythm-and-blues CDs.

They met at the cash register, made their purchases, and left the mall to head home.

When they got to Julie's place, she invited Mike to make himself at home while she started dinner.

He wandered here and there in the living room, glancing at the bookshelves, studying the pictures on the mantel, wishing all the while he was at her own place so that he could collect a more intimate insight into her private side.

When she came out of the kitchen, she carried two glasses of white wine, one of which she handed to Mike.

"Let's make a toast," she suggested. "To a great day and a new beginning toward friendship."

"Let's make a truer toast," Mike countered. "To a great day and to an equally great discovery that no matter what, the least we can be is friends."

Julie's gaze was pensive as she raised her glass. He'd told her only yesterday that beyond a certain point he wasn't willing to go. She used that now to temper her leaping response to his proffered words. Touching her glass delicately to his, she smiled and murmured, "Cheers."

The evening was only slightly cool, but Julie impulsively lit a fire in the fireplace anyway, knowing the open circulation through the house would keep the temperature down and the gesture atmospheric.

Mike watched her and smiled indulgently, understanding the romantic impulse that drove her, wondering idly where it might lead before the evening was through.

When the fire was ignited, Julie made herself comfortable on the floor, bracing her back against the sofa. Mike sat in an adjoining chair and sipped his wine, enjoying the nondemanding peace of the moment. With other women this same sort of mood had been more calculated, more knowing. The easy sensation he was enjoying now was rare.

He liked it immensely.

"Tell me about yourself, Mike; you never really have. Do you have family?"

He felt the first twinges of tension intrude on this otherwise effortless day, threatening to burst his bubble. He sighed.

"I don't have siblings, if that's what you mean. My father is dead."

"And your mother?"

"Is a very important lady back in Chicago, I suppose. She's the owner of a very pricey chain of import/export ventures."

Julie was intrigued by the way he categorized his closest living relative by what she did, not by what she was to him. "Are you close?"

"Enough," Mike answered. He stared into the flames, thinking of the gully that evasion encompassed. He raised his glass, found it empty, and set it down on the table at his elbow.

"Here, I'll get you a refill." Julie started to rise.

"No, that's okay. I can wait for dinner."

Julie nodded and settled back down. "So I already know something about what motivates the cop. Tell me a little about what shaped the man beneath the badge."

Distinctly uncomfortable with the turn of conversation, Mike reached for a little flippancy. "Does my manner suggest to you, child, that I was born in the proverbial barn?"

At least as well versed in deflection as he, Julie kept her tone light but her focus serious. Mike's dodging of what should have been a simple topic only whetted her curiosity.

"Far from it," she said. He must have caught something in her tone because he threw her a look that was just the slightest bit sharp.

"If you really want to know, were I to take a guess, I would venture to say that either you're on the take or you have been somewhat to the manner born."

"Well, I sure as hell am not on the take," Mike said, bristling a little.

"No, Michael, I never seriously considered for a moment that you were." She lifted her glass. "Which brings us to option two."

"And upon what basis have you selected that option?"

"Your car, for one thing. Somehow I don't think Jaguars fall within the salary range of any cop I ever heard of. Your clothes, for another. They're casual enough, but their cut and quality are hardly inexpensive. And, as I mentioned once before, the cost of living here is hardly cheap."

A corner of Mike's mouth quirked with the barest humor. "All right, I didn't starve growing up. What else?"

Julie debated about how far she should push. Mike was a proud man and, despite his easygoing good humor throughout the day, past encounters she'd shared with him, little things he'd said, reminded her he was also a guarded one. Because he was, she guessed he wouldn't take too kindly to her continued third degree. She was thinking about how to proceed when she was literally saved by the bell.

"That's the timer on the microwave," she said, unfolding herself. "I'll be right back."

"No, wait," Mike said, rising himself, "I'll come and help."

Julie remembered what had happened the last time he had invaded her kitchen. Involuntarily she shivered but managed to say evenly enough, "Fine. You put together the salad, and we'll get it done twice as fast."

They worked side by side. Mike prepared the greens while Julie pulled chicken breasts from the oven and topped them with an aromatic, heated wine sauce. She popped two fat potatoes into the oven next, and by the time she and Mike had finished preparing the table and setting out the food, they were done.

"Lord, girl," he said between bites a few minutes later, "you ever think of hiring yourself out?"

Julie smiled at the compliment and forked off a portion of her potato. "The real thanks go to Aunt Peggy. She taught me all the tricks I know."

"Not your mom, huh?"

Now it was Julie's turn to clam up. "No," she answered quietly, "not my mother."

Mike paused in his chewing to look up, wanting to know what he'd said to take away her smile. "I'm sorry, I've said something wrong."

Julie finished chewing and glanced briefly across the table, telling herself to get it together. "No, you didn't." She willed her smile and her good humor back into place. "In fact you've been saying the right things all day."

"Oh, yeah?" Mike raised his napkin to his mouth. "Like what?"

Julie got up and stacked her plate with his. She took them both to the sink and then turned to him and said softly, "I would suggest we carry this conversation back to the living room."

All of Mike's senses came to attention at her seductive inflection. He followed.

She walked over to the CD player, inserted one of the Billie Holiday disks she had purchased, and then punched up the fire until it was steadily burning again. This time when she seated herself on the sofa before the softly shifting flames, Mike followed her.

When he took her in his arms, she didn't protest, and he sighed, allowing himself free reign to finally kiss her the way he'd been wanting to do all day.

Julie let herself be pressed back into the cushions. When she felt Mike's warm, hungry lips parting hers, she allowed it. His tongue was a hungry marauder, but after the first insistent kiss it gentled and coaxed hers into play with a finesse that left her gasping.

Julie sighed as his mouth casually left hers to trail a leisurely path of nibbling kisses down her throat. He stopped at the top of the soft row of lace that edged the scooped neckline of her cotton camisole.

Julie was half reclining beneath him, luxuriating in the feel of his hands on her body, in their delicate caress of her breasts, when she felt his hands still on the pearl buttons across her chest. He unfastened them one by one. When he gently parted the fabric, baring her soft flesh to his gaze, her breath suspended. When his hands shifted once more, this time to anchor themselves in her hair, the air escaped her lungs in a shallow rush.

She read the question in his soul-deep eyes, could feel the growing evidence of his need pressing low against her stomach.

She wanted him, but now that he was giving her time to think, she started to question the wisdom of giving in to her desire. They were still the same people, and though today they'd given each other a glimpse of how they could be together, Julie knew that when the sun rose in the morning their fundamental conflicts would remain.

"Mike—" she began, not even sure if her head was really going to win out over her heart, when for the second time that evening she was saved by the proverbial bell. It was the phone.

Her editor was the only one who had the number to the beach house, and if Hank was calling her, it had to be urgent.

Mike read the cooling in her eyes, felt it in her body, and let her up. Beneath his frustration was a niggling sense of relief. He'd been rushing headlong in a direction his saner self was reminding him he wasn't at all sure he really wanted to go.

"That's all right, Hank, he and I are old acquaintances, remember? I know the number."

Mike listened to Julie as she stood across the room from him looking decidedly grim. She had fastened her camisole, and now she depressed the button on the receiver that severed her connection. She immediately started to press in another set of numbers.

Watching her intense concentration, Mike felt his professional instinct snap to full alert.

"Where is it?" Julie yanked open the drawer to the phone stand and felt around until she pulled out a pen and pad of paper. She jotted something down then hung up.

"What?" Mike was on his feet.

"There's been a gang shooting. Some seniors at a neighboring retirement home close by have been hit. One is already dead."

"Are you the first to know it?" Mike thought of the other crime scoops she had been on top of before other reporters had even had the chance to get close.

"Probably." Julie looked across the room at Mike, into his eyes. She didn't have to see an essential part of him pulling back; she could feel it. "Yes, this"— she gestured at the phone—"was another tip, just like all the rest. Too late to save lives, but right in the nick of time to get me to the scene to mop up."

"Well, this time you aren't going to the scene alone, I'm coming with you."

"So you can keep an eye on me?" Julie knew she snapped, but she hated the subtle mistrust that was seeping back into Mike's demeanor just as she hated the defensiveness she felt she needed to counter it.

"Whatever," Mike said noncommittally. "Come on."

It was literally a bloody mess. Three teens were dead, one old man's body was being transferred to a waiting body bag, and several other senior citizens were standing around badly shaken.

Julie swallowed the nausea that rose inside her at the thought of all the senseless waste, always the senseless waste. But that was why she was here, to profile it, to spotlight it, to make it live in all its senseless brutality for those who ignored it out of fear or dispassionately viewed it through a glaze of insensitivity.

Taking out her handheld recorder, Julie started doing her job.

And Mike started doing his. He watched the crowd in general and the crowd around Julie in particular. He was looking for a lingering glance, an out-of-place concentration of interest not on the scene of violence but on the reporter who covered it.

Who this mysterious informant of hers was was something Mike wanted to know. His gut hunch was that if he could discover his identity, he could also discover his reason for continuing to string Julie along. He suspected it had little to do with the perverse kick Julie seemed convinced it gave him to play on her emotions and sense of scruples. He suspected it had more to do with the deaths of Phillip Blakemore, Pete Henry, and now Del Evans.

Mike's gaze drifted to his left. A casually dressed middle-aged man was separating himself from the crowd, making his way toward Julie's back. He wore an intense expression of concentration, and as he moved, Mike found himself moving too. Automatically he reached for his gun, belatedly realized he didn't have it, and cursed.

The danger signal was sounding loud in Mike's head, and by the time he reached the man, the man was less than a foot away from Julie. Snaking out a grasping hand, Mike was able to intercept the man by grabbing hold of his collar and yanking him off his course.

A couple of people gave the two startled looks and backed off as Mike dragged the man away from the mob.

"Hey, what the hell is the matter with you?" the man squeaked.

"What the hell is the matter with you? You get a kick out of stalking lady reporters?" Mike demanded. His tone was hard and uncompromising and he gave the man a little shake for emphasis. *"Talk!"*

Clearly thinking he had been grabbed by a lunatic, the man glared at him. "I saw two of the kids who ran away, that's all. That's all I wanted to tell her!"

"Why not the cops?" The man hesitated, turning his head to look at the media hullabaloo just now arriving. Julie was snapping off her recorder and closing her notebook. Mike shook the man again, snapping his attention back around to him.

"The cops already got what they need. I just thought—"

"You could get your name in the paper," Mike said with dawning disgust. "You damned parasite. Skitter back to your hole before I kick you there."

The man started to back away, but before he had backed completely out of sight, he gave Mike a lingering, sulky, mean-spirited look.

"Jesus Christ," Mike muttered.

"Who was that?" Julie wanted to know as she came over to his side.

"Slime," Mike answered briefly. "You get what you need?"

"Yeah, I got it. Let's go."

"Yeah, let's. I've got something I want to run by you, and I already have a feeling you're not going to like it."

Julie looked at him, trying to read his closed expression. "Well, if it's another lecture, odds say you're probably right."

"Odds say you'd better listen to me or, as that wonderfully succinct little saying goes, your ass could be grass, sweetheart."

Chapter

TEN

"I think you ought to start letting this source of yours pass his tips on to someone else."

Julie dropped her purse onto her aunt's living room coffee table and faced Mike, her hands on her hips. "*You* think? And why is that?"

"Because every time you light out of your office, your house, or wherever the hell else he manages to track you down, you're setting yourself up as a target, lady. That's why."

"He doesn't track me down, and he didn't this time. My editor took a message and 'tracked me down,' if you'll recall. But besides that minor point, I'm guessing you have some other tangible reason for advising me to back away from him?"

Mike's face hardened. "Some creep came rushing almost within spitting distance of you today. Luckily he wasn't your friend, slash, a psycho; he was just a glory junkie. The point is, if he had been a psycho and nobody had been with you, watching out for a nut like him, you could have been hurt. Your editor would have only known you were on some hot news trail. But neither he nor anybody else would have known where that trail was, which means nobody would have been able to back you up in a situation you knew beforehand could be volatile."

"Nothing has ever happened to me—"

"Whenever you go storming off with your informant's wink and smile to these crime scenes, you willingly stick your neck out, plain and simple. Just to carry out your little journalistic crusades."

The possible dangers of what she did occurred to Julie frequently, but for her own reasons she always refused to dwell on it. And so instead of blowing up at Mike now, she turned pensive and walked past him into the kitchen.

Mike found her getting a glass of water. He'd expected more resistance, more of a fight. He was relieved she'd been thinking enough not to give it to him, but her subdued restraint in the face of his censure disturbed him.

"So why do you?" he asked, leaning a hip against the sink where she stood.

Julie set down her glass. "Do what?" She looked at him. "You do that a lot, you know, sidle up to your point in half sentences."

Mike was undeterred. "Let this guy manipulate you? It has to be for more than the sake of a good story."

"How do you know? Maybe that's precisely why I do it, for the sake of a good story."

Mike just looked at her.

She sighed and walked away from him to sit down at the kitchen table. A fatigue of spirit descended upon her, much as it had the night before when she'd debated whether or not to speak of Adam.

"I do it because I have to, that's all," she said. "But since your mind seems prone to seek the more

Machiavellian cause for things, you probably wouldn't understand."

Joining her, Mike sat too and folded his hands in front of him. "Try me."

Julie looked up, wishing there was some way she could avoid this particular conversation. She'd been suppressing the sense of guilt that drove her for years. It would be infinitely more comfortable to go on doing it, but she knew she had reached a point in her relationship with Mike that demanded more frankness from her.

"I do it because I can. People in our town, in our society, need more than the knowledge of the ugliness that surrounds them. They need to taste, hear, see, feel it. If they don't, the meanness out there just goes on unchecked, and as a society we never advance. We never acquire a frame of reference for our fears, and it becomes increasingly easy to lose sight of the evil we need to guard against."

She leaned forward, wanting, needing, to make him understand. "For so many, life isn't a pretty, neat little package they can unwrap at leisure and enjoy like a box of candy.

"I can hold a mirror up to those things because I've been blessed with a facility for words and an intelligence to use them."

Her sincerity was as plain as her passion. Mike thought of how it was the same winning combination that made her newswriting so evocative. Yet she was uncomfortable bearing these inner thoughts to him. She'd done it only because he had asked it of her. More than his respect, he felt his affection for her go up another notch.

But he still sensed he hadn't really gotten to the core of his primary question.

"But why *you*, Julianna Connor? You've offered me an explanation, but somehow I still don't think I've gotten the reason."

Julie looked away.

Mike studied her, then ventured, "It has more to do with the woman behind the reporter, doesn't it? With that 'holy terror' you mentioned once before."

Julie's laugh was abrupt. "No, Mike, I'm not an ex-juvenile delinquent trying to make good. Try again."

"I am trying, I'm trying to understand you," he answered quietly. Her wall was going back up with a vengeance, but now that Mike had had a solid glimpse behind it, he was unruffled and greatly intrigued.

"All right. You want to know why I put my neck on the line to do my job? I'll tell you. The reason is, I owe it to myself, but maybe even more importantly, I owe it to this community."

She pushed away from the table and headed back through the dining room into the living room. When Mike found her sitting on the floor with her back against the sofa, she seemed to be a hundred miles away. Her knees were pulled up against her chest, and her absent gaze was riveted on the now-darkened fireplace, whose ashes had gone cold.

Although he wanted to take her in his arms, he sensed her greater need now was for distance. So he sat on the end of the sofa apart from her.

"I can't imagine your having committed some grievance so grim that you're tied to this town to do penance." And as he said the words to her, he acknowledged what his heart had come to terms with long ago.

Somehow Julie Connor was a victim here, not of

her own making and certainly not of the spirit. Rather, she, like him, was caught in some impenetrable web of intrigue. But the difference in their situations was what concerned Mike most, because whereas he was searching primarily for enlightenment that would help him solve a crime, Julie was searching for something a lot more essential to herself.

Survival, maybe. That that survival could be figurative as well as literal had not really occurred to him until now. Now that it had, his need to know why was as imperative as his increasing need to be with her. He couldn't shake either.

"I wasn't as fortunate as you when I was born." Julie spoke without bitterness or ire, just reciting the facts.

"My parents weren't rich, and my circumstances weren't cushioned. I wasn't more than a baby when they died. But from all my childhood memories and the gaps that have since been filled in about them for me by the people who knew them, I've learned that when they died, they weren't necessarily missed.

"They were grifters who got through life using anything and anyone they could in order to fashion for themselves their vision of the high life. By the time I was born, they had their routine down. A child, apparently, was nothing more than a detriment to the plan."

"Detriment?"

For the first time, Julie turned her head to look at him; her study, like her words, was detached. "Do I have to spell it out, Mike? You're a big, bad cop well versed in the ways of the world. Surely you can read between the lines I'm giving you. No? Well, let me help you understand."

"Julie, don't," Mike said. Whatever he'd thought he was asking, he hadn't anticipated this. Now that he had her talking, he hated hearing her pain.

"They ignored me," she said, "and when the couldn't, they lashed out at me, repeatedly." What she didn't tell Mike was that it had taken another attack of brutality from Del Evans to act as the catalyst to open the locked drawer of memories she had successfully hidden from herself for most of her twenty-six years.

"They earned a reputation for being trash, and naturally as their little girl the same reputation, instead of a helping hand, was extended to me. When Peggy came along and insisted on forging the relationship she had missed with her sister as well as with the niece she had never met, I was in heaven. Mama didn't care about that, but since Peggy's doorstep was a convenient drop for me, Mama didn't disregard her completely.

"When she and Daddy were finally killed one night in a drunken car accident, I was glad." Again she turned her gaze back to the empty grate. "I know that admission should make me ashamed, but it doesn't. I was glad."

Mike heard what she was saying and regretted the pain she had suffered as a child. But her story was also causing him to look inward into a parallel, sheltered recess of his own.

No, his parents hadn't been abusive drunks. But they had nurtured a virulent and abiding hatred for each other. What was worse, they hadn't been above shamelessly pulling their only child apart between them as a frequent way to score points.

He'd forgotten the exact age at which he'd finally learned to dissociate himself from their corrosive arguments; what he did know was that no child should ever be forced to equate survival and emotional isolation at an age that young.

How often had he turned to his mother, seeking some outward expression of love, and later to his father to garner some acknowledgment of the apology that routinely lurked in his eyes? At least, Mike recalled ruefully, as often as he had been rebuffed by both and, as always, compelled to find answers that he could live with on his own.

In fact, though his mother used to tease him about it facetiously, she could, Mike often thought, cheerfully have killed his father and never lost a moment's sleep within the battlefield of their home. He supposed his father's desertion proved that at the time he'd felt pretty much the same way.

He was so lost in thought that Julie's next words startled him slightly.

"Of course, someone like you probably can't understand what I'm saying. Just suffice it to say, I know where I've come from, and because of it I know where my social obligation lies."

In atoning for the sins of her parents? Perhaps at any cost? That was crazy, but it was obviously a point of huge vulnerability for Julie, and Mike doubted if he could even begin to make her see it. There was one thing, however, that maybe he could make her see.

"I can understand more than you think, Julie, and I think there's a particular point you should consider."

"Which is?" Julie murmured.

"This guy, this source, could be tied to the Blakemore murder. And he could be using you."

Julie turned sideways to face him, lowering her knees to the floor.

"We still don't know what his motives are," Mike continued gently, "but I think your own motives place you in a very vulnerable position to be manipulated by him."

"That is ridiculous," she said, violently resenting the suggestion of his assessment. "I am not an emotional weakling, Mike, and I'm certainly not stupid."

She was upset. He didn't blame her; what he had suggested was disturbing. But because he could see a little more objectively into Julie's vulnerability, and because he was genuinely unwilling to minimize any new sensitivity to danger he might have alerted her to, he didn't back down. He merely decided that for the time being a change of subject was prudent and needed.

"I want to start looking at Roy Bronson tomorrow. As I said before, I'm betting he has something pertinent he can tell us, and I'm ready to start working on him to get it."

Julie wasn't quite ready to let the previous conversation go, but on another level neither was she equipped right now to pursue it.

"How?" she asked, making a conscious effort to shift her concentration into another gear.

"I'd like for you to do a check into his business connections and acquaintances, past and present. Let's see if we can't spot at least a paper trail that might lead to something interesting."

Julie thought about it and nodded. "Sounds like that should make for a busy day. You'll be wanting to head home to get some sleep."

Mike looked at Julie, thinking of events that had

transpired earlier in the evening, thinking that if reality had not intruded upon their decision to carve out a space of their own little world, the rest of this night might have turned out very differently.

With more than a little regret, he rose and walked to the door. Julie sat where she was, watching him.

"I'll be in touch," he said softly.

Julie let him get the front door open and his hand on the screen door before the turmoil of her emotions urged her to give in to impulse just once more.

She got smoothly to her feet and made her way over to Mike, feeling hesitant yet determined. Mike appeared to regard her approach just as hesitantly. When she reached his side, she clasped her hands at her waist and rose on tiptoe.

The light kiss she placed on his cheek was, she knew, less than they both wanted. But too much had transpired in the course of the day.

She saw the smile that never really reached beyond his eyes; nevertheless, it was enough. She released a slow sigh of relief, knowing he understood, feeling that with his quiet acquiescence it was all right.

"Bye, honey," he murmured, and then he walked out into the night.

The next two days suggested what Julie had pointed out once before and Mike had hoped wouldn't be the case. Roy Bronson seemed to be a small businessman whose professional and private dealings were strictly legitimate.

It was on the third day that Julie and Mike got

lucky. Julie was doing a check, per Mike's suggestion, into small business ventures that had been established within five years of Phillip Blakemore's relocation from Chicago to Michigan City. She wasn't necessarily expecting to find anything significant and, in fact, had suggested to Mike that they combine the check with another that took a look into Blakemore's professional connections in Chicago.

Mike was willing, but the Chicago connection was put on hold when they discovered through local real estate records that within a year of his arrival in Michigan City, Blakemore had purchased a commercial property with which to create a modest antiques dealership called Charles Field & Co.

The business still existed, and Julie decided to visit there, posing as a customer. Curious to know whether "Charles Field" was a business front or a real live person, she asked to speak with Mr. Field and was informed that he was out of the country indefinitely and, unfortunately, unreachable. The evasion kicked Julie's professional curiosity into overdrive.

She next called in a favor from a friend who worked for the Internal Revenue Service and discovered that the dealership was, in fact, a partnership. However, the name appearing legally along with Phillip Blakemore's was not Charles Field.

It was Roy Bronson.

Additionally, Julie was told that the partnership had been a limited one, leaving Bronson free to manage the store's daily operations while Blakemore primarily contributed capital and little else. Upon dissolution of the partnership, Bronson had turned management over to the shop's current manager.

Given Bronson's murky background, Julie and Mike easily agreed that Bronson had created the pretense because, quite simply, he had something to hide. What they specifically wanted to know was why the eminently upstanding Phillip Blakemore would have entered into a professional association with Bronson, who was something of an unknown element even back then.

"I'll go talk to him," Julie told Mike. It was early evening, and they were at his place sharing a pot of chili. "I've got a plausible in. I'll simply explain to him that I'm doing a follow-up profile of Phillip Blakemore that requires more in-depth coverage of the man behind the attorney.

"I'll tell him that through land records I've discovered Blakemore started his professional life here in Indiana as an antiques dealer. I'll say that in light of that I'm approaching him because the dealership's present manager has informed me that he was the store's first manager. As such, and as an early acquaintance of Blakemore's, he can probably lend an insight into the young, struggling businessman that few others here today are in a position to."

"Sounds plausible enough to fly." Mike took a last bite of food and pushed his bowl away. "But what's your backup plan if it doesn't?"

"It will," Julie said confidently. "I'll simply push if he gets stubborn. And if he does get stubborn, that resistance in itself will be insightful, because on the surface of things there's absolutely no reason for him to hedge."

Mike thought about it and nodded. "All right, Connor, go get 'em."

———

The next morning she did. She called Bronson at his bar first thing. He sounded receptive to the idea and invited her to come by within the hour.

Bronson's place was designed as a popular sports bar. At ten o'clock in the morning it seemed a bit forlorn with the big-screen corner television silent and the chairs upended on the little tables scattered across the hardwood floor. Bronson's manager was preoccupied with an inventory check, so he didn't immediately notice Julie when she walked in. She was making her way to the bar with a pleasant smile when the man looked up.

"Hi, I'm Julie Connor. I have a ten o'clock with Mr. Bronson." She held out her hand.

"Ed," the manager said simply with a reciprocal smile that seemed more like a facial tick. "I'll take you back."

Ed led her to a narrow hallway whose walls were lined with placards boasting beer slogans and sports trivia. Interspersed among them were framed photos of local and national sports personalities, along with corresponding news articles. Ed stopped two doors from the rest rooms, which put them at the end of the hallway.

"In there." He nodded toward the closed door and then turned around and walked away.

"Thank you, Ed," Julie murmured in an amused undertone and reached out to knock lightly before opening the door.

Roy Bronson didn't look shady. In fact he was better looking than Julie had remembered in a silver-haired, grandfatherly sort of way.

"Julie," he said, rising from behind his large, cluttered desk. He held out his hand as he walked around it. "Long time no see. You're looking great. Have a seat."

"Hello, Mr. Bronson." She glanced behind her and saw an empty high-back chair propped against the wall. Pulling it over, she settled it right in front of Bronson's desk and seated herself. She dropped her purse at her feet.

"No reason to stand on formality; after all we aren't quite strangers. Make it Roy." He smiled again.

Julie nodded. "I'll get to the point. I know you're a busy man, Roy. As I said over the phone, I'd like to talk a bit about Phillip Blakemore, but not about the successful attorney everyone knew by the time of his death. I'd like to get a more informal portrait of the young man, the young businessman who arrived here twenty-five years ago to make a go of things outside the legal profession."

Bronson had seated himself again during Julie's explanation. He leaned back in his swivel chair, his leg bent across his knee, his hands steepled beneath his chin. He appeared to be listening very carefully and periodically nodded his head at what Julie was saying, as if recollections were occurring to him as she talked.

"So where in all that, exactly, can I help you, Julie?"

"Start by telling me what you recall about Blakemore's reasons for wanting to enter into the antiques venture. How did you meet him? Why didn't he simply attempt to reestablish the law practice he'd left in Chicago? You were one of his first friends, What did he tell you?"

"Well," Bronson said at length, "I was one of the first contacts he made here in Michigan City, yes.

Phillip was in the midst of a separation from his wife back in Chicago. He met me at a small business association meeting he attended to get the lay of the land, opportunity-wise. We hit it off right away, and not long after that decided to work on his antiques venture together.''

"I wasn't aware of the fact that Blakemore had a background in antiques."

"He didn't, really. But he had the backing. He'd made some good investments with the money he'd made from his practice back in Chicago, and he decided to use a chunk of it for start-up capital in partnership with Mr. Field."

"So Blakemore had the means to sail pretty effortlessly back into the sort of legal work he knew and had been successful in. Why didn't he? It strikes me as strange that he would decide to make such a drastic switch in the middle of a stream that was already running pretty smoothly for him."

Bronson nodded. "I wanted to know that too when he talked about bringing me into the business. You see, I was just struggling back in those days, and I really didn't have the patience to start over and make another go at things if the venture failed. I didn't want to be taken on by someone who was just going to get restless on me and move on. Mr. Field, you see, had already made it clear to Phillip that his primary interest in the business hinged on the money it could net for him.

"Phillip said he had gotten burned out with law, plain and simple. He said he came to Indiana because it was still close enough to some of the trappings he wasn't sure he wanted to let go of completely back in Chicago. But aside from that he wanted to make a very clean break, which included,

he said, a new career direction. As for why Michigan
City, he said he'd become addicted to lakeside living
and didn't want to give that up."

Julie encouraged Bronson to talk a bit more about
his friendship with Blakemore. He recounted some
youthful escapades they'd shared around town as
well as a couple of amusing anecdotes about experi-
ences they'd had trying to get the business off the
ground. Julie assured Bronson his recountings would
give her story good color, but shortly thereafter decided to home in on the real point of the interview.

"So the shop lasted as a joint venture with Mr.
Field for about two years, yes?"

"Yes."

"And it was at that point that Blakemore decided
to sell his portion of the business to Field, retain you
as manager, and leave to go back to the law after all.
What happened?"

Bronson shrugged. "What I'd figured might happen back when we entered into the partnership. He
got bored with the life of being a small businessman.
He said he missed the one-on-one interaction with
people he'd enjoyed as a lawyer. In short, he felt he
was stagnating without his practice.

"Fortunately, the business was successful, so his
departure didn't really put me in a bad spot finan-
cially."

"So you would characterize your association with
Blakemore in all the years that followed as pretty
close? You guys remained friends, yes?"

Bronson shrugged again. "Yeah, you could certainly say that, friends."

Julie nodded and regarded Bronson with a gently
puzzled expression. "Isn't it funny, then, that when
I profiled him last year he never once mentioned

your name when he talked about his old friends and acquaintances?''

Bronson steepled his hands again and regarded Julie over them. "Not really that strange, I'm sure, Julie. Surely you didn't expect him to list every single friend he ever had in this town during a what, thirty-minute, hour-long interview?''

Julie smiled and leaned back in her chair, prepared to enjoy this first spark of defensiveness.

"Of course not, Roy. But don't you find it unusual that he elected to leave out in its entirety a significant chapter of his settlement here? He never even mentioned the business.''

"Well, Phil was pretty much a legal bigwig when he died. In comparison, the association we shared was probably, for him, pretty small potatoes.''

"And as for not discussing his relationship with you,'' Julie went on, "well, I have friends I haven't seen in years whom I consider significant influences on my early life. Their names come to mind readily when I think of those days. Blakemore was a man trying to rebuild his life in the wake of a broken marriage. He was a stranger in town and he was embarking on a major decision to scrap a successful law practice to begin a new and unfamiliar professional career basically from scratch.

"Then came you, his first close business associate and first real friend. If I were recounting the story of my life as a benefactor for this town and I were in his shoes, I certainly would have mentioned someone like you.''

Bronson's smile chilled. "Well, what can I say? Things happen. Sometimes the best of us forget the little people in the wake of success.''

"Yes, but forgetting little people is hardly in character with the man I profiled, with the man I knew. In fact, he built a reputation that spanned his life-time here for exactly the opposite reason, for being the sort of man who never forgot the little people. In fact, he was admired precisely for that, for bending over backward to help them, wouldn't you agree?''

Bronson's features, which had been so open at the start of their interview, flattened out so that now they were nearly expressionless.

"As I said, Julie, we were friends, and now Phillip is dead. It's too late for anybody to get inside his head to figure out why he did or didn't choose to include me in his stroll down memory lane a year ago when he talked to you." He made a point of looking at his watch. "Now, is there anything else? I've got to help Ed with inventory before we open this afternoon."

Julie reached for her purse, feeling a rush of success. There was definitely something more to Bronson and Blakemore's relationship than met the eye. Bronson was too irritated suddenly, and Julie felt sure it was because their split had been far from amiable.

Most importantly, he had, by his silence, sustained the lie of Charles Field.

She held out her hand to Bronson. "Thanks for your time, Roy. You've given me some good stuff. I'll be sure to send you a copy of the article."

Bronson took her hand but kept the contact brief. "I'll look for it. You have a nice day, now." He smiled again and Julie found herself suppressing a shiver.

For a split second the predatory quality of it had reminded her of Mike's warning about Jimmy Sales.

Chapter
ELEVEN

"So you think he was stonewalling you, huh?"

Mike asked the question from where they were sitting together on the beach, watching the sun set. He had been preoccupied for the day with his own investigatory activities, and Julie hadn't rushed this meeting, knowing he'd contact her when he could.

When he'd shown up at her place a short time ago, she'd poured two glasses of sun tea from a pitcher she'd had chilling in the refrigerator and suggested they take the conversation outside to enjoy what was left of the day. Now Julie sat beside him, enjoying his companionship, realizing how much she had looked forward to it since the night before.

She glanced over at Mike, who hadn't bothered to open his eyes or shift his position since he'd spoken. He was still reclining on the sand, his hands clasped beneath his head. He was clad in only a decidedly disreputable pair of cotton shorts.

Julie smiled, taking into pleasurable account the way his relaxed posture threw into prominent relief the tapered, muscled expanse of his dark torso, the slight concavity of his stomach that rose and fell with his gentle breathing, his slim hips as they narrowed into the low-riding waistband of his pants.

Swimmer's body, she mused, wondering if the activity kept him in shape or if he was just the product of fortunate genes that had combined with superior conditioning to give him the appearance of a toned athlete in his prime.

"He tried to stonewall me at the end," she said, drawing another cooling sip from her glass. "It only convinced me that he and Blakemore very likely fell out about something, and Blakemore severed the relationship completely. Businesswise and personally."

"Any thoughts about what that could have been?"

"My guess would be some point of ethics. Blakemore was an honorable man. I don't think Roy Bronson has much honor now, and I doubt if he did then."

Honorable? Damn, his old man must have experienced an epiphany on the road from Chicago to Indiana. Honorable men might have divorced their wives, but they rarely walked out on their bewildered children without so much as a real good-bye or explanation for what was going to amount to a lifetime of severed contact.

Mike sat up and wrapped his arm around a raised knee. "I contacted my federal colleague today. We talked about Roy Bronson and the Charles Field alias. I figured Bronson would get squirrelly about anything linked to his business that you might be able to take away with you to trace.

"My colleague is using his federal resources to test out a couple of avenues. He should have something to tell me by tomorrow." Tom had done a good job digging out the information about Del Evans. If

Bronson had any links to organized crime via Chicago, Tom was the man to ferret that out as well.

"Good," Julie said. "In the meantime, I'm going to do some follow-up work on the paper trail connected with Bronson's antiques shop. It can't hurt, and who knows what it might yield?"

Mike reached over and caressed Julie's slender back. It was just an impulse to touch, and he followed it. She started a little, then leaned back into his hand.

Encouraged, Mike shifted to his knees and moved behind her, gently drawing her back into the vee of his body. He wrapped his arms around her shoulders, enfolding her in his embrace. When she lifted her hands to clasp his wrists closer to her body, he smiled.

"I missed you today, woman," he breathed.

Julie tilted her head to meet his gaze over her shoulder. "Me too. It surprised me."

"What!" Mike's smile widened into a grin of amusement at Julie's guileless faux pas. Her shoulders vibrated with gentle laughter.

"That sounded awful, didn't it. What I meant was, I didn't realize I had gotten so used to expecting you to be with me, to wanting to be with you. We've known each other such a brief time. It surprises me, that's all."

Mike's grin dissolved into something more pensive. "Yeah," he murmured, pulling her closer, "I know what you mean."

What Julie had just expressed sounded like more than expectation. It sounded an awful lot like need. He felt it just as strongly for her, and therein lay his dilemma.

He'd spent a lifetime building his defenses against

that particular emotion. Initially it hadn't been his choice, it had simply been a reflex arising from a childhood with a father who obviously didn't care enough to stay and a mother who was oddly disinclined to take up the emotional slack his departure had left.

He thought again of how wrong Julie had been when she'd assumed he couldn't understand the barrenness of her childhood. Yes, materially, his upbringing had been oceans away from her experience. But on an emotional level, where it counted in the end, he had been just as abandoned as she.

Consequently he had learned to rein in his wants beneath a mantle of control. Self-sufficiency had been the byword he'd chosen to live by, and it had stood him in good stead throughout his childhood and through his years with the police department, where he knew he'd earned a reputation as a stand-up guy who, even so, was something of a loner.

It had also sustained him in his relationships with women. He'd enjoyed them, but he'd never let the entanglements progress to a point that was more than pleasurably casual. He hadn't wanted to deal with the possibility of their coming to mean anything.

And if the trade-off for the control was occasional loneliness, he accepted it because in the end it was a whole lot less painful than setting himself up for a fall.

Only now, with Julie, he felt the rules of his life shifting. The frightening thing was that it had started so insidiously he hadn't even known it. He didn't want to fall in love with her; he didn't want to be in love. He wanted . . . what? he countered honestly.

To go on drifting without a longtime purpose for tomorrow?

The simple truth was, he was already half in love with her, and he was scared to death that giving in to an emotion that encompassed all he had spent a lifetime avoiding would leave him an emotional mess.

"Mike, what's wrong?"

The question nudged Mike into realizing how long he'd been silent. "Nothing, just thinking."

Julie wondered, but she let it go. She knew she'd imagined neither the subtle tension that had crept into his arms nor the slight stiffening of his hairdusted wrists beneath her fingers. But she did sense he was grappling with something major, something having to do more with her than with the Blakemore case.

Eventually the beach started clearing for the day. Julie and Mike took it as their cue to part as well.

"Do you want to come in for dinner?" Julie half expected him to decline.

"Let me take a rain check, okay?"

Mike's answer was easy enough but distracted, Julie thought. He seemed restless suddenly, as if he was anxious to get away. She tried not to be hurt. He'd told her in plain terms that despite what he felt for her, his limitations existed.

"Sure," she said with forced casualness. "If I come up with anything by tomorrow, I'll let you know." She started to walk away.

Wanting very badly for him to call to her, Julie kept her steps measured and slow, but Mike didn't say a word. When she couldn't stand it a moment longer she turned to see what he was doing. He was halfway down the beach.

The only consolation she took with her as she

walked the rest of the way up to the house was that his bent head, his slow stride, the hands he had shoved low into his pockets, conveyed an air of dejection she thought matched her own.

———

The next day Tom came through. What he found pleased Mike, but it also disturbed him. The circle of crime that had consumed his father still couldn't be defined, but Mike had the feeling it was closing.

Roy Bronson, alias Charles Field, had shared business ties twelve years ago with a Chicago textile entity that had been suspected at one time of fronting a drug-trafficking operation.

Bronson had conveniently severed his own ties with the owners of that venture just before its mob links had been confirmed and it had been brought down. Mike didn't believe for a moment that Bronson could be an innocent when he had been professionally involved with those criminals.

What he needed to do was to get close to the man. He needed to put himself into a position to watch him. When he phoned Julie with Tom's news, which he presented as his fictional colleague's findings, she provided him with the means of proximity.

"I saw an ad in the paper yesterday. The bar is looking for a bartender. You could make that your ticket in."

"Yeah, you're right," Mike said. "How about you? Have you turned up anything else on your end?"

"Not so far, but I'm hardly finished looking."

He came to a decision. "How about dinner tonight?"

Julie hesitated.

"My treat. I'll take you out."

"Mike, I don't—"

"I want to talk, Julie. We—need to talk."

"We have talked."

"All right, dammit, *I* need to talk."

Julie let that settle. "Six o'clock?"

Mike released a breath. "Yeah. I'll pick you up."

———

They went to a nearby bar and grill Julie was familiar with. Mike approved of her choice. The dining room was softly lit and, combined with the booth they were shown to, conducive to privacy. The food was simple but good, and once it was served their waiter, for the most part, left them alone.

By unspoken consent, they eased into their meal, enjoying their food while they talked of inconsequential things. Early on, Mike mentioned that he'd gone over to Bronson's and had succeeded in talking his way into the evening bartending job they were hiring for.

After that the conversation drifted until finally the meal was done and Julie fell quiet.

"When I walked away the other day, it wasn't because I didn't want to be with you."

"Then why did you?" Julie appreciated his coming straight to the point.

The admission wasn't easy, and Mike needed to take a breath before making it. "It was because I did want to be with you, Julie. I didn't know how to handle it."

That surprised Julie. Not what he had said, rather

his candor in admitting it. She had wondered at something of the sort at the time. But as the night and the following day had passed with no word from him, she told herself that her own emotions had fooled her into wishful thinking.

"If it gives you any comfort, this—whatever it is between us—has thrown me too. The only thing I know for sure is that I can't stay indifferent to it." She added more softly, "Or you."

Mike nodded, though deep down inside he wanted to bolt. At similar junctions in other relationships he had always interpreted like noises from his companions as his cue to leave. With Julie, the juncture was turning into something completely unique to his experience.

It was becoming, quite simply, a situation he couldn't run from. Not even temporarily. He pushed his napkin aside and leaned slightly across the table.

"I can't tell you what I want, Julie." He laughed gently, with more irony than amusement. "I honestly don't know myself. The things I feel when I'm with you are . . . well, I'm not even sure I really want to rationalize them anymore."

"So what do we do?"

As heavy moments ticked by, Mike searched inward for sudden insight, for something that would transform his anxiety into something comforting for Julie to hear, something comfortable for him to say.

Julie's ponderment of him was no less thoughtful, no more filled with answers.

In the end, because he sensed that whatever he said would become the turning point for whatever happened afterward, he chose simplicity.

"We play it by ear, I guess. The only rules are no expectations and no promises."

Julie nodded, a little saddened that he'd needed to voice the restrictions. But because she too had existed as an intensely private person for so long, she empathized with his need for restraint.

Relatively little had been said, but Julie knew that miles had been crossed. She was both terrified and strangely relieved.

"So," she said, needing to lighten things a bit, "does all this mean we can date, or what?"

Mike chuckled, feeling his tension start to ease, feeling that though he'd come here about as emotionally equipped as a man about to jump off a cliff, perhaps—just perhaps—he'd done the right thing.

"Yeah, it probably does," he answered. "How do you feel about that?"

"Comfortable. How do you?"

He smiled. "I'll live."

Julie slid her hand across the table.

Mike gripped it.

Shortly thereafter he paid their bill and they left. A brief while later he pulled up behind Julie's house and cut his engine. He sat looking out into the darkness, then turned slightly so that he was facing her. He searched for a way to break the stillness.

Julie understood that she could invite him in or she could ask him to go. He would abide, taking whatever she said as the measure of the pace with which she wanted to advance their fragile understanding.

She knew what she wanted, but she questioned the wisdom of taking it so soon. She raised her hand to his cheek, thinking, hesitating.

Mike read the need, but he also felt Julie's caution. Raising his own hand, he settled it upon her fragile wrist and leaned in toward her until his lips touched hers. When he heard her sigh, he slid his hand slowly, gently along her arm until her shoulder was under his palm. He tugged softly, urging, asking, and then he released a sigh of his own when Julie complied.

Mouths merged, tongues tangled, breaths mingled. Mike felt himself sinking into her. She turned pliant and giving beneath his hands, and his senses hummed. He loved the little sounds she made as his mouth left hers to nuzzle at the smooth, fragrant base of her throat. He loved the feel of her, loved the taste of her, loved the urgency he felt to give even as his body pleaded with him to take.

"Julie," he murmured when he could. Her eyes, light and seductively magical in the moonlight, opened slowly, as if she were rising out of a dream. Their focus, when they locked on to his, was misty, watchful, aroused. Definitely aroused.

"Ah, God," he groaned, pulling her to him again. "Sweetheart, I want you. You know that I want you."

Julie's mouth lifted to his, seeking the sweetness that had engulfed her with his first touch.

When his broad hand tangled in her hair to anchor her more firmly in his embrace, she allowed it. When his other hand drifted down to soothe her already sensitized breasts, to rest briefly at her waist, to come to a breathless pause at that achy feminine part of her that also yearned for his caress, she melted. And when she felt the weight of his body pressing insistently against hers, needing room, seeking purchase to take more, she understood.

She wanted more pleasure too.

But she also wanted the fragile promise they'd just discovered in each other to survive the impulsive heat of tonight. Their bodies were ready, but she seriously wondered if their hearts could take the strain.

And so she resisted her desire and released her mouth from his. She summoned every ounce of will-power inside her to murmur against his throat the words of sanity they both needed to hear.

"Mike, this isn't right." She felt his hands still and mentally sighed when a different kind of tension suffused his body.

"It's too soon," she continued, willing him to understand, leaning back in the seat as he slowly levered his body from hers. He stared at her for the longest moment, his emotions unfathomable, his silence broken only by the slow evening of his breathing.

And then something flickered in his eyes, and Julie's stomach dropped. She could see an essential part of him, something vital, pulling back, pulling inward away from her. Impulsively she reached out to him, but her gesture was stayed by his hand's catching hers.

Instead of pushing her away as she feared, he laced his fingers through hers until, together, their hands formed a fist. And then he surprised her and touched her unbearably by drawing the fist to his mouth where he brushed each of her curved fingers with his lips.

"I know, honey," he breathed. "I do. It's just . . ."

She threaded the fingers of her other hand into his thick, springy hair. "Yes," she breathed back. "It's just." She took a breath and waited for him to look up, waited for him to see as well as hear what she was saying. "But this time there's more. Isn't there?"

Mike knew what she was asking, knew what she was saying. And like a bête noire the old fear arose to hover along the edge of his consciousness. And then he became aware of the solidity of Julie's touch and the strength it gave him for the first time in his life to push his fear away.

"Yes. There's more." There was, he realized, or at least there could be. If he would let it. If they both would let it, in its own good time.

Sitting up completely, Mike helped Julie do the same. He helped her pull her clothes back together, a small wistful smile touching his mouth as he did it.

When the repairs were done and there were only the parting words left to say, Mike was the one this time who found the strength to say them.

"Go on inside, sweetheart. I'll see you tomorrow."

Julie looked at him, wanting to say something more, wanting to know if, despite his tenderness, he needed her to. And then he answered her by smiling. It was a gesture meant to reassure, to send her into the night with the confidence that his reassurance had been tendered with good faith. But it was shadowed with such unguarded vulnerability that it nearly broke her heart.

"Good night," she finally whispered, and stepped out of his car. This time, when she walked away, the fact that he let her didn't hurt. This time she understood that he wasn't letting her go, he was only grabbing what, at that moment, he needed more: time to realign his old perceptions.

Time to give them both room to breathe.

Chapter

TWELVE

"What's happening with the Connor thing, Paul?"

From his luxury apartment window, Simmons gazed out over the downtown Chicago skyline. "She's staying pretty low," he told his boss. "Only thing of note she did was go to see Bronson to do a little up-close and personal probing about Phillip's early years."

"And?"

He adjusted the receiver more comfortably against his ear. "Nothing. Bronson told her enough to pacify her about Phillip's settlement into the community, acclimatizing to his adopted business, you know. Fluff. Fortunately, he didn't know enough to inadvertently spill any of the heavy stuff about before all that."

"Are you sure?"

Simmons thought through a pause. "What do you mean?"

"I mean I don't want any more snags in this thing. I think the fact that Julie Connor has been asking around at all about Phillip since his death is sending

up flags we should be paying particularly close attention to."

"Well, in the eventuality that that's the case, I've
alerted Roy to stay on his toes. He's served us well
all these years. I don't doubt he's fully equipped to
keep doing it."

"I'm trusting you on this, Paul."

Simmons smiled. "When have I ever let you
down?"

Caution was evident in the answer. "As you say."

———

"Pretty much, your primary duties here will be to
keep the bar clean, the conversation supplied when
it's wanted, and the customers wet." Ed handed
Mike his this-is-to-get-acquainted beer and downed
the final contents of his own. They were sitting at
one of the tables in Bronson's bar thirty minutes before opening, engaged in a final orientation.

Mike took a drink from his mug and sat back in
his chair, crossing his leg over his knee. He was
thinking, as he had about two minutes after "Big
Ed," as he'd privately dubbed him, had hired him,
that the man was almost a walking personification of
the stereotypical big lug.

A nice enough guy, Ed was a man who knew how
to do his work, maintain his loyalties, and keep his
mouth shut when it was warranted. Mike had encountered men of his type before and knew that if
you played them right, they could be extremely useful. Mike intended to bide his time so that when the
opportunity was right, he'd be in a prime position to
strum Ed's strings.

"So, you say despite the other odd jobs you've

done you've always ended up tending a little bar. I was pretty rushed other day; tell me about it again. Where is it you say you've been?"

"Here and there," Mike said. "I started doing it while I was in college. I've done it when I've needed extra cash ever since."

"College, huh?" Ed said. He got up and walked over behind the bar to draw another beer from the tap. "What's a smart guy like you doing here in this little backwater town hauling beer for a bunch of mugs like me?"

"There are worse places, Ed," Mike said simply.

He had considered what his cover story would be. In the end he'd decided a nonstory would provide the most solid protection. A man with no tangible past provided fewer tracks to cover. Neither did he provide any curious tidbits of information or facts that would inspire a discreet search later on.

Ed considered what Mike had told him and appeared to let it go. It didn't surprise Mike; true to type, Ed was probably figuring the fewer complications his life took on, the easier it would remain to live it.

——

Eight hours later the hands on the clock above the bar edged toward midnight. The end of Mike's shift was near. The night had been relatively quiet, the customers modest, and significant enlightenment into what made Roy Bronson tick nil.

Bronson had come in to do some paperwork at about eight, exchanged a few polite words with Ed, introduced himself to Mike, and retreated to his office in the back. Mike's gut impression of him had pretty much echoed Julie's description.

The man was congenial enough, but there was something cool about him, something watchful that had Mike instantly on his guard and certain that Mr. Roy Bronson was most probably a man of interesting secrets.

"The challenge," he told Julie several nights later, "is to find the most expedient way to tap into his secrets."

Mike had developed the habit of checking in on her after he finished work the three evenings of the week he tended bar. The first time he'd shown up, she'd been surprised but obviously pleased. The second night, though they'd parted the first time with no subsequent agreement, she'd been expecting him.

By the third night of the second week, she had a late light supper waiting for him that only needed heating up in the microwave. He'd accepted it and her welcoming kiss with the same quiet ease with which she'd offered them.

And now she was sitting with him, patiently sharing a plate of shrimp, while he shared his night with her again, including his newly forming plan on how to force a closer access to Roy Bronson.

"I need to get into that office," Mike said, thinking out loud.

"You're right there on the premises," Julie pointed out. "What's the problem?"

"There isn't one during the course of my shift. But I have a feeling that what I want to hear or see doesn't necessarily correspond with the hours of my job. At any rate, I need to be able to conduct a private search without the threat of interruption."

"Is Bronson the only one with the key to his office?"

"No, Ed has a set. Ed explained that the boss provided him with them in case there's an emergency and Bronson's not around."

Julie chewed thoughtfully, then said, "So, is there any chance you maybe could temporarily—"

"Lift Ed's keys?" Mike supplied.

"Yeah." Julie smiled.

"Yeah." Mike smiled back. "It occurs to me that that's one possibility."

"And once you've done that, there's probably the chance that you can hold on to them long enough to make yourself a spare?"

Mike leaned back on the sofa, pulling Julie with him. Playfully he said, "Are you sure you've really left your wild and wicked ways behind, woman?"

Julie didn't take offense as she once might have; her growing trust in the man who teased her was overriding the need. "Look who's talking, cop. Doesn't that old saying involve something about the pot calling the kettle?"

Mike chuckled, dropped a kiss to her mouth and held on to her loosely, comfortably. This felt so right, he thought. She felt so right.

———

The next afternoon Mike got his chance at the keys. Or rather, he created it.

Ed had just finished mopping the floor. He was hauling a bucket of water in one hand and a bottle of disinfectant in the other to the back storage room when Mike intercepted him.

Flinging the rag he'd been wiping the bar down

with across his shoulder, Mike tapped Ed on the back as he was passing.

"Hey, Ed, man, I've got a favor to ask you."

"Yeah, what? This water's heavy."

"It's kind of embarrassing. I left my shift keys at home and I need to get into my register to pull out the cash report for you."

"Dammit, Quinn," Ed growled. "I hope you're more conscientious when it comes to handling the cash I'm trusting you with."

Mike assumed a properly abashed expression.

Ed set down his bucket and fished inside his back pocket. He pulled out a small set of keys. "Here." He separated one from the rest though he didn't pull it from the ring. "It's this one. I'm going out back to dump this."

Ed picked up his bucket and continued on toward the service door in the rear, which led to a back parking lot and Dumpster. Mike fingered the keys and watched him retreat.

Sometimes when your luck was in, it really did get as easy as it looked in the movies, he thought ruefully.

He literally didn't have a moment to spare, so he moved. He walked down the back hall to Bronson's office and started trying keys. He got through the entire ring before he accepted the incredible: None of the keys fit Bronson's door. What the *hell*?

The sound of the back door opening threw his brain into hypergear. He wouldn't get a better chance . . . maybe, if that luck he'd thought he'd had a minute ago was really in—

He stooped down, squinting through the hallway's dim light, peering intently at the lock on Bronson's door. And smiled. It was there, a code number.

Quickly he straightened back up, knowing he had maybe one second to get back to the register if he wanted to save his bacon. He made it just before Ed emerged from the hallway.

"Here you go," he said to Ed, handing over the keys. "You'd better check them. The register key didn't work." Mike hoped that was true or he'd look even more foolish after Ed contradicted him and questioned his second mistake.

Ed grunted, looking at Mike in confusion. Then a disgusted look crossed his face. "Dammit, I hate it when I do that." Reaching back inside his other jean pocket, he pulled out another ring.

"Sorry," he said. "Here are the keys. I gave you my house ring. Sometimes when I'm in a hurry I get'm mixed up."

Mike took the ring from Ed's hand, thanking the good Lord all the while for the man's slow wits. After he'd opened the register and pulled the report that Ed needed from it, Ed headed back toward his office to do his daily work with the business financials.

Mike bypassed the lakeshore after his shift ended and headed to the edge of town. Thirty minutes later, he left the twenty-four-hour locksmith's shop with the key Bronson's lock code had produced.

All he had to do now was sit tight until the time was right to capitalize on his access to Bronson's office.

———

"Mike, look at this," Julie said the following evening.

He sat down on Julie's porch steps and took the

set of papers she handed to him. They were copies of twenty-year-old financial reports and tax statements belonging to Charles Field & Co.

Mike regarded Julie curiously. "How did you get all this confidential tax stuff?"

"Privileged information. Just read it."

All of the information appeared to be pretty routine until gradually, as Mike scanned the sheets, a common thread began to separate itself from the more uninteresting data.

"Tell me about this Micah Ltd."

"It's a very active antiques subsidiary of a very large commercial conglomerate based in Chicago," she said. "It's nationally prestigious despite its low profile, and it's been a solid money maker for its parent company for nearly thirty years. At first glance everything about its connection with Bronson's business appears to be absolutely unremarkable."

"Seems to be," Mike agreed.

"Take a closer look," Julie urged.

Mike did and at length frowned. "Some of this Micah merchandise is extremely upper-end stuff, not the sort of stock you'd think Bronson's modest little collectibles enterprise could support as consistently as these reports indicate."

"So why would Micah keep cropping up as a dealer for such a relatively modest businessman as Bronson?" Julie asked rhetorically. Mike regarded her thoughtfully, and she said, "Take a look at this."

Mike accepted another printout, this time of an annual report. "Shit," he murmured softly.

"Yeah. For the past twenty-five years the chief operating officer of Micah Ltd. has been one James Bronson. He has a brother named Roy."

While Mike digested that, Julie continued, "His record has been impeccable, with one exception, which occurred in 1965.

"He was subpoenaed for questioning in connection with suspected business improprieties that had cropped up as an adjoining issue to a federal organized crime investigation. He managed to talk his way out from under a racketeering accusation, and the business wasn't hurt. Nevertheless, one could argue that the suspicion established a possible connection with the mob, and by association, for his parent company also."

"What's the parent company?" Mike wanted to know. "Who runs it?"

"The company is Blakemore Industries," Julie said. "The CEO is a man named Paul Simmons. But this entity has so many layers to it I wouldn't be surprised to find that his title is titular only. I'm still working on it."

A moment passed before Mike could speak. "Who knows you've been digging for this information, Julie?"

"I've been discreet. Most everything I've gotten here I acquired through public records and business histories accessible to any citizen who could have an interest and expertise in knowing how to look them up."

"Aside from the IRS, did you go through any other channels at all that were out of the ordinary?" Mike persisted. "Law enforcement, private, anything?"

"No, Mike. The only other private channel I used, if you could classify it that way, was a friend of mine at the paper. Margaret O'Brien. She's a crime reporter who also used to work in Chicago before she came here.''

Heading off whatever Mike's look of irritation warned her he was about to say, Julie added, ''It's okay. She's also my best friend. I gave her absolutely no reason to believe the Micah stuff I asked her for wasn't related to another story I'm researching.'' Julie laid her hand on Mike's wrist. ''I'd trust her with my life.''

Mike turned his attention to the beach and the scattering of sunbathers lying on it. Eventually he released a heavy sigh.

Julie knew he wasn't comfortable with her having brought a third party into what they were doing, no matter how peripherally. He didn't, however, comment further, and she was relieved.

''All the same,'' Mike told her, ''I want you to stay alert. Watch out for anything, *anything* unusual around you. That includes conversations and questions from people you know as well as people you don't. Do you understand?''

''Yes, Mike.'' Julie was a bit subdued at the urgency of his request. She knew he knew she was aware of the danger attached to what they were doing. Why was he suddenly so intense?

She squeezed his wrist, distracting his thoughts a bit from the inward place they had shifted. ''What's wrong?''

The connection, Mike thought. Was his parents' organization linked to the tainted Micah by unlucky happenstance only? Or did a more sinister relationship exist? If his mother was truly in danger, as his father had said, then the latter couldn't make much sense.

''Mike?'' Julie urged again.

"It's nothing." He draped an arm around her shoulders and pulled her close, stalling. "Nothing. I just want to make sure you stay safe."

"How much safer could I be? I've got my very own live-in cop, so to speak."

Mike let a beat pass, then said, "That might not be such a bad idea."

Julie leaned away from him to better gauge his expression. "You're serious, aren't you?"

"Yes." And even though the offer had been an impulsive outgrowth of what was bothering him, he realized he had been deadly serious as he'd said it.

Julie pulled away and leaned forward. She rubbed her arms and turned her own gaze outward toward the same view of beach and water that had seemed to so fascinate Mike earlier.

With her silence Mike realized she was reading all sorts of connotations into his offer, connotations that went way beyond the one that had inspired him to speak.

"I was only making a suggestion for protection, Julie. Nothing more."

Oh, but it was that something more that was pressing her to hold her silence now. It was that something more that she desperately wanted.

It was that something more that she had been sublimating, with Mike's tacit agreement, ever since that night of awareness when they had admitted to each other just how incendiary their unchecked feelings for each other could be.

She heard herself say, "I don't think the idea would be very wise, do you?"

Did he? For days now, they had been abiding by their understanding not to complicate their tenuous relationship with anything physical. But for days now, he was also honest enough to admit that the understanding had become strained with another unspoken agreement.

What he felt for Julie and what Julie felt for him was clearly moving out of a safe realm of friendship and intimate companionship into something more. Into something neither one of them obviously yet had the courage to confront.

And so he considered her question very seriously. Despite his need to protect her, despite her increasing willingness to let him, he didn't want to make the wrong move.

"All right. But I'm right here whenever you need me. And I still intend to stay close."

Julie let her disappointment war with relief as she listened to his words and understood what he was telling her.

"I'm counting on it," she said.

Mike laid a caressing hand against her throat and tilted her head back for his kiss. She responded fully, letting her tongue slide along his. Mike knew he had better get them onto safer ground or else all of their good intentions were going to go sailing right out there into that lake.

He broke the kiss and said, "Come on, go put on your shoes. I'm taking you out to dinner."

Julie reluctantly let her stirring passion dissipate to a faint wisp of regret. She even dredged up a smile because she knew exactly what Mike was doing.

"Dude," she answered quietly, "you're on."

———

The next evening wasn't nearly so relaxed for Mike. It was a nasty, rainy night following what had been a nasty, rainy day. The mood of the customers at the bar seemed to reflect the weather. The conversation was sparse and the drinking was steady.

Ed seemed to be in a particularly taciturn mood, which meant he spent the entire night communicating with Mike in words of one syllable instead of two. Of Bronson, Mike caught a glimpse only when he walked into the bar around nine. He headed directly to his office with hardly a word of conversation for anyone, let alone a greeting.

The rain drove on and the time crawled by until finally the customers started trickling out, seemingly one by one, until at last it was midnight and time for closing. Mike called a cab for the last customer, a regular who was really little more than a drunk, at about twelve fifteen. He poured him out of the door and into the waiting car roughly ten minutes later.

"You don't have to stay, Mike. I'll clean up if you want to take off," Ed said to him. Mike looked up from collecting the few soiled glasses still scattered across the room. It was the longest sentence the man had uttered all night.

Bronson still hadn't budged from the office. "I don't mind, Ed. I don't have anything to do. In fact, if you want to take off instead, I'll do the entire cleanup tonight."

Ed leaned against the bar. "Well, Betty Lou did get her shift changed to days, which means when I don't have to be here, I get the chance to see her more often."

"That settles it then, man. Take off. I've got it covered here."

Ed grinned a very male grin, and suddenly Mike was amused to think that he could probably make a good guess as to what had been getting Ed down tonight. It was the same thing that was kicking his butt into gear now.

"See you," he called to the man, and Ed lifted a hand to say good-bye. Mike shook his head and took another look at the clock behind him. Twelve thirty-five. How much longer was Bronson going to be?

At one o'clock straight up, Bronson appeared. He was lugging the same briefcase he had come in with, his intention to finally leave for the night apparent.

"Hey, Quinn, you still here?"

He sounded tired, Mike thought. With those red eyes he looked it, too. "Yeah, I'm just about done though. I'll lock up and be right behind you."

Unexpectedly, Bronson set his briefcase down on the floor and leaned against the bar. Mike gave the final touches to polishing the bar and wondered what Bronson was up to. He was pulling open the cash drawer to count and record the night's intake when Bronson offered a clue.

"Ed tells me you're from around here. Says despite the fact you're neither down on your luck nor unmotivated, you like to drift and tend bar."

Mike pulled out a stack of bills and started counting. "Ed didn't seem to have a problem with that." He paused to look up into Bronson's inquisitive eyes. "Do you?"

Bronson watched him in return, taking his measure. Then he smiled. "No, no. Whatever works. Ed says you're good, says he's got no problems with you."

Mike went back to his counting. Bronson continued to lean.

"How long you planning to stick around, Quinn?"

Mike put down the last notations on his report.

"Awhile, I don't know. Don't worry, I'll give you plenty of notice before I go."

"Uhm." Bronson lightly slapped the bar and picked up his case. "Like I said, no problem. 'Night."

" 'Night," Mike murmured. Once the door shut behind Bronson, Mike snapped off the lights and grabbed his own keys. He let Bronson get to the end of the lot before he slipped out the door, locked it, and jogged to his car.

There was no traffic to contend with this time of night, and the trail Mike initiated upon Bronson was launched easily.

Mike had been put on his guard by the man's little inquisition. He didn't know what could have triggered it tonight aside from maybe Bronson's general criminal instincts. Nevertheless it had told Mike that now was as good a time as any to start looking into what Roy Bronson did with his downtime.

Somehow Mike hadn't expected Bronson to head home, and he wasn't disappointed. Fifteen minutes into the drive Bronson pulled into the large parking lot of a collection of specialty shops.

Mike had cut his lights at least a mile back, and now he cut his engine, staying well back from the lot on the opposite side of the road. Bronson walked to the door of his antiques shop, went through a procedure obviously intended to disengage the alarm, and juggled his keys until he found the one he wanted. He inserted it into the lock and walked inside.

When a dim glow from what had to be an electric light appeared, Mike put his car in reverse and backed down the road until he could be reasonably sure the car was completely out of sight. He flipped on his headlights, turned around so that he was again facing north, and headed back to the bar.

Whatever Bronson was doing this late at night was probably going to occupy him for a while since he'd chosen the wee hours to do it. Well, it would probably take at least long enough, Mike thought; he wanted to see inside the man's office, and now seemed like a choice opportunity to do it.

Mike parked in the rear lot. Before he got out of his car, he unlocked his glove compartment and pulled out a fully loaded 9mm semiautomatic.

When he'd let himself into the building, he locked the door behind him and made his way through the darkness. He didn't want to use any lights that could catch the attention of anyone who happened to be driving by.

At the locked door of Bronson's office, he pulled out his key as well as a penlight. He inserted the key into the lock and it turned easily.

Closing the door behind him, Mike secured the lock again and went to work. He put on a pair of thin leather gloves and walked over to Bronson's desk. It was unlocked and therefore, Mike was certain, sure to yield little in the way of what he wanted to find.

He was right. The primary drawer revealed a disorganized clutter of rubber bands, paper clips, Post-it Notes, pens, and pencils. The double rows of adjoining drawers on either side contained only employee files, administrative files, and equipment operations manuals.

Mike closed the drawers without disturbing the arrangement of anything and made a slow, careful scan around the office. His eye fell on a shoulder-high metal fire file. If anything of use was going to be found, he figured, sure as hell it was going to be sitting inside there.

He pulled a picklock from his back pocket. Less than thirty seconds later he'd manipulated the tension tool and rake in efficient conjunction and re-pocketed his tools.

Ah, now it gets more interesting, Mike thought as he opened each of the four levels of drawers, forgoing an immediate examination of their contents. He wanted to get an idea of how they were organized first. The method was the simplest of all. Everything comprising Bronson's loose papers and files was divvied up and slotted into alphabetical dividers.

Mike thought that if he was lucky, mostly everything he was looking for would be stashed within the first two drawers. He started with the logical first choice: *B.*

And hit pay dirt of a sort.

There was indeed a *B* file stuffed full of news clips, notes, and photos spanning most of the adult public life of Phillip Blakemore. The puzzling thing was that the file wasn't dedicated to Phillip Blakemore alone. Just as prominently profiled, along with Blakemore, was his wife, Donna. The clips highlighted her successes as a society wife and as the business maven she later became.

Mike pulled the file from the drawer and walked over to the desk where he could spread its contents out for a more careful study.

He found a yellowed 1961 newspaper clip detailing the announcement of Phillip Blakemore's engagement to Donna Morris, both native residents of Chicago. An actual announcement of the wedding was clipped to the back. There were subsequent clips of legal victories won by Phillip Blakemore, along with the simultaneous growth of the flagship textile company he and his wife founded.

Mike continued to flip through the files. As documentation of the passing years continued, the progress of that company as it grew into a corporation was noted. Interspersed with the brief snippets of acquisitions and mergers that contributed to its growth were personal interviews with both Blakemores.

The angle, not surprising considering the times of the news being made, focused repeatedly on the newsworthiness of local blacks who were slowly making their way into Fortune 500 status. The theme of the articles continued on that way until Mike flipped to one, dated in April 1970. It noted the fact that Donna Blakemore, CEO of Blakemore Industries, was filing for divorce from her equally prominent husband.

The printed reason for the divorce was irreconcilable differences. It was the blanket reason most splitting couples gave to the media, Mike thought. In this case it was a sterile summation of the bitter arguments and even colder silences he could still vividly remember from his childhood.

Mike shut the folder and went on to the second that had been present in the *B* file. This one was of Phillip Blakemore's activities alone. All of them were ones that had taken place after he had come to Indiana.

Mike read through them, feeling an odd mixture of emotions. It was like reading through the panoramic life of a stranger, and yet this stranger was his father. A number of articles detailing services and donations to the community dominated the file.

As Mike sifted through them, pausing to read

some and bypassing others, he was also struck by the fact that finally, after twenty-five years, he was being allowed the opportunity to watch his father age in front of his eyes.

He was Phillip Blakemore's son, and the first chance he was getting to live out a lifetime with the only man he had called Father was through the impersonality of a stack of flat black-and-white news clips.

Mike shut the file. What the hell did his parents have to do with Roy Bronson? He picked up the folders and put them back inside the fire file. On a hunch he flipped through to the C section.

Connor. A file existed.

Mike pulled it out. Though it was thin, it was no less disturbing to see. Inside was a collection of clips of the stories she had written within the past two months, all having to do with escalating crime within the city. Most of the stories cited were ones she had told him were the result of tips forwarded to her by her mysterious source. At the bottom of one of those clips, a word that Mike couldn't make out had been scribbled in ink.

Holding his penlight a little closer to the newsprint, he stared at the poor handwriting until the word before him started to take on coherent form: CLOSURE, he read. Below the terse word was printed Monday's date. Today was Tuesday, which meant the date could have been relevant for yesterday . . . or it could be some sort of marker for the week.

Slowly a chill came over Mike, and his own words, words he had hurled at Julie in frustrated anger, came back to him.

". . . *Every time you light out of your office, your*

house or wherever the hell he manages to track you down, you're setting yourself up as a target. . . ."

And as clear as a bell, Julie's words came back to him, words she'd uttered much earlier but with dark conviction as if even then she'd sensed some inevitable danger.

"They're going to send others."

"Jesus." Mike wasn't even aware he'd expelled the oath, or the fact that in his sudden apprehension it had sounded more like a prayer.

He restored and locked the fire file as quickly as caution permitted, then let himself out of Bronson's office and the building. As clear as any warning of danger he'd ever had on the streets was the one his gut was giving him now.

Julie was in jeopardy and needed him.

He sprinted to his car and gunned it out of the lot.

Chapter

THIRTEEN

A sedan, its headlights dark, was pulling away from the curb across the road from her house just as the house came into Mike's sight.

He pulled up and cursed again even as he cut his motor and jumped out. He rapped hard on Julie's door.

"Julie! Let me in." He knocked hard twice more and groped inside his pants pocket for his keys. His heart accelerated and he was about to start hammering again when he heard movement on the other side of the door.

Julie pulled open the door. Her brow was creased with consternation.

She was okay. Mike's relief was instant and consuming. He knew what had happened. She had been watched, not attacked. Not yet.

He shouldered around her, catching her gently by the waist once she'd shut the door. He just held her. She raised her hands to his waist after a moment and hugged him back. "What in the world is wrong?" she demanded.

Hell, no doubt he was giving her the fright he

wanted to avoid. He couldn't help it. His fear had been too real, and now his relief was too profound.

"Nothing, sweetheart. It's okay."

Julie pulled away, trying to read the truth in his face.

He decided right then to delay telling her that she had been under surveillance. He caught her hand instead and pulled her to the kitchen.

"Sit down," he instructed her. "I'll make some coffee."

Julie walked over to him and put her hand on his wrist, stalling him. "You'll do no such thing. Not until I get an explanation of why you came here practically bursting in like a wild man."

Why had he thought even for a minute that he could put her off? "I'll tell you. But not until I've made the coffee. So please, sit down."

He was brooking no resistance, and she wasn't going to get anywhere until Mike allowed it in his own good time. She sat.

Mike brewed the coffee. After it was done, he carried two mugs to the table and joined her.

"I got into Bronson's office after work tonight. I got into his files. I didn't like what I found; that's why I double-timed it over here."

"And you found?"

"Two files. One keeping track of Phillip Blakemore and his wife." He raised his mug and drank, studying her over the rim. "The other was keeping track of you."

Julie's own mug hit the table with a thud. She looked solemnly up at Mike. Her voice sounded thin even to her own ears.

"What about me? What kind of file could there be?"

"One that presented a meticulous record of not only the investigative crime stories you've been writing, but also the accolades you've been receiving in their wake."

Julie's thoughts raced back to the conversation she and Mike had had about her putting herself in danger by continuing to put herself into the hands of her silent informant in order to have access to the stories she wrote. She raised her eyes to Mike and knew that he was remembering too.

"I don't have to say it, do I, Julie. Will you admit now that this snitch thing is dangerous and that it has to stop?"

Julie pushed herself up and walked over to the counter. She leaned her rear against it and crossed her arms around her middle. She wasn't admitting anything without thinking it through, and she couldn't do that with his dark, troubled eyes boring across the table at her like an inquisitor's.

"Am I going to get an answer?" he persisted.

"Just hold on. I'm thinking."

"About what? *Dammit*, what am I going to have to do to get through to you!"

"Bloody well stop shouting for starters!" Julie shouted back.

"Well, you make me shout." He was only able to tone his voice down marginally. "I have never in my life met anyone more stubborn, more *pigheaded* than you. Doesn't the fact that a creep like Bronson is keeping tabs on you tell you all you need to know?"

"No, it doesn't. I don't know *why* he's keeping tabs, and if you'd calm down long enough to think with your head instead of your emotions, you'd realize that that's the case with you too."

Mike's expression didn't soften.

Julie's imposed calm seeped away in the face of Mike's unrelenting harshness. "Or do you know something that I don't?"

Mike swung his head away and ran his hand across the back of his neck.

He did and he didn't. Some game was definitely afoot; he just didn't know what it was. But he'd never get anywhere with Julie if he didn't get a rein on his fear for her and, accordingly, a rein on his temper and control.

"Listen, I'm sorry I shouted. Come back over here and sit down and I'll promise to make another effort to discuss this calmly."

Julie pushed away from the counter, gathering her short cotton wrapper closer around her night-shirt. She pulled her chair back out and sat.

"Thanks," Mike said. He reached a hand out across the table, palm up. After a moment, Julie's joined with it and Mike curled his fingers around hers.

"Okay," he said on a controlled exhalation. "Let's begin again. A man was murdered. He may or may not have had ties to organized crime; neverthe-less the possibility that he had some sort of involve-ment is likely, seeing as how he contacted you, boasting supposed information he was willing to share with you just prior to his death."

"And that death was very probably murder," Ju-lie continued, picking up the thread. "If indeed it was, we have to assume it was perpetrated in order to keep Blakemore from revealing to me or anyone else whatever he knew."

"Right. Only the attack upon you by Del Evans suggests that perhaps those who perpetrated the murder on Blakemore aren't sure what it is you know and were looking to silence you too."

"Either silence or find out," Julie amended, ignoring a frisson of fear. "I would suggest that if they wanted me dead, they probably would have succeeded by now, or at least they would have certainly been making more of an effort."

"Which in turn suggests that the likelihood is, they don't know what you know and are biding their time until they can find out."

"Which keeps me in danger—"

"And explains the surveillance I intercepted when I arrived," Mike interrupted her.

"Surveillance?" Julie's tone was mild; her watchful attitude was anything but.

Mike let go of her hand and got up to get himself some more coffee. "I'm pretty sure of it." He poured himself a second cup. "We'll come back to that. For now, let's stick to the evidence trail we're plotting. Okay?"

Julie nodded her assent.

"In a mere matter of months," Mike resumed, "before Blakemore makes contact with you, you start receiving anonymous phone calls from a man who won't leave his name but who seems determined to act as your very own personal informer."

"And the stories he seems determined to put me on to all have to do with violent crime or the victims who have been the targets of gang violence. My snitch's motives remain unclear, but the frequency of his tips doesn't cease to abate. Which suggests his motivation could be—?"

"Diversionary?"

Julie looked into Mike's eyes, giving the notion time to sink in. His steady regard, the quiet certainty in his tone helped lend credence to his guess. It just as successfully helped erode Julie's already tenuous peace of mind on the subject.

"From what?" she wanted to know.

"Obvious answer. Something bigger that's going down in this town. Which, in all likelihood, brings us back to the tie-in with organized crime."

Julie dropped her head and fought the sinking feeling in her stomach. What if he was right? What if she had been letting herself be used by her source to, in effect, assist the establishment of a criminal organization in her own backyard? The irony would be too terrible.

The only justification that had kept her talking to her informant had been her certainty that the good she effected in exposing the crime outweighed the ethically questionable manner of how she obtained her information.

When Mike had suggested before that she might be putting herself into just such a sling by the choice she had made, she had railed at him. She didn't have the heart to do so now because all of the satisfaction she had taken from the stories she had written was turning to dust.

It wasn't hard for Mike to figure out the direction in which Julie's thoughts were taking her. Her stillness was very reminiscent of that which had gripped her the last time they had gotten on to this subject. And because he knew how close to the bone all of this hit for her, he waited for her to give him a lead on how to proceed.

Eventually Julie rallied from the darkness of her thoughts. Brooding wasn't getting her anywhere except deeper into the hole of her own dark uncertainty. She needed to be more constructive. She needed to be a partner to Mike, not a pseudoneurotic hindrance.

"Let's get back to the surveillance," she said briskly. "Why are you so sure it was one? You could have just stumbled across Joe Blow, who happened to be lost. It's not hard to do if you're not familiar with these back roads."

"Joe Blow wouldn't have been parked in the shadows with his dome light off and his headlights dark. If he were lost, he would surely at least have been parked because he was trying to read some sort of directions or map."

Julie didn't have a viable argument for Mike's logic.

"So what do you suggest we do?"

"I think the time has seriously come for what I suggested the other day. I think I should move in here with you. I think I should put myself into position to be your around-the-clock bodyguard."

Julie could already feel the comfort of that suggestion even as her heart stuttered at the much more personal apprehension that had stopped them both from pursuing it before. The problem was, the situation had, as of tonight, taken them beyond that, and she wasn't stupid.

Someone had been lurking outside her house. Mike was more capable by training and inclination to deal with the potential threat of that situation than was she. What he suggested made her nervous. But more importantly it made sense.

"Would you want to move in tonight?"

Mike nodded. "I think that would be good."

Julie took a breath and expelled it. "Fine, then. You go get your stuff, and I'll make up the spare bedroom." She didn't meet his eyes as she got up to go to the sink and rinse out her mug. She could feel Mike's eyes on her back as he sat where he was, choosing not to move immediately. Clearly he was weighing, thinking.

As the silence stretched on she turned to face him. His features were calm and inscrutable. The heat she could see in his eyes, just barely banked, was not. He said nothing, however. He just pushed himself up from the table and with a casual "I'll be back" was gone.

Julie turned back to the sink and leaned her hands upon the edge for support. She wasn't really surprised to see them tremble since her insides were shaking like a leaf.

Lord, if she could just make it through this night, she might be okay.

She pulled linens from the closet in the back hallway and took them to the spare bedroom. It adjoined hers and overlooked the swath of beach that stretched to the east. She had the west view. Carpeted and papered in tones of wheat and brown with splashes of green for accent, it seemed a more masculine room than hers, which, she supposed, was fitting.

She had the bed made and fresh towels hanging in the half bath that opened off the rear of the room when she heard Mike come back into the house. Her hands faltered a bit with the soap she was unwrapping, and she gave herself a hard mental shake. They were adults, for God's sake, not impetuous children. Absolutely nothing was going to happen that they didn't want to happen.

Giving the room a last check, she walked out and went back into the living room to join Mike.

He was standing in the middle of the floor studying the duffel he'd dropped at his feet. At her approach his head jerked up and the frown that had drawn his brows together immediately smoothed.

"Just show me where to go and you can go back to bed," he said easily. "I'll check things out, make sure the house is secure, before I turn in myself."

Julie nodded. "This way."

She led him down the hall, noticing how his glance took in the rumpled bed she'd been sleeping in as they passed by the open door to her room. When she stopped at the threshold of his, he stopped behind her and for a moment was standing so close she could actually feel his warm breath caress the back of her neck.

He said nothing and she stood absolutely still. The moment was charged. And then he moved around her, still saying nothing, and she breathed again.

"I've already stocked your bathroom with linens and toiletries. If you need anything else, the linen closet is in the hall."

Mike dropped his bag on the bed and turned to face her. He stuffed his hands into his windbreaker's pockets, looking for all the world as if suddenly he didn't know what to do with them.

"I'll be all right, Julie, thanks."

Julie looked around the room and then down at her bare toes. She tugged at her hair, which had come to rest over one shoulder. "If you wake up first, it's all right to fix yourself something for breakfast. You already know where the coffee and everything is in the kitchen, and—"

"Go to bed, Julie." His interruption was soft yet firm.

Julie swallowed and backed out of the room.

"Right," she murmured. "Good night."

She shut his door behind her and walked over to her own. Debating, she finally pushed hers shut as well, but she didn't let it catch. She just wanted to be sure she'd be able to hear the comforting settling noises of the house during the night, she told herself.

Shedding her wrapper, she slipped back under the covers and snuggled down to go back to sleep. She could hear Mike moving around next door, opening and shutting dresser drawers. She turned and smoothed her pillow, trying to get it more comfortable beneath her head. She heard the shower in the adjoining bathroom switch on. Unaccountably, her own cool skin grew slightly warm.

"Dammit," she murmured, rising to grab the covers so that she could straighten them around her. All of a sudden they seemed to be tying her up like a straitjacket. She flopped back down, closed her eyes, and tried again.

His shower switched off, and her eyes popped back open to stare into the darkness. Her gaze was drawn to the little ribbon of moonlit hallway, visible between her cracked door and the wall. Abruptly Mike's door opened, and his shadow moved across that ribbon of light to continue down the hallway.

Long minutes passed, during which Julie heard him opening and shutting doors, rattling windows, completing the circuit of his house check. When he walked back into his room shortly thereafter, his door closed and didn't open again.

Julie lay where she was, doggedly courting the sleep that wouldn't come, until, giving up, at least temporarily, she threw the covers back and padded into the kitchen. Hot cocoa had always been Peggy's remedy to cure whatever ailed her when she was a child.

Julie pulled the canister of chocolate powder down off the cabinet shelf and scooped the necessary amount into a large mug. She had to smile at herself. *So, Connor*, she thought, *we're dealing with an ailment, huh?*

Words from one of her favorite songs suddenly came to mind, and her smile widened: "I've got a bad case of loving you, do I?" she murmured as she lifted the teakettle from the burner and poured water into her mug.

Julie carried her drink back out into the living room. Leaving the lamps off, she walked over to the venetian blinds and lifted them, letting the moonlight pour in. The illuminated night provided all the light she needed. She curled up into the sofa, putting her feet under her, and sipped at her chocolate until it was gone.

She curled her arms against the armrest and pillowed her head down upon them. Her last thought as the sleep that had remained elusive in her bedroom rushed to meet her was that she was safe, absolutely safe. Not only in body but also in soul.

The chocolate was warm in her stomach, and her mind was at peace. Her faith in the man down the hallway turned out to be the most effective sedative of all.

———

Mike was running, running down a long, dark tunnel. Total darkness hemmed him in from the left and from the right. Some unseen force was pushing him down the tunnel, pursuing him, threatening to hurt him if he didn't run. And so he did, and when the flames shot up to block the precious light at the end of the tunnel, still he ran.

Sweat was pouring off him as he got closer to the heat. He tried to stop, to stand inside the darkness where it was safe, but his feet kept moving him closer to the flames. And then he was there, throwing his hands up against the searing wall of death.

But just when he thought he was done for, the flames dropped away, as if they had been sucked down into some vortex beneath him. In their wake, he saw his father lying bloodied and bruised on the deck floor. Mike ran to his side, noting that the tunnel had somehow transformed into his father's yacht.

He knelt beside his father, trying to comfort him, trying to shield him from some unknown death that lurked just behind them . . . over them . . . at his shoulder. Mike jerked his head up and saw his mother. She was holding a gun on them both. Her smile, the smile that he had grown up with, wasn't really a smile at all, but some gross rictus of hatred.

"He's dead, Michael," she said, "dead. And I killed him. And now I'm going to kill her"—a hooded figure materialized out of the darkness; in its grip was a struggling Julie, looking very vulnerable and scared in her thin cotton nightshirt—"and then I'm going to kill you."

His mother's soundless laugh drifted out over the night, no less terrifying for its silence. Mike looked down at his father, and his horror grew. His father was dead, his skin ashen and cold, but he was laughing too.

"You let me die, boy," the corpse said. It and his

mother were both laughing together as if they shared some great joke.

Mike dropped his father's body to the deck and jumped away. Still the ghoul laughed.

"No!" Mike screamed. He tried to run to Julie, tried to reach her, but suddenly his wrists and ankles were shackled and he couldn't move. He watched helplessly as the hooded executioner leisurely raised a gun to her head.

"No!" Mike screamed again, helpless to move, helpless to save her. He struggled against his bonds, but he was helpless, helpless . . . the gun fired . . .

"Jesus, no!" Mike reared up and fought at the manacles binding his wrists. He kicked at the darkness that continued to swallow him. "I'm sorry. Dad, I'm sorry!" he gasped.

And then through the mist of his terror he started to realize it wasn't the darkness that enshrouded him, it wasn't a metal binding that was holding him down. He was in bed, fighting against the covers, fighting against Julie's soothing hands, hands that were trying to calm him as surely as the firm gentleness that was modulating her voice.

"Mike, it was a nightmare. Come on, honey, wake up, it's over now. It's over. I've got you. It's over."

What she was saying began to fully penetrate the mist, and he stilled, falling back against his pillows, gasping, needing to suck in deep breaths as if he were a marathon runner who had just come to the end of his race.

His heart was still pounding, his skin was still damp with the sweat of his fear, and, God help him, he couldn't push it away. The echo of that gunshot kept repeating and reverberating in his brain.

Before he was aware of what was happening, he felt the cover beside him shifting and lifting off him completely. Its light weight was replaced by a warmer one as Julie climbed up onto the bed beside him. She pulled him close and draped her arms around him until he turned enough to put his arms around her and return the embrace.

"Oh, God," he breathed, "it was so real. It was all so damned real."

"Shh, I know. But it's all right now, I've got you. Just rest."

Grateful for her presence, touched that this slight woman had come running to his side to slay his night dragons, Mike shut his eyes and pulled her close. He willed his heart to slow, his breathing to even, his senses to clear.

"I've got you," she repeated again, like a litany. She offered it to him like some verbal talisman he could carry with him into the night. And as its magic began to soothe, Mike's fears about his father and mother and Julie's safety all began to recede beneath a greater urgency to draw comfort from the protector he held in his arms.

"Julie," he breathed. He wasn't sure what he was saying, he just needed to say it.

"I'm right here. I'm here."

He pulled back a little to look at her, asking, wanting. Her eyes slowly answered, and when Mike erased the last bit of distance separating them, her mouth opened beneath his.

Julie let him shift their positions, let him press the slight weight of her deeper into the pillows, drawing the essence of her closer into his arms because he needed her. But he wasn't the only one taking. He sensed that she was setting aside her own fears because she too needed to be needed.

Mike's lips lifted from hers and sank to her throat. He nibbled and trailed the caress over to her soft, fragrant shoulder. His tongue glided across her skin, heightening the touch, and he heard Julie's answering sigh.

"Mike, Mike," she whisper-chanted, and the plea in her voice urged him on. Drifting a hand down to her waist, he tugged aside a handful of the cotton shirt that shielded from him what he desperately needed to bring into view. He dragged it up until the warm juncture of her thighs was bare and cradling the hard part of him that burned to make her his.

He pulled a little more, and Julie shifted until her body released the nightshirt and her sensitized, sleep-warm skin was at the mercy of his persistent touch.

Mike suddenly turned until he was on his back and Julie was draped across him. He urged her up a little so that he could reach the waistband of his pajama pants, and when he did, her hands were there with him, helping him, wanting him, driving him insane with their urgency.

"Honey," he managed to say, "I'm not sure that I can go slow. I'll try, but I—"

Julie placed a delicate finger against his lips. "You're not going to hurt me." Her voice was low and husky and aroused. She'd never wanted a man this badly in her life, and the need to have him was carrying her outside her body, carrying her beyond caution and fear until there was only need. Only need.

She pushed the covers down to the end of the

bed, and as she did, Mike kicked his pajama bottoms out of the way until the cotton fabric joined them.

Julie was pleased and unbearably touched when he found, even through the heat of his passion, the sanity to reach over to the night table and pull from its drawer the precaution that would protect her. And when moments later he reached down to pull her back up to him, positioning her until she was straddling him and just short of taking into her body the passion he was so ready to give, she came eagerly.

For a breathless moment, Julie sensed an odd resurgency of his hesitation and his reluctance inspired her to take the initiative. She reached down between them and cupped him in her hand, luxuriating in the warm, tensile strength that greeted her. She rejoiced in the urgency that made him arch into her hand over and over as the drive for fulfillment reclaimed him.

She watched his pleasure-tortured face, and the realization came to her that for this first time with him she wanted his satisfaction perhaps even more than she wanted her own. And so she stroked him, stroked him lovingly, stroked him mad until she knew he had climbed to the brink and was ready to take the tumble.

"Julie!" he gasped. And she was there for him, there with him when he surprised her. He reared up and grasped her arms, pulling her forward, lifting her up so that she was left in no doubt that because it was their first time, he wanted her to be with him.

She shuddered as he filled her, and when his hands closed around her breasts, she felt her senses explode. She was still coming down when, again, she felt herself cradled against him, and their positions reversed until she was cocooned in his damp warmth, her thundering heart a companion to his.

He was still hard inside her and she wanted him to experience the same joy. And so she started to undulate her hips, slowly at first, coaxing him to take what he needed, telling him that though she appreciated his gentleness, it was okay to be strong.

Mike's answering groan seemed to rise from the depths of his trembling body. Julie sighed with the emotion he inspired within her and dropped her hands down to his steely buttocks to urge him along.

When he started to move, her breath suspended. When his own hand reached down to slip beneath her hips and draw her harder against him, she expelled it on a gasp. And when finally he lost himself to the rhythm of his own body, when he could only pump deeply against her, inside her, her legs involuntarily widened to receive his thrusts.

She felt herself quickening again, and then she was clinging to him, holding on for dear life when the second eruption gripped her. She cried out and heard Mike's answering groan as his body tensed for one pulsing moment before he shuddered uncontrollably against her body, and then more gradually as his spent body sank down upon hers, against her heart.

She held him in the silence that followed. And eventually, as breath returned to him, he gave the pressure back. Neither found words adequate to complement what had transpired, and so they said nothing into the long moments that passed between them, content to offer a kiss here, a caress there. He left her but briefly, and when he returned, he felt his contentment grow utterly complete when she smiled into his eyes and nestled smoothly back into his arms.

And when the dawn finally started to break over the horizon, they watched it through the window until, just as easily as they had come into each other's arms, they slept.

Chapter

FOURTEEN

When Julie woke, the sun was high and she was alone. Turning to her side, she ran her hand dreamily over the space where Mike had slept. It was still warm. She smiled.

She had her shower and went into the living room to find him. Everything was quiet and she saw that the back door was open. She walked over to it, peered out, and saw Mike sitting on the porch step.

His back was braced against a railing post, and his legs were stretched out in front of him, crossed at the ankles. He was barefoot, clad only in khaki shorts. A mug of coffee was cupped in his hands.

Julie pushed open the screen door to join him.

"Good morning," she said, kicking his feet over a little to make room.

"Hey, girl," he responded softly. Reaching over, he ruffled her hair. When he drew back, Julie caught his hand for a moment to give it a squeeze before letting go.

"About last night," he began.

"I'm all right with it, Mike," Julie interrupted him. "It's all right."

He smiled slightly, letting his eyes drift over her, taking in the way the healthy glow of her brown skin seemed to be creamily highlighted by the red polo shirt she wore and the waving blackness of her hair.

"I was about to say that I'm not sorry about it either. It was special, and I'm glad it happened." He took a breath. "I need time with it, though, Julie. I think both of us do." In the wake of her silence, he felt compelled to push a little. "Am I wrong?"

Julie looked deeply into his eyes while she searched her own heart. What she found compelled her to be just as honest. "No, you're not wrong."

Mike nodded and looked away. "But that doesn't mean that I want to give up what we have today, nor the possibility of where it might lead us."

Julie scooted over on the step so that she was sitting directly in front of him, so that she was able to lean back into the arm he wrapped around her shoulder.

"Neither do I." She lifted her hand to cover the one at her shoulder. They sat that way, together yet lost in their own individual thoughts, for a long while, letting the sun bathe them, letting the morning take on life.

Eventually some of the things that Mike had said last night before they'd made love came back to Julie. The curiosity she felt about them then rose anew. As did the apprehension.

"Mike, did the person you saw watching the house last night see you before he took off?"

Mike felt the sudden tension in Julie's body and pulled her closer. "I don't think so, hon. He was already moving pretty quickly down the road by the time I came into plain sight."

Julie digested that, then asked, "What do you

think it means, Mike, the fact that Bronson has been keeping files on both Phillip and Donna Blakemore? Do you think it's he who's behind Phillip Blakemore's murder?"

"If he is, he wasn't acting alone."

"How can you be sure?"

"His connection to Micah and Micah's connection to organized crime. The fact that the shadow of the mob is all over this thing. And besides, Bronson has always been a small-time operator. He still is. I can't see him orchestrating that scenario of Blakemore's murder all alone."

Something about what Mike had just said struck Julie as odd. She turned her head to look at him.

"Scenario? You say that as if you had specific knowledge about how it was done."

Mike looked down at her, damning his relaxed guard and the subsequent slip, which could still be salvageable.

"Just a figure of speech. All I meant was, the murder involved probable sabotage, and nothing about Bronson sways me into believing the man would be willing to single-handedly take on something that complex."

Julie seemed to think about it, then she slowly turned back around. "Then if you think his murder was planned by the mob, do you think their motive was truly to silence him about what he knew, or do you think it was maybe some sort of act of revenge?"

Mike relaxed again, glad that Julie seemed to have accepted what he'd told her. "To my knowledge, the activity of the most powerful syndicates is rarely marred by brutal sentimentality." That much about the particular syndicate that increasingly looked to Mike to be behind his father's death was the truth.

"They tend to like to keep their business clean, simple, and precise. No wasted actions, no ambiguous motives."

"So you're suggesting that Blakemore's murder, if syndicate related, which it would seem to be, was purely a precautionary measure."

"Yes." Against what, Mike wondered bitterly? And then he was snapped away from that thought with Julie's next musing.

"Then if he knew something, he must have been involved in it. Men who seem to be as upstanding as Blakemore don't just happen to innocently acquire information that could get them killed in the normal scheme of things." She gave it some more thought. "And if that's so, what do you think his wife's link could be to all of this?"

"I don't know yet, Julie. I have to think about that."

She must have heard something in his voice because she turned her head again to look at him and asked, "What? Are you all right?"

"Yeah, I'm fine. Listen, I think we need to escalate things a little. I want you to see what else you can find out about Micah and about Blakemore Industries. Any other subsidiaries of the Industries, any hush-hush business moves, any silent partners who may have once been or are now on the scene. Anything, everything."

"Okay. And what will you be doing?"

"Stepping up the surveillance of Bronson, I think. That man has something to tell, and I'm going to find out what it is."

"Fine. I'll get started right away. This is going to take a lot of work and—" She expelled a sigh. "Oh, Mike, I'm just ready to see it ended."

"Me too, babe." The problem was he was beginning to be afraid of where the ending might lead.

———

"I want her brought in."

Simmons faced his boss, who was seated behind a massive desk positioned the width of the study across from him. "She will be, soon. Bronson already has a handle on it."

"No, I mean as soon as possible."

"What's happened?"

"Roy thinks his files have been tampered with. Nothing blatant. Just a couple of inserts he thinks have been shuffled around inside one of his folders."

"Nothing's missing? Nothing has been damaged?"

"He says not."

Simmons expelled a sigh. "You handle things enough and you're bound to shuffle them. He's never been concerned about this before. Why now?"

"He says he's got some new help he's uneasy about."

"Uneasy how?"

"The guy rubs him wrong, stays too quiet, too much to himself, which wouldn't be a problem except for one thing."

"Which is?"

"Bronson says he watches everything. Bronson doesn't conduct organization business from the bar very often, but when he does, this help seems to be nearby wherever he moves. The guy is making him nervous."

"So why doesn't he fire him?"

"Because if the guy's carrying around something

Bronson thinks he ought to know, he'd rather have him where he can get to him than have the guy circling around somewhere out of reach.''

"Well, I'll put somebody on to watching him too. What's his name?"

"Quinn. Mike Quinn."

"I'll take care of it. In the meantime, you want the Connor woman brought here to the estate?"

"Yes. It's safe here, and there will be no interruptions when we interrogate her to get what she knows."

"About the organization and Phillip Blakemore's role in it."

"And about one other disturbing little thing that's come up."

"What's that?"

"Her newest fascination."

"Which is?"

"Micah, Paul. Micah. It's only a matter of time before she makes her way to Santos. That can't happen."

"Are you sure about what you're suggesting? He's been loyal to us for a lot of years."

"Not suggesting, Paul. Stating. His company's profits have been especially good, lately. But I somehow tend to think that even his luxurious style of living has undergone a significant elevation above and beyond the allowance for what he's taking home every week."

"You know he's stealing from us, then?" Simmons settled back a little further in his chair.

"No, that's been checked. But it would appear that he's pulling in an additional income for some sort of extracurricular service rendered. Combine that appearance with the fact that for the first time in our acquaintance, I'm getting reports that he's been showing an inordinate amount of interest in the working end of a variety of business operations that don't directly concern him."

Simmons's relaxed posture abruptly dissolved, and he leaned forward. His expression was intent, his voice controlled. "You think he's informing, then."

"I think his behavior is raising too many questions, and that the imminent intrusion on the situation by Julie Connor is making the solution to a dilemma I've been wrestling with increasingly desirable."

With perfect understanding, Simmons gazed into the eyes that regarded him steadily from across the room. "You can consider the solution in motion."

———

"Roy! It's for you." Mike held the receiver up above the heads of the guys lining the bar, just in case Bronson hadn't made out what he'd said amid the noise from the television, the laughter, and the loud talking.

Bronson turned his head away from a customer he'd been chatting with. "I'll take it in my office, Mike."

"Sure." Mike pressed the hold button and went back to filling another mug from the tap. That was the third call tonight. Same caller, same intensity when he'd asked for Bronson.

Mike glanced at the phone console and saw the flashing red light go still, signaling that Bronson had picked up the call. He noted the time. Ten oh-five.

Ten thirty rolled around and Bronson's line was

still lighted. Mike wondered what the voice-activated cassette recorder he'd concealed on the bookshelf behind Bronson's desk would reveal after he retrieved it tonight and played it back.

Last evening's observations demonstrated clearly that time, particularly for Julie, was running out. Mike intended to rush things to a head tonight, including some insight into when Bronson's "closure" was coming.

Five minutes later Bronson's line went dark, but Bronson didn't come out of his office for the rest of the night. About five minutes before midnight rolled around, the line lit up again. The last customer walked out, and Ed started the routine of his nightly cleanup.

"Hey, Ed?" Mike called.

The man looked up from the pile of dust he'd swept up and was picking up to dump into a trash can.

"How's Betty Lou been treating you?" Mike narrowed his question with a smile.

Ed grinned back. "Ain't got no complaints, man." He went back to sweeping.

Mike's eye touched on the phone console again. Bronson was still talking.

"Sounds like you've been taking good advantage of that new shift of hers."

"Yeah," Ed mumbled. He was still grinning.

"Listen, man, it's the weekend. Why don't you take off. I'll finish that."

"Nah, not your job. I'm almost done."

Yeah, dammit, Mike thought irritably, *so is Bronson probably*. "Really, man. You go visit your girl. Shit, you can bet I'd be out of here on a Friday night if the offer was reversed and I had a girl of my own."

Ed's broom paused. He stood gazing at the second pile of dust he had collected, apparently, Mike thought hopefully, mulling it over. Finally Ed said, "Well, if you really don't mind . . ."

"It's done. Get on out of here."

Ed leaned the broom against a table and, with a definite pep in his step, trotted over to the bar, untying his apron on the way. He folded it neatly, placed it on the counter, and turned to leave. He'd taken two steps when he hesitated and turned back.

"Mike, are you—"

"Yes," Mike attempted to soften the sharpness of his response with a chuckle. "Good night. And give her a kiss for me."

"Yeah." His certainty restored, Ed saluted and left. When Mike heard his car rev up in the lot, he dropped the rag he was holding and popped open the cash register. From the recesses of it behind the cash tray, he pulled out his gun, which he had stored there when he'd come in this afternoon, checked the clip, and snapped the drawer closed.

He walked lightly down the hallway, taking care that Bronson wouldn't detect his approach. When he reached the door, he could hear Bronson talking although he couldn't distinctly make out what he was saying. What he could make out was the fact that Bronson was upset.

Taking a chance, Mike held the gun behind his back and used his other hand to delicately test the knob to the door. It moved easily, and Mike turned it as far as it would go. Then, carefully, he eased the door away from the jamb just a crack, just enough to provide some clarity to Bronson's side of the conversation.

"Yes, yes. But the fact remains that maybe Phillip

didn't have to die," Bronson was saying. "I don't care, he could have been taken instead."

A gap of silence followed, and then Bronson said, "Maybe Pete Henry didn't talk because he really didn't have anything to tell. Connor should have been the focus all along. Maybe somebody else could have seen that. Maybe we need a younger man to start doing your job—what? No, *you* go to hell, you bastard!"

That cinched it. Mike started to force his way inside, but Bronson's next words held him where he was.

"He must have taken the money and run after he did Blakemore; he didn't return to the pickup point after the hit, and nobody's heard from him since. 'Course, the other possibility is, maybe he was unlucky and got torched too. That explosion wasn't in any plan that I knew of, unless our boy decided at the last minute to get a little creative on his own."

Bronson listened for a moment, then continued heatedly, "Listen, I don't know why you decided to make the approach anyway. Blakemore had kept his hands clean for the whole twenty-five years he was here. You should have believed him when he said he didn't want any part of the action anymore. All of us should have."

Mike felt numb. What he'd been trying to tell himself wasn't true very clearly was. Not only had his father had knowledge about the crime syndicate that had killed him, he had, at least at one time, been part of it. And if that was true of him, and his mother was still active in running the family business, which Julie had discovered could have a link with organized crime, then his mother—what was Bronson saying?

"When is that backup going to get here to help me with this Quinn? Something isn't right. He smells like a cop."

Mike pushed his way inside. He took the time to enjoy the satisfaction of Bronson's startled gaze as, first, it registered him, then, second, the gun. Mike had it pointed at his face.

"Shit, man, I told you—" Bronson didn't get the chance to say any more because Mike was across the room snatching the receiver out of his hand and slamming it down.

Mike hauled the older man to his feet and positioned his body behind him. The hand holding the gun wrapped around Bronson's throat and Mike tightened his arm to secure the man in a hammerlock.

"All right, old man, now you can start talking to me." His voice sounded alarmingly cool, even to his own ears. "Who killed Phillip Blakemore? Who's trying to hurt Julie Connor?"

"Let me go, punk!" Bronson struggled against the hold, and Mike increased the pressure against his throat for the trouble. Bronson coughed and spit out a string of oaths, but he stopped struggling.

"Now, we'll try again," Mike said. "Tell me who arranged Phillip Blakemore's murder." He cocked the gun beside Bronson's ear for good measure. "Did you?"

"No!" Bronson raised both hands to pull against the vise Mike's arm had become. Mike didn't give an inch. The man had room to talk. It was enough.

"Then who? Come on, dammit!"

"The organization," Bronson gasped. "Phillip knew too much. He always had, ever since he left us. But he was also just as culpable as us, which kept him from threatening to spill it all these years. Until now."

Mike blinked as the ugliness of what Bronson was revealing struggled to sweep away his concentration. He fought it with everything inside him, knowing he needed to stay focused on this moment, focused on learning what he needed to keep Julie and maybe his mother alive.

"What did he have to spill? And who was he going to spill it to?"

"The approach. We approached him to join us again. He declined years ago after he moved here, but we knew he wasn't a threat to us then because ratting on us would have been like ratting on himself. He'd been in too deep. He had too much to lose.

"So we let it lie until a few months ago when we decided to expand our operation into Indiana. He was our natural contact. The decision to try him again was made. He refused."

"And instead decided to talk anyway, despite the legal repercussions he knew he was inviting, to say nothing of the retribution from you guys. Why?"

"Let me *go!*"

Mike clipped him on the ear with the gun. "*Why*, you scum?"

"I don't know! He said he was tired of living with it! He said he was getting too old, and it was weighing too heavy on him. He said something about wanting to make amends with his son, that whatever happened after that was out of his hands."

Every word Bronson uttered battered Mike's consciousness like sharp stones. Holding it together in the face of what he was hearing, what he was relearning about his father, was arguably the hardest thing he'd ever had to do in his life.

"Who was he going to tell?"

"The reporter. Julie Connor. Liked her. Thought he could trust her."

"Why not the cops?"

Incredibly, Bronson chuckled. "Like I said, he used to be one of us. He obviously still remembered which bases get covered first, and the old bastard wanted to live long enough to win."

Now came the hardest question because it could lead to the hardest answer of all. "Who's threatening my mother, Bronson?"

"Your mother? What the hell are you talking about?"

"Before my father died, he told me to protect my mother. Tell me who's after her?"

As what Mike was saying hung in the air, Bronson's struggles lessened. His voice sounded strained.

"*Jesus Christ*, you're the kid. You're supposed to be on vacation, not here meddling in this! How do you know—? Why are you—?"

"Answer the question, man!" Mike's patience was gone. The second clip he gave Bronson was not gentle, and the man went down. "Get up," Mike snarled. "Get up or so help me I'll hurt you."

Bronson lay on his side, looking up at Mike with wary eyes. And then those eyes flickered to the desk drawer that was level with his face. before Mike could intercept him, Bronson had the drawer open and was fumbling to pull out his own gun.

Mike rushed him and Bronson's gun clattered back into the drawer. But that didn't stop Bronson from trying to get control of Mike's. They struggled and Bronson made it to his feet. Mike had youth on his side, but the old man was strong, and as they struggled they lurched awkwardly across the room, each straining for dominance.

The room's single unshaded window was at Mike's back when the old man managed to get his fingers curled around Mike's fist that held the gun. Mike resisted him, but Bronson was able to take away Mike's advantage when he swung his own hand, smashing Mike's closed fist back into the wall behind him.

Mike grunted with pain but held on. Bronson was so intent on taking the gun that he was unprepared for Mike's knee smashing up into his crotch. The old man went limp, and Mike lunged away from Bronson and the window, leaving the old man sagging in front of the window's metal grate.

The lunge saved Mike's life. In what seemed like less than a split second after he moved, a bullet smashed through the grate, somehow missing the metal and making deadly impact with Bronson. It took him cleanly in the face.

Mike didn't have time to be shocked or even to think; he reacted.

Whirling away from Bronson's gory corpse, he shouldered past the half-closed office door and hit the hall running. The shot had come from the back, but he'd seen no car parked in the lot. The shooter had lined up the kill on foot.

Mike figured he had maybe a thirty-second advantage before the assassin made it around to cut him off at the front. He put on a burst of speed, trying like hell to cash in on that advantage.

The front lot was empty, the only car parked his. He made for it and had the door open when he heard another car careening around the building.

Mike threw himself inside, jammed his key in the ignition, and gunned the car out of the lot. The killer was close behind him.

It had rained during the night, and now the street gleamed blackly beneath Mike's screaming tires. He had to get to Julie and pray that it wasn't already too late. But he had to shake this killer first or sure as hell it would be.

Mike accelerated to a dangerous pace, taking a series of twisting and turning two-lane roads. The killer was good. He didn't seem to be closing the gap significantly, but neither was he being shaken. And then suddenly he was gaining ground and Mike kicked his car into gear, giving the vehicle its head and hoping it would live up to its performance reputation.

The killer was closing, and Mike was grimly assessing his options when fate gave him a break. The killer was advancing and then he was skidding, the car going sideways, obviously wildly out of control. Through his rearview Mike could just make out the killer wrestling with the wheel before the careening car's tires went off the road. The last thing Mike saw was the slow-motion rotation of the car as it slammed sideways into a stand of trees.

. The actual impact was frightening, and Mike could imagine the car and its driver smashing through bark, metal, and glass until both came to a mangled rest at the side of the road.

Mike decelerated and reversed long enough to confirm his guess, then he changed his direction until he was heading north toward Julie. Others would be after them. Perhaps they already were.

He just prayed to God that when he reached Julie he wasn't too late.

Chapter

FIFTEEN

The house was dark when Mike pulled up outside it. His heart thudded painfully as he vaulted out of the car. Running up the steps, he had the presence of mind this time to use his key to let himself in.

"Julie!"

"I'm back here."

"Thank God," Mike whispered. She sounded absolutely fine, and he followed the sound of her voice to the den in the rear. She was seated at the home computer station she'd rigged up since she'd been sitting the house. And now she appeared to be waiting for a printout to finish spilling from the laser jet beside her.

"Mike, I—what's happened?"

"Come on, honey, we have to get out of here."

"Why?" But even as she asked she was standing. His face was closed and hard and it was frightening.

"Bronson's dead. There was some trouble at the bar tonight. Our secrecy's blown. We've got to get out now."

Julie was smart enough not to ask questions. The

time for answers would come later. "What do we do?"

"We throw together what we need and we move."

Julie didn't waste time. She ripped the printout from the printer, folded it, and slid it into her pants pocket. Then she went to her room and pulled out an oversized carry-on and started emptying T-shirts and shorts from her drawers. Toiletries, lingerie, and casual shoes rounded out the haul. She met Mike in the front room in ten minutes.

Without a word, she followed him outside, locked up the house, and then hesitated. She wanted to leave word for Peg that she would be out of touch for a short while. But even as she considered doing it, she knew she couldn't invite the danger of leaving such an obvious flag behind them.

Unhappy but resigned, she turned to Mike and they were on their way.

Julie waited until they were on the toll road headed toward Illinois to ask him where they were going.

"To a safe house I know. We'll be all right there temporarily, until we can get some bearings and figure out our next move."

Julie accepted that. "Why is Bronson dead?"

Mike spared her a brief glance. "I'm pretty sure it's because someone was trying to kill me."

"Who?" Julie was making a monumental effort to maintain her calm, to keep her voice steady. Though she felt close to panic, she knew the last thing Mike needed to contend with was her fear.

"The same people who killed Phillip Blakemore. The same people who were responsible for the attack on you. The same people who murdered Pete Henry."

"How do you know?"

Mike recited everything Roy Bronson had said. He omitted his own apprehensions that Bronson had been skimming the tip of the iceberg, that before this matter was through they would both come to learn there was much, much more.

"Oh, God." Julie turned her head away from him to look out of her window, to focus on the darkness as it raced by.

Mike reached over along the seat and took her hand. It was still and cold. "We'll be all right for tonight. No one is on our tail right now, and I know exactly where to go."

Several more miles passed and both Julie and Mike sat quietly in the dark, formulating their thoughts, dealing with their fears. And then Julie said, "I've learned something more. Something to complement what you've already told me."

"And that is?"

"There's a definite connection between Micah and Blakemore Industries that extends beyond what's strictly legitimate. At one time briefly in the past they were jointly suspected of having affiliations with underworld crime figures."

Mike felt the same sense of unreality that had overwhelmed him as he'd listened to Bronson's spiel grip him again.

"Go on," he said levelly.

Julie explained how she had gotten in touch with some newspaper people she knew in Chicago who had not only a history with the city but a detailed knowledge that went back way before her time as well. She explained how one source had recalled a murder that had garnered some notoriety because key players who had been implicated also had business ties to Micah and Blakemore Industries.

"It was in 1969," she told him. "Myron Hammond, a drug lord, was murdered in his home in late May. At first, the police got nowhere with it, no leads and no suspects. They could only assume some motive having to do with syndicate war or gang interplay. And then they got a break. Forensics turned up some evidence they had missed the first time around and they found their guy. It was his story that made the headlines."

"And it was?"

"That he'd received his orders from a man named John Santos. Santos had ordered the hit, allegedly because Hammond was trying to encroach on some drug-smuggling action controlled by another entity."

"Micah?"

"That's what he said."

"But as we both know, the business is still operating today, so obviously his allegations didn't stick."

"Nevertheless, it was the common opinion of law enforcement as well as the media that the allegations at least merited serious consideration."

"So why didn't they go anywhere? Was it because of Santos? What happened to him?"

"He was able to beat the allegations by thoroughly discrediting his accuser with the assistance of some pretty slick lawyers. Charges were dropped, Santos stayed free, and Hammond's murderer got life for first-degree murder."

"And Santos?"

"Is still comfortably ensconced today where he was then. As a very active vice president with Blakemore Industries."

"And the connection between Micah and Blake-more Industries?"

"I had a time getting through those incredibly complex layers I told you about, but the bottom line is this. Micah has a very intimate, you might say in a sense, familial, history with Blakemore Industries. John Santos's first noteworthy professional assignment was as the acting CEO of Micah before he was brought over to Blakemore Industries.

"He was answerable then to the true driving force of Blakemore Industries, who, the bottom of my paper trail indicates, is still the real driving force behind the organization today: Donna Blakemore."

Julie's voice seemed to be coming from a distance, and Mike struggled to hold on to the thread of their conversation even as he reeled. It didn't make sense. His father had told him with his dying breath that his mother was in danger. Or had he been trying to tell him that his mother *was* danger? There had to be an explanation. There had to be.

"What about Phillip Blakemore?" Mike held his breath, waiting to be punched again by this one.

"It's shadowy. The only thing I could confirm was that while he and his wife retained joint ownership of their company, he acted as its chief legal counsel. His professional services were officially severed with their divorce in 1971."

"So, there's another probable link between Phillip Blakemore and his executioners," Mike stated.

"You'll have to contact your federal source when we get to where we're going. The feds ought to be brought in on what we know."

"I'll notify who has to be notified in due time."

Julie looked over at him, a little thrown by what sounded like his distinct evasiveness. "But—"

"Look, let's just get through tonight, Julie, okay?"

Julie let Mike's sharp words hover in the air between them, wondering what he wasn't telling her, knowing that while he heard her words and gave appropriate responses, he was grappling with something more.

"All right, Mike," she said finally. "We'll get through tonight."

He didn't say anything more, and Julie could see by way of the watery moonlight that his jaw was set like granite.

They passed the rest of their journey in tense silence until finally they hit the outskirts of Chicago. Mike drove them to a suburb west of the city and entered a tidy residential area, distinguished by row houses and well-manicured lawns, none of which ran more than a few yards deep.

He found the one he wanted and pulled into its drive, cutting first his lights, then his engine. Julie looked at the illuminated face of her watch. It was going on three in the morning.

A soft porch lamp was on, and after they rang the bell, the resident of the house obviously used it to discern who was crazy enough to be at the door so early in the morning. Julie and Mike didn't have to wait long before inside latches were thrown and the door was swung open to them.

A tall, pale man of medium height stood before them in pajamas, which were covered by a plaid flannel robe. Both had obviously seen better days. His light brown hair was mussed from the sleep they had dragged him from, and his lean jaw was darkened with stubble.

But for all the fuzzy externals of his appearance,

his eyes were sharp, and after glancing at Julie, they settled on Mike with intensity and demand.

"Tom, man," Mike said.

It was the only address and clue to the man's identity Mike offered. Julie was about to take charge of the introductions and rudely ask Mike who the man was when Mike reached over to take her hand.

"We're in trouble," he told Tom. "We need a place for the night."

Tom seemed to weigh that before he spoke. "You got it." He stepped back, letting Julie and Mike walk in.

The house was dark, and Julie couldn't make out much except for the fact that the space was compact and economically furnished. Mike was speaking.

"Tom Redman, this is Julie Connor. Julie, Tom's my partner here on the force."

Julie held out her hand and Tom took it. His grip was firm and his study of her comprehensive. "So, you two are together?" He was gently digging, obviously wanting to be brought out of the dark.

"If you don't mind, I'll explain the particulars in the morning," Mike stalled. "Right now, we're just looking for someplace to crash."

"Okay. Do you need . . . ?" Tom was obviously trying to proceed delicately. "I can make up the sofa through there"—he gestured into the darkness behind him—"and the room in the back—"

"Not necessary," Mike helped. "The back bedroom will do fine."

Tom's glance went from one to the other, and he discreetly held his curiosity as well as his tongue. "Fine. I'll get you the sheets and stuff you need to make it up."

Mike headed toward the rear of the house, and

Julie followed. Tom met them at the bedroom door and transferred an armload of bedding to Mike.

"Will that do it for now?" Again Tom looked them over.

"Yeah," Mike answered. "Good night. And thanks."

" 'Night." Tom nodded. He seemed to be debating about whether to say something else, and apparently decided against it. He nodded once more, then faded away.

Mike stepped aside to let Julie go in before him. He followed her and shut the door, turning the lock. Julie dropped her bag to the floor and heard Mike hit a wall switch. A table lamp flicked on, throwing a soft, warm glow across the room.

She looked around tiredly and noted that the window was shaded. She walked over to it and lifted a corner to look out. Their room overlooked the backyard, which, even though it was shrouded in darkness, seemed to be a bit larger than the front. It was raining again.

She dropped the shade and turned back toward the bed, intending to help Mike make it up. He already had most of it done, so she grabbed a pillow and stuffed it inside a case, then she grabbed a second and did the same.

The house was air-conditioned, and though it wasn't cold, it was cool enough to make the prospect of curling up under the summer-weight blanket Tom had given them attractive. Mike offered her a corner of it and she took it. Together they shook it out and arranged it over the full-size bed.

When that was done, they looked at each other with mutual fatigue and started to remove their clothes. Mike stopped at his briefs and sat on the edge of the bed waiting for Julie to finish.

Julie unzipped her bag, reached in, and pulled out an oversize thin cotton T-shirt with the name of her paper and the accompanying word DEVILS embossed across the front. She glanced over at Mike and, reading his interested look, murmured, "Softball."

He nodded tiredly, but a corner of his mouth kicked up.

Julie discarded everything but her underwear and pulled the shirt over her head. When she joined Mike on the bed, they slid under the covers together. The lamp was on Julie's side, so she hit the switch and again threw the room into darkness.

When she turned back over to settle down, Mike's arms were waiting, and she scooted close, letting herself be enfolded within them. He dropped a kiss to her forehead and held her tight. Almost immediately, they both dropped off to sleep.

———

Julie opened her eyes abruptly. She wasn't startled exactly, but she did feel that something was a bit wrong. She was all alone on her side of the bed, for one thing. Turning, she saw Mike, sitting up against the headboard. She could just make out his silhouette by the faint, predawn glow that was dimly starting to seep into the room.

His arms were crossed in front of him, and one knee was raised beneath the sheets. His head was turned away from her, but she didn't need to see his expression. The same tension that had held him during the latter portion of their drive into the city was back again. Despite the brief time they'd succumbed to sleep, Mike seemed to be no more relaxed than he had been when they'd gotten here.

"It's all going to turn out all right, Mike. I believe that, and you've got to believe it too."

He didn't acknowledge her immediately, but when he did, he merely turned his head to look at her, offering no response.

"Today, we'll go to the police, and they'll help us out of this maze." Julie laid a hand on his arm, trying, maybe, to transfer a little of her positive assurance to him. Or maybe she was just trying to get him to talk to her.

What could he say to her? He knew she wanted to hear him reaffirm her assertion that things were going to turn out all right. But the truth was, even though his father's murder might get solved, things, at least for him, were going to turn out far from all right.

He'd been awake for a while, hadn't really been able to sleep, and in the darkness many things had begun to seem clearer.

For instance, the reason why his father had just taken off as he had all those years ago. If he had wanted to escape from a life, from an existence he had come to find intolerable, it did make sense.

It might not have been the right thing to do, and certainly leaving his only child might not have been honorable. But his father, like everyone else, had been human enough to make a mistake. And again in that light his leaving had been understandable.

And in the end, if Bronson was to be believed, and there was no reason why he shouldn't be, his father had reached out to him to atone. He'd attempted not only to make amends to his son, but also to come clean about his life, despite the fact that he had to know the mob was going to catch on and that talking to Julie was going to kill him.

Julie had just been an innocent bystander, caught in all of this because she happened to be the one his father had chosen as the conduit for his public confession and the public exposure of the rottenness that had invaded her town.

The more enigmatic puzzle piece to all this, of course, was his mother. She was the indisputable head of Blakemore Industries and had been for years. How could she allow the continued reputation of her organization to be jeopardized by a prolonged affiliation with a subsidiary that invited such public scrutiny of its suspected links to organized crime?

Unless of course, and this was what his mind was so unwilling to accept, she had full knowledge of that link and encouraged it. Had been encouraging it for years.

"Mike?"

He looked down at Julie again, wanting to talk to her, afraid that if he did open up to her, revealing his fears would make them more real.

"You can still grab at least a couple of hours of sleep before we have to get out of here," he told her. "Why don't you, honey."

"And what about you? Please tell me what's wrong."

"I will, I promise I will. But all in good time. You'll have to trust me on that, okay?"

No, it wasn't okay, but he didn't want to talk, so what was there left for her to do? She drew her hand away and lay back down, turning away from him.

Dammit, he thought with weary frustration. He slid down beside her.

"Julie, don't." He reached out and tried to coax

her to turn back over. She resisted. "There's nothing you can do."

"But there's something you can do, Mike," she said. "You can trust me."

"I do." He did, perhaps more than he had trusted another human being in his life. But, God help him, he was battling a lifetime of habit, and she wanted so much.

Or perhaps, he told himself honestly, she wanted nothing more than a measure of proof his professed trust entailed. Did he have the courage? More importantly, did he have the love?

Because love was exactly what he had been tumbling headlong into with her for the longest time now. Here in the dim hush of morning, that was another truth that had come to him. It unsettled him, but it was undeniably there, just the same.

"Julie, I've been living a lie," he heard himself say.

Julie didn't respond at first, but when she did, it wasn't with words. She simply turned over.

"My name's not Mike Quinn," he went on slowly, feeling as if he were excising every word from some rusty place locked deep inside him. "It's Michael Blakemore. I'm Phillip Blakemore's son."

Julie's features remained smooth, her gaze steady as she looked up at him, telling him to go on.

Mike studied her reaction, or rather, lack of one. His brow furrowed. "How long have you known?"

"I didn't for sure. I only started to suspect something was out of kilter the night you had your nightmare. Some of the things you said while you were caught up in the dream made me wonder."

"And yet you didn't confront me with a thing. Why?"

Again Julie gazed quietly up at him. And just as quietly, Mike knew. Because despite everything, despite her suspicion that he was on some level deceiving her, she still trusted him.

She realized the full danger of the game they were playing. She fully realized that he had basically stood between her and peril, maybe even death. Knowing that, she would have been fully justified in going to the police, in challenging his story in the attempt to ensure her own safety.

But she hadn't.

Because she had trusted him. More than he had trusted her. He felt humbled. He felt like a fool.

But beneath the enormity of all those realizations, he felt loved. For the first time in his life unconditionally loved.

"Oh, God, Julie," he whispered, reaching down to pull her close, "I'm sorry. I—I love you. I'm sorry."

She held on, but still she didn't say anything, and Mike pulled back hoping he'd see why.

He did. She was crying.

She reached a hand up to cup his jaw. "I love you too. I didn't say anything, ask any questions, because I needed you to come to me. I needed to know that you would take that step, and now you have. Now you have."

She pulled him down to her and kissed him.

A rush of tenderness flooded through Mike, and he returned her kiss, sharing it and deepening it until, at length, he made it his own.

"Julie," he murmured once, and then he pressed her more deeply into the pillows beneath them. He needed to be a part of her, truly a part of her, but the need was strangely without urgency, without haste.

He reached between them and caressed her slender hip, eventually tangling his hand in her silken panties and easing them off. And then he reached for his own briefs and discarded them as well.

When he returned to her arms, he started kissing her and caressing her, but for now he did no more. There was no hurry. No hurry.

He rose a little, so that he could gain fuller access to her body, and when he had, he trailed his mouth down to the base of her throat. There he dropped a kiss. He detoured over to her collarbone and dropped another kiss. And then he wandered back on course until his mouth was at a tender breast.

Not bothering to remove her T-shirt, he kissed her through the fabric, found her tautening nipple, and used his tongue to wet the caress.

Julie's hands came up around his shoulders, and she was aware of little else but the spiraling curls of pleasure each sweep of his tongue pulled from her womb.

When he widened his mouth to take in more of her breast, she gasped and let her legs shift against his. When he moved on to the other, seemingly intent on making it just as wet, its peak just as hard, Julie released a breathless little moan and arched her back at the raw pleasure.

Mike smiled against her shirt and carried on, ignoring the pulsing heaviness between his legs, intent at this moment on just making her feel good.

He loved her, and there was no hurry.

He pushed up her shirt a little, just enough to give himself access, and let his mouth move on. He stopped once to lick at the faint indentations of her of ribs, dallied once more to dip inside her soft little belly button, and then very deliberately hesitated at the barrier where her soft curls grew and shielded from him what he wanted.

Very casually he lowered his head a fraction and touched his tongue to that moist barrier, swirled it along her damp skin, testing her readiness, gauging her love.

He needn't have worried. She was weeping for him.

Julie's fingers curled in his hair, and she tugged, wanting the sensations he was creating not to stop but wanting the sensation of having him inside her more.

At her urging, Mike hesitated, but he didn't stop. Only when she was on the brink of release did he comply, but not as she had envisioned.

He took the time to reach inside his duffel, which rested beside him on the floor. And after his loving precaution had been taken, he climbed up her writhing, panting body, briefly blanketing it with his own. And then, very gently, he turned her over.

Julie was beyond coherence, lost in feeling, lost in love. When his strong hands delicately parted her legs, she didn't protest. When she felt him lift her hips slightly to position her, she wasn't afraid. And when she felt his hair-roughened body curve around her buttocks and back with soft abrasiveness, she could only sigh and concentrate on how she wanted more.

Mike gave it to her, easing into her that first tiny bit, sliding his hand around her and down between her legs to supply an invasive counterpoint to the thrust and then the slow, rhythmic movement of his hard body.

Julie's world narrowed to the pinpoint of sensation between her legs, hovered on the brink of something more, and then expanded into a throbbing fireburst of feeling. She gasped, then gasped again with the force of it, shuddered as the intensity of it pulsed on. And only when the pleasure started to fade that first tiny bit did she realize that Mike was still moving against her, moving with her, moving inside her, holding off his own climax.

She could feel his heat surrounding her like a furnace, feel his sweat trickling down her body, feel his need growing even larger inside her. Not wanting him to hold back, not wanting him to deny her the pleasure of his release a moment longer, she reached a trembling hand behind her and touched that wet, heated place where they were joined.

Mike trembled as if he had been electrified. A low, agonized groan tore from him and he shoved himself into her twice, then again, and then he climaxed. His orgasm seemed endless, depthless, and when it finally abated, he could barely breathe.

They collapsed together, Julie willingly bearing the weight of his spent body, Mike having not the strength to move.

"Oh, God," he managed, "oh, God, Julie. I love you."

Julie smiled, but she couldn't dredge up the energy to answer. She was already half asleep.

Mike was feeling drowsy too, and so he shifted his body just a fraction in order to give her breathing room, and then he linked his hands with hers. Shortly thereafter, they slept once more.

Julie dreamed she was being bathed in a shower of light. She was floating in some nebulous place as comforting as a womb, as beautiful as a vortex of kaleidoscopic colors. She thought that surely it was into such a sphere that she had been tossed. Her mind felt at peace, and her body tingled with contentment. She sighed with the fullness of it. The vibrations of her sighs woke her up.

But the tingling didn't fade away. It only increased, and with slow awareness Julie realized it was Mike who was sustaining the feeling.

She lay partially on her stomach and his wrist was nestled between the mattress and her lower body. His hand was stroking her. And when one finger gently inserted itself inside her to slowly slick across the sensitive nub of her femininity, she delicately convulsed.

"Mike," she whispered as the peak of the crest took her. But when her heart stopped pounding, the pleasure was already building again.

"Shh," she heard him murmur, and she did. It was so easy to obey when her very skin felt as if he had possessed it and made it his own. When the second climax washed over her, she whimpered. With the third, she could only shudder, her capacity for speech and thinking blown away by his touch.

Finally Mike withdrew his hand, saying not a word. He shifted them a little until her back was cradled against his body, until his hardness was cushioned against the soft flesh he had just loved.

Julie really tried to move, knowing he needed to be eased, but the warm band of his arms stayed her attempt. "It's all right," he mouthed against her nape. "You've given me all I need. Sleep."

And for the final time that night she did.

Chapter

SIXTEEN

When they awakened, the darkness of the night was completely gone, and a watery sunlight was breaking through the gray clouds hanging heavy across the sky.

Julie knew that Mike had things to tell her, apprehensions about his parents and the criminal organization so many indicators suggested both of them were part of. But they both agreed to postpone the venting until after they'd had their shower and joined Tom for the morning.

When they walked into Tom's kitchen, they found that he had obviously been up for a while because he had a platter of bacon and home fries and toast already cooked and warming in the oven for them.

Mike squeezed Julie's hand before taking a seat across from her at the kitchen table. As he sat, he saw Tom notice the gesture, and he met his friend's eyes with a slight nod and even slighter smile.

Tom reached for a piece of toast. "So, much has obviously happened, friend, since we last talked. Fill me in.''

With Julie's assistance, Mike did. They left nothing about what they'd uncovered out of the telling, and Mike ended the recitation by punctuating it with his very personal concerns about what role his mother might have been playing in the whole mess.

"Whew," Tom said softly. He snapped a piece of bacon in half. "I think your best option is to take all of this to headquarters, man. It's too big, and you can keep yourself alive only so long as a force of one."

Mike pushed his food around distractedly, accepting the logic in Tom's advice, wise advice that was hardly news to him. Assuming, of course, that he could trust the hierarchy he needed to talk to on the force, which was by no means certain now.

On the other hand, he'd stake everything he had on the trustworthiness of his lieutenant, who had long been a respected friend. That could, at least, be the place for him to start. But even accepting that, Mike's hesitation to contact his superior was strong. Furthermore, he couldn't rationally excuse the hesitation away.

All he knew was that despite the professional and procedural ramifications he would incur, this was about his family. That made it, at base, his problem to deal with. It was that simple. And that complex.

By now Julie was getting good at reading the intractability behind Mike's silences. "What are you going to do?" She was sure she wouldn't like it, but she had to know.

"The only thing I can do. Nothing irreversible, not until after I've confronted my mother."

Julie had been afraid he was going to say that.

"After all, when you look at all of this stuff that points to a link between her and Dad and criminal doings, it's nothing that's really concrete. Everything we're supposing here could still have a legitimate explanation."

"Here," Tom said, passing Mike a carafe, "have another glass of orange juice to wash your rationalizations down with."

Mike gave Tom a suggestion that was anatomically impossible.

"Boys," Julie intervened mildly, "let's stay constructive."

"I'd rather we stayed safe," Tom said. "The same people who killed Bronson, who would have killed you, Mike, had his timing been worse, are still after you now as far as you know. How long do you two think you can evade them?"

"It doesn't have to be for long. I just want to buy enough time to get to the core of the truth of all this for myself," Mike insisted.

"And that means hashing it all out with your mother in a face-to-face," Julie said.

"I've already said so. What concerns me right now is making sure you and Tom are not endangered by this. I need to get away from here, find someplace else to hole up until I can determine the best way to approach my mother."

Mike looked up at Julie, who was regarding him steadily. That she was reading into his declaration what he wasn't saying was evident in her eyes, in the set expression on her face.

"I'm staying with you, Mike, whatever you decide to do, so you can stop thinking about abandoning me for my own good right now."

"Tom was right about one thing, Julie. I am an army of one." It galled him to say it, but her safety was too important to him. "There's only so much I can do to protect you from what we may be up against."

"You haven't done so badly so far. No deal, mister. I stay."

Again Mike looked deeply into her eyes, giving her another chance to do the sensible thing without fear of hurting his feelings. She didn't budge.

He'd die for her, he thought.

"All right then, let's move. Tom," he said, pushing himself up, "we'll stay in touch. I don't know where we're going to be. And I guess even if I did, it would be safer for you if I didn't tell you."

"There's nothing I can do to sway your determination, then?"

"No. This is something I have to do my way. I'm sorry if you can't understand."

Tom rubbed his jaw and frowned down at the table. "As a cop, I think you very well might be crazy. But as a man, I'm not sure that if I were in your place I wouldn't do the same." He looked up, encompassing them both in his parting comment. "Take care and keep your heads up. I'm here if you need me, however I can help."

Mike walked over to his friend. Tom got up from his chair and the two clasped hands. Then turning to Julie, Tom surprised her by enfolding her in a big friendly hug.

"I have a feeling I could really come to like you," he told her. "I'm counting on getting the chance to find out."

Julie smiled, touched by his generosity. "Me too, Tom."

"All right then, you two." Tom nodded at them and looked down at his watch. "It's about nine o'clock now. High time you got your stuff together and took off."

Five minutes later, they did. Tom stood behind his screen door and waved them off as they backed out of his drive.

———

Their first stop was a car rental where Mike exchanged his car for something a bit more understated.

"So where are we headed?" Julie wanted to know once they hit the streets again.

"You've heard the saying 'hide in plain sight'? Well, that's where we're headed, somewhere invisible that's right in plain sight."

That somewhere turned out to be a motel not far from downtown. The most charitable way to describe it, Julie thought, was as a three-story functional.

Mike parked, and she grabbed her bag and got out of the car to join him. Eyeing the clientele trafficking in and out of its scarred doors, Julie raised her brow ruefully and thought it best not to dwell overmuch on what function the joint probably served.

Mike took her hand as they reached the doors. Julie didn't balk.

"Yeah?" The manager, a squat and startlingly hairy little man, regarded them without interest.

"We need a room," Mike said.

The little man looked them over, giving lingering attention to Julie. He shook his head and muttered, "They need a room, they say. Who doesn't?"

Julie struggled not to smile.

The man stated how much and Mike paid him and took the key.

They gave up on the elevator after three minutes and spied the service stairs about a foot down the hall to the right. Their room was only two doors down from the landing of their floor. Julie braced for what she would see inside.

Brown. The muddy paper on the walls was fading into brown. The chipped dresser and cheap wooden bed frame had no doubt started life that way; extensive scraping and scarring were now eroding the fact.

The naked shades at the window were an indiscriminate beige. They should have provided a bright spot, but they succeeded only in filtering the sunlight that struggled to seep into the room until it was muted too. Checking out the adjoining bath accommodations was a joy Julie elected to forgo until later.

She was thinking that things couldn't get any stranger when her attention was pulled to the wall separating their room and the adjoining one. Something was hitting it. She listened, puzzled for a minute, but as the noise took on a regular rhythm she realized what she was hearing and didn't know whether to be amused or embarrassed.

She looked over at Mike, who had hefted his duffel onto the bed. He was smiling and swept the room with an encompassing glance.

"At least it's clean," he suggested.

"Dare I ask compared to what?"

"No."

Julie heaved a long-suffering sigh, grateful for the undeniable humor of the situation. It was doing a fair job, for a few moments anyway, of lightening their load.

She put her own bag on the bed and looked over

at the dresser. On second thought, she let go of the zipper tab and left it closed, then walked over to the TV instead to flip it on. It was almost time for the news. Maybe they'd see something interesting. Maybe they'd see something about Bronson.

The possibility brought back her low-grade fear, and she unconsciously crossed her arms and rubbed them.

Sensing her mood, Mike walked up behind her and enfolded her in his arms.

"Why don't you lie down and get a little more sleep," he said against her hair. "We're not going anywhere for a while."

Julie started to protest, but she couldn't through her sudden yawn.

"What are you going to do?" she asked instead.

"Some thinking. Figure out a game plan."

"You're sure you want to handle it this way?"

"I have to."

She said nothing.

"It's still not too late for you to go to the police," he reminded her softly.

"I'm staying with you."

He was staggered all over again. That simple statement embodied such an enormous amount of trust. What had he done to earn it? No one had ever offered so much of it so freely to him before.

"Why?" He needed to hear a tangible reason. He needed reassurance that he was doing the right thing in not making her go.

"I have to," she said, echoing the same gut certainty he'd voiced moments ago.

"I love you, Julie."

"I know."

She looked back over her shoulder and let the

breadth of that statement take hold. His eyes gentled as he watched her, and she knew he was remembering everything that had transpired between them during the last forty-eight hours.

"I know," he echoed. And suddenly, the abilities and strength he knew he needed to protect her, the confidence that had momentarily faltered, making him worry that they just weren't there, were within his reach again. Her unconditional love had put them there.

He'd face down the whole damned mob for her because for the first time in his life somebody else's well-being, Julie's well-being, had become infinitely more important to him than his own.

"Go ahead," he said, setting her away from him. He turned her toward the bed. "Take that nap. We'll talk when you're done."

Julie moved her bag to an adjacent chair and lay down. The last thing she heard before she drifted off was a perky-voiced weatherman droning on about the warm front he was expecting to drift in.

NINE TWENTY P.M.

"Do they know?"

The speaker, a rangy, dark young man, waited with his fair-haired associate for a quartet of little kids, obviously defying their curfew, to get their bikes across the intersection. Once they had and were rushing down the road amid bursts of laughter and nervous chatter about how one was going to get it worse than the other, the two men walked on.

They were headed for Redman's house.

"Simmons has to; he gave the order. As for the boss, I can't say, man."

"Has to." The young one grunted. "What a bitch. Nobody would ever think to ask me, but if they had, I could have told 'em it was coming all along."

"Maybe. Maybe not. Wraps have been kept pretty tight on things since I been here. The oldsters say it was tight even before that. This was just bad luck, that's all."

"Yeah," the darker one murmured, unconvinced. "More like, inevitable, you mean."

The blond thought about it as they walked up Redman's drive. "Maybe," he said again. But he wasn't really listening anymore.

He was focusing on the task ahead. He flexed his hands, which were stuffed deeply inside his windbreaker pocket; then he curled his right one back around his gun. He knew without looking that his partner was doing much the same.

They were very familiar with each other's abilities and routines, had been for years. It was why they always worked so well together.

The blond's companion knocked on the door. He and his partner stepped out of the direct spill of light falling from the porch lamp. The door opened.

"Can we come in, man?" the Hispanic asked.

Tom opened his door wider, then stepped back to let them in. "I thought you guys were on until midnight."

"Nixed at the last minute, and since it's so rare we're all off duty together, Ed and me thought we'd come by to take you up on some of that poker you promised us."

Tom smiled. "Beer's through here."

The blond closed the front door behind him and glanced at his partner. They both watched Tom turn and head back toward the kitchen at the rear of the house.

Tom was shouldering the refrigerator door closed with his hip when the two men joined him. In one hand he held two cold bottles by their necks; he held his own in the other.

"Where's, Mike, man?" The Hispanic perched one hip casually on Tom's kitchen table.

Tom looked over at him in mild surprise. "I'm not his keeper. Far as I know, he's still on leave. Good thing, Jake, yeah, since he's always the one to whip your ass."

"So you're telling us you don't know." Jake's partner didn't sit and he didn't relax. He moved closer to Tom, thinking what a shitty assignment this was. Tom was another cop and a friend.

The first tendrils of unease started to stir inside Tom. "What is this?" He was setting the bottles on the counter when it registered that Jake's right hand stayed fisted inside his pocket.

For one flashing moment Tom felt disoriented. In the next he felt horribly naked and exposed, which he was, he realized through a wave of disgust and fury.

"You're with them, aren't you?" He jerked a drawer beside him open by feel. He groped for a knife. It gained him a frozen moment of surprise from his two colleagues, but the moment wasn't enough.

Tom felt a slashing pain across his left cheek and went down. He raised his hand to block the second vicious blow from Ed's pistol. He was no match on his back for the third when Jake restrained his arms and made the attack dual.

"Tell us where to find Mike and the girl and we

won't have to kill you. . . ." Ed paused in the beating, urging Tom to answer.

Through his tearing eyes, Tom could see his own blood smeared on the other man's fist, could see it dripping a little as Ed motioned to Jake with his gun. Tom's arms were finally loosed, and he tried to catch his breath, tried to pull forth the energy to counter this assault that was surely going to kill him.

On the streets he faced death nearly every day. Now that it hovered near, he was grimly aware of never having imagined the scenario in which it arrived wearing a trusted smile to blindside him in his own home.

"I don't know," Tom uttered through his dimming consciousness, around his pain. Then he heard the crashing of furniture, crockery and china and realized his house was being carefully ransacked.

Robbery, he thought grimly. The setup was being put carefully into place.

Ed and Jake knew him and had quickly made the determination that he wasn't going to tell them anything. And so they were embarking on phase two of the plan, arranging his murder, as they had the inside expertise and knowledge to do, to look like another statistic, a random break-in and assault.

"Go to hell, both of you," Tom gasped. "Burn with the high-priced scum you sold out to. None of you are going to win this thing."

"Wrong answer, bro." An ephemeral flash of regret was the only emotion Ed felt as he cocked his gun.

ELEVEN OH-TWO P.M.

"Oh, my God." Julie put down her fast-food hamburger, the product of the meal run she and

Mike had made twenty minutes ago. She watched the live-eye news report unfold with increasing horror and called out to Mike to hurry.

He came quickly out of the bathroom, alarmed. Seeing that her attention was riveted to the television, he turned his there too. He sank to the bed, settling in close beside her.

". . . Officer Horton, can you bring us up to speed on what's happened here?" the eager news reporter was asking.

The departmental spokesman, whom Mike knew well, looked back at the crime scene that had been cordoned off around Tom's house, then back into the camera. He looked furious but resigned. "From the mess inside it appears robbery may have been the motive, but we really don't have any firm indications supporting that assumption at this time."

"And how soon will you be able to confirm something from Redman?"

Horton fixed his gaze upon the pretty young man much as he would a scuttling bug, Julie suspected. "If Officer Redman lives, that confirmation will be ascertained as soon as possible."

"Do you have any suspects?" the reporter pushed on, undaunted.

"Some neighborhood kids saw two men out in the neighborhood earlier, but their descriptions are vague. Another neighbor may have seen something through her window. We're checking it out."

"Thank you, Officer Horton." The reporter turned a hard, glittering smile into the eye of the camera.

"As you can see, an awful, senseless tragedy has befallen one of our city's police officers, but not in the way one might most expect it. To recap, a savage act of violence just a few hours ago, apparently perpetrated in his home, has left Detective Tom Redman in extremely critical condition with a gunshot wound to the head. According to investigators here on the scene, the attack on the officer could be random. Gang violence hasn't been ruled out. . . ."

Julie scooted around Mike and got off the bed. Two steps later she was over at the television shutting it off. She heaved a sigh and turned back to Mike. His expression was frightening. The rage emanating from him made her catch her breath.

"It wasn't random," he said. "It was a warning, plain and simple."

"But how—"

"Because they know it's me who's on to them." Mike looked up. "She knows."

Julie joined him back on the bed. She put her arm around his shoulders. The tension threading through them hardened them like granite.

"Whoever Bronson was talking to that night only needed to hear his suspicion about a cop to put it together. Phillip Blakemore is killed, his wife has in all probability sanctioned the murder, and their son, who happens to be a cop, conveniently drops out of sight on an extended vacation.

"All she needed to do was send someone down to Bronson's with my photo, asking if this guy has been nosing around. The ID is made, and I'm a cop on the run."

"And they thought they could force Tom to tell them where we are."

Mike's face was set like stone. "They didn't think any such damned thing. They knew Tom wouldn't give me up. They did him to send me a message, to tell me they know the guy who's onto them and

Blakemore's murder is me. They did him to show me they're ready to start playing hardball."

An awful thought occurred to Julie. "Peg!" she whispered.

Mike nodded. "I'm calling my lieutenant. I'll keep the communication as safe as I can, although nothing at this point can be guaranteed. I'll fill him in, and he'll contact who needs to be contacted in Indiana so that safety precautions can be put into place to protect your aunt."

"And what about us? We can't sit still any longer. One way or the other, we have to move."

"I know. There's only one place to go, babe."

"To your home?"

He nodded. "To my mother."

ELEVEN THIRTY P.M.

Donna Blakemore leaned over to tap her cigarette out in a crystal ashtray. She stared unseeingly for a while at the television set she'd just snapped off with the remote. Eventually it became impossible to sit still, so she got up to pace.

Another mistake had been made. This time it might prove critical. Tom Redman wasn't dead, dammit.

The real quandary that had her on her feet, however, was not that Tom Redman wasn't yet dead. That could still be remedied; he would be. The real problem was the inescapable fact that before too much longer her son could be dead. More precisely, he would need to be, both he and the Connor girl who was with him.

The day she had dreaded since Phillip had left,

the day she had known in her heart would have to arrive, was finally here twenty-five years later.

Her son was on to her, and to keep all she had worked for, all she had sweated for for most of his lifetime safe, she was going to have to break the primordial bond between a mother and son.

She was going to have to betray her only son's trust. Brutally.

She swore just as the scrape of a key in her lock turned her around.

Paul Simmons stepped into the apartment. She'd known he would come, known he'd understand that he need wait for no invitation to meet her in the penthouse she used as her base when she was doing business in the city.

She knew, as she pulled him into her arms, that he understood he had much to answer for, but that for the moment this, *this*, was what she craved first. This was what they both needed most.

The sex between them had always been good. No, Donna thought as Simmons crushed her mouth beneath his, better than good. Electric.

She let him lead her to the sofa, let him open and then peel away the thin silk wrapper she wore. It was all that covered her. She took satisfaction in his visual appreciation of her still-trim body and palmed her own breasts, lifting one so that he could suckle it.

Simmons didn't bother discarding all of his own clothes. He took the time only to open his pants. Then he was against her, upon her, inside her. He rode her hard and fast, and when she moaned at the height of her climax, gritted her teeth with the force of it, he tensed, swallowed deeply, then came as well.

She lay there absorbing the aftershocks of her pleasure, letting the man who had been her lover for more than thirty years rest against her body. And then when she gradually felt her strength returning, she pushed him away.

Simmons didn't resist. He sat up and let his eyes follow her easy movements while she retrieved her wrapper from the floor.

When she was clothed again and Simmons's own clothes had been repaired, Donna moved away from him to sit on a chair across the room. Before what was going to be said was said, she felt it necessary to create a distance.

"Where are the two who handled Redman, Paul?"

"Ready to step back into uniform tomorrow. The shooter can't understand why Redman isn't dead. He said the bullet he emptied into the man was fired at damned near point-blank range."

"He couldn't spare the extra time or measure of caution to make sure he was dead?"

"Redman's girlfriend was knocking on the door. Came out of nowhere on this particular night just in time to fuck everything up. They had to get out. They were lucky they could make it out the back. It was bum luck, Donna."

"Theirs. I want them dead. If another piece of 'bum' luck should surface and Redman gets to talk before we nail him, it could become a disaster."

"They've served us effectively for ten years."

"Are you refusing to obey my order, Paul?" Donna's tone remained mild.

"No. I'm just thinking of how sanctions have always been carefully thought out or avoided if other options were there. I don't think we ought to get anxious about this thing and initiate a wrong move. The result could prove to be too intense."

"I don't believe I've ever been a rash woman, Paul. This organization has not grown and thrived because of my foolish decisions."

"Donna, relax. I'm not trying to offend. I just want to make sure that before we embark on any more"—Donna's brow rose, and Simmons carefully sidestepped the word *murders*—"absolutes, the reasoning we choose to justify it is clear."

"I suppose that's an oblique way of leading up to what you really came here to talk about tonight, hmm?"

Simmons paused delicately. "Mike?"

Donna steepled her fingers beneath her chin. "Yes, Paul. My son. Mike."

"What do you want to do about him?"

She smiled. "Meaning you want me to officially issue the call."

Simmons merely waited.

Donna looked away. "All those years ago before Phillip left, even before he found out about us, you wanted me to send my son away. I told myself it was because you were jealous of Phillip's child and wanted the boy out of our lives."

She looked across the room at him. "And so I didn't listen. I could have sent him away then. Phillip would have taken him.

"But I kept Michael because even though I had fallen out of love with his father, I needed Phillip's son to grow up healthy and to thrive so that I could make my point."

"Which was?" Even after all these years, Simmons had lacked the courage to really challenge the convoluted logic that had driven the woman he loved to make the choices of life and death she had in regard to her husband and her son.

"That if Phillip ever spoke out against us, if he ever in the slightest way indicted anything we had done, I would take from him the greatest thing a man can stand to lose. I would forever take away from him his son."

"But he's your son, too," Simmons answered slowly, trying to understand.

The expression on Donna's face remained illusive, as if she had retreated someplace deep inside herself. And then she seemed to shake herself a little, and she focused on Simmons again, focused as if she really saw him.

"He was the product of an act of jealous anger perpetrated against me by his father. I never told you that, did I, Paul? Never told you about the night Phillip raped me after he accused me of being unfaithful with you."

Simmons's brow knitted. "No, Donna. You didn't."

"Doesn't matter now," she said tonelessly. "It's all too far in the past. The point is, I have an errant son who needs to be kept quiet about all it is that by now he surely knows."

Simmons repressed a shiver at the facility with which the woman before him could so abruptly shut off her emotions in order to concentrate on a professional choice, a matter of business. The ability had always been her strength. But in the back of his mind he had always wondered when the day would come when her eye would turn on him.

"We still don't know where he is. But this town isn't that big, Donna. If tonight's summons doesn't work, we'll find him."

"It'll work. He'll come looking for me. He likes to think of himself as an honorable man, as an honorable cop."

She laughed a little bitterly. "Jesus, after all these years that one still gives me a laugh. My son, *my* son, the cop, can you believe it? No cute little boy trotting home to say, 'I want to be a lawyer,' or 'I want to be a doctor' from him. Oh, no. Some cosmic jester must have gotten a big laugh at the recitation that spilled out of my little boy's mouth, 'I want to be a cop, Mama!'

"He's the sanctimonious embodiment of everything that was foolish and sentimental in his father, everything that turned Phillip against the sheer magnitude of what we did, everything that turned him against us. Against me."

It was Simmons's opinion that the resourceful man and smart, obviously dedicated cop who had developed from Donna and Phillip Blakemore's little boy was hardly a lightweight matter. But he wisely refrained from pointing that out.

What he did point to was the question out on the table. "So what do we do when we find him, or when he comes to us, as the case may be?"

Donna peered at him as though he had failed to grasp the easiest solution in the world.

"We kill him," she said.

Chapter

SEVENTEEN

The dull glow of early morning was struggling to push its way into the room when Julie stirred. She was hovering between sleep and wakefulness when the low rumble of Mike's voice pulled her into full consciousness.

She turned on the bed to look over her shoulder and saw him sitting a slight distance away from her in the room's single threadbare chair. His ankle was resting across his knee, and the telephone was sitting in his lap.

"Yes, sir, since my father's murder," Mike was saying. "I understand. But my answers lay in Michigan City, and I had to be the one responsible for finding them."

Julie watched Mike as the silence on his end strung out. His brow creased, and he started kneading the lines that appeared there with a tired hand.

"It wasn't an intentional deception. I asked Tom to give me his word. Other than using departmental resources to pull up some background information for me a couple of times, he's been out of the loop.

Yes, sir. Yes. No, sir, she's with me.'' He sighed, raised his eyes heavenward and listened some more.

Julie threw back the covers and scooted down to the end of the bed. She rested her elbows on her knees and absently noted the contrast her toes made against the indiscriminately colored nub of the carpeted floor.

"This afternoon. I'd like some backup. I hope I won't need it, but I have reason to suspect there's a good chance that I will." For the first time, Mike's attention shifted over to Julie. "She won't come in, sir."

Julie met Mike's gaze and smiled slightly when he winked. The worry lines didn't leave his brow. She got up and walked into the bathroom.

Fifteen minutes later she stepped from the shower and wrapped herself in a towel before walking back out into the room. Mike had finished his conversation.

He was still sitting in the same position, and his gaze was focused on the day's street scene slowly coming to life outside the window. He didn't turn his head when he heard her entry, and Julie didn't disturb him.

She grabbed a T-shirt, some khaki shorts, some undergarments, and her cosmetic bag. Carrying them all back into the steamy bathroom, she closed the door behind her and allowed Mike some more time to brood.

The second time she emerged, she found him making a sweep of the room to ensure, she guessed, that they weren't leaving anything behind.

Silently she joined him. While he walked into the bathroom, she began stuffing everything she'd used this morning back inside her oversize shoulder bag.

Mike carried a couple of toiletries back into the room and finished packing his own.

"So what's the plan?" Julie sat on the side of the bed and looked up at him. He walked over to join her. Instead of answering immediately, he wrapped an arm around her shoulder and tugged her to him.

"Good morning," he murmured. He kissed her gently, taking his morning sustenance from the touch.

Julie sighed against his lips, and then she kissed him back. She braced one hand upon his jean-covered thigh and leaned into him a bit, deepening the contact briefly before she drew back. Her hand cupped his bearded jaw as she smiled into his eyes.

"Good morning," she finally replied, and then she sobered a little. "Or is it?"

"My lieutenant knows the story. He isn't happy with it, but it isn't anything I can't tamp down later. The important thing is that he knows that by one o'clock we're going to be headed over to my mother's place."

"And in the interim?"

"I want a Q and A with the former Micah Ltd. I'm going to beard that old lion, John Santos, in his own home today; his receptionist says he's off sick. Aren't we lucky."

———

Royce Manners was pleasantly tired. Though it was only nine in the morning, he didn't mind. He'd been running for about an hour, and now that his body had gently told him it had reached the end of its endurance, he sat thinking as well as recuperating his strength on a park bench overlooking the endless blue water bordering Lake Shore Drive.

Two weeks after the Evans gig, they'd brought him out of Indiana and into Chicago. They'd installed him in his own modest apartment, and though it wasn't quite in this ritzy district, it wasn't so far away that he couldn't carry his exercise across the boundary. It wasn't so remote that he couldn't pretend it was among these other upper-crust joggers that he really belonged.

He raised his face to the gently shifting early-morning breeze, appreciating the way it cooled the sweat on his skin, enjoying the way it sifted through his gray hair. When the rush of it eased, he turned his face idly to his left and opened his eyes. Another jogger, a well-toned young man clad in a thin blue tank and some clingy-fabric running shorts, both obviously designed to display his conditioning, was coming his way.

Royce smiled and nodded at the man, who smiled back as he ran past. *Ah, the life*, Royce thought. A pretty young blonde on a skateboard weaved and swayed artfully past a moment later. She was totally preoccupied with maintaining the smooth rhythm of her board and almost barreled into two joggers, who broke apart in the nick of time to avoid her. She sailed on, never looking up.

Royce smiled, trying to remember what it had been like to be that young, wishing he were again so that maybe he could go skating off behind her. Her two would-be victims intercepted his gaze and nodded to him, sharing rueful smiles of male understanding and resigned shrugs. When Royce chuckled, they slowed and with a gesture asked if they could share his bench.

"Hey, it's a free park, guys. Come on over and take a breather."

"Thanks, man," the taller one said. He was breathing hard with exertion. But it was as obvious with him as it was with his friend that the exertion was a healthy one having everything to do with conditioned effort and little to do with overtaxation.

The three sat in companionable silence for a while and watched the other passersby, the day, and the water.

"You guys run here every morning?" Royce encompassed both of them with a friendly runner-to-runner glance.

"Frank does," the taller one said, tilting his chin to motion over at his friend, who sat on Royce's other side. "I'm usually on my way to the office by now. But this morning he convinced me to run, so I'm taking it slow before the day's craziness begins. How about you, man? This your regular beat? You look like you're in pretty good shape."

Royce leaned back, lifted his elbows to the bench back, and all but preened. These two obviously prosperous, active, and attractive young men hadn't even thought to question whether he fit into this scenario.

"Every morning I'm here. I'm starting to get in about two hours now. It's not hard for a mature guy like me to hack it if I take a little rest, like now, between runs."

"Hell," Frank said, "you look like you could take us both on if you put your mind to it"—he paused teasingly—"old man."

The three laughed softly, and Royce's contentment went up another notch.

"In fact, Royce," Frank continued, "maybe you'd like to think about giving it a try."

Royce, belatedly realizing he'd been addressed by the name he hadn't given them, was the last one to stop laughing. By that time it was too late. The taller man had leaned in close enough to Royce to conceal from other passersby that he had taken Royce's left arm in a viselike grip. To his right Frank had pulled from his nylon jacket pocket a syringe and angled his body in toward Royce's in a manner that shielded it.

Royce had managed only a startled squawk when he felt a sharp stinging under his right breastbone. Almost immediately he felt his brain go fuzzy and his limbs go numb.

Frank and his companion gently lowered Royce's arms so that they rested in his lap. The slight, sudden slump of his body and bowed head aided the illusion of slumber.

As another runner approached from the distance, he took in the tableau of the two young relaxing runners who quietly flanked the sleeping older man. Public park or no, old people ought to stay more alert, he thought. No doubt, though—he nodded as he passed by—those two guys would provide a benevolent safeguard until the old guy woke up.

It was another hour before a pretty young college girl who was walking her dog studied the old man sleeping alone on the bench long enough to get suspicious. It was another ten minutes before she spotted a squad car cruising by and flagged it down to investigate.

———

Mike and Julie were roughly ninety minutes out of the city when Mike turned onto the tree-lined drive that flanked the mansion where John Santos lived. It was shortly before eleven in the morning, and the street was relatively quiet, all of the daily commuters having gone off to work hours ago. Here and there, a retiree or a trim young housewife with her child in tow worked at landscaping a lawn.

Mike cut the engine on his rental and waited for Julie to join him at the front door before he knocked. They both took in the expansive front lawn and the aesthetically pleasing yet thorough way it was enclosed within a wall of flowering shrubbery. Mike turned back to the door and rang the doorbell this time. When another minute passed, he got a bad feeling.

Frowning, he pushed Julie behind him while he pulled his semiautomatic from where he'd concealed it, beneath the cover of his nylon windbreaker inside the back waistband of his jeans.

Julie took in the way Mike made the weapon an easy extension of his hand and swallowed.

Mike tested the doorknob. It turned easily, and his bad feeling increased. "Stay right with me, sweetheart," he murmured over his shoulder at Julie.

"Don't worry about it," she murmured back.

Mike eased the door open and they proceeded cautiously inside. The day's brilliant sunlight spilled down from a beveled cupola that hung over the flagstone entryway. Huge potted ferns flanked the entrance on either side of them and created a gracious invitation toward the sprawling spiral staircase directly before them.

There wasn't the slightest sound coming from anywhere within the house. Mike reached down with his free hand and enfolded Julie's within it. There was a single room opening off the entryway to their right. They made their way toward it, and just before they walked into the splash of light spilling from it at their feet, Mike cocked his gun.

"Jesus!" Julie gasped, her hand involuntarily jerking in Mike's.

Mrs. Santos had never gotten the opportunity to finish her breakfast. She lay slumped across her plate. One side of her beautifully arranged white hair was lying in a puddle of spilled orange juice. The artful effect of her cheerfully arranged flowers that graced her cheerfully appointed morning room was marred by the stain of blood spilling from the head shot that had killed her.

For months afterward Julie would remember with horror the startled surprise with which the woman's open eyes stared blindly across the room.

"Come on," Mike said, ushering her out of the room, hating like hell the ugliness and undoubted continuation of violence his mission was bound to expose Julie to.

They checked out the rest of the first floor, which consisted of a living room, a kitchen, and a large formal dining room. They found nothing. Back at the front of the house, Mike held Julie's hand tightly and led the way up the spiral staircase.

The landing ran in a dual north-and-south direction. Mike turned south. Two doors down he found John Santos. He was as informally dressed as his wife and just as dead. Perhaps he had been preparing to go join his neighbors outside shortly to work on his lawn.

Instead, he lay where the bullet had dropped him, on the floor of his study, his blood soaking through the silky luxuriance of his Aubusson carpet.

"Shit," Mike murmured.

He let go of Julie's hand and walked over to the body, which lay facedown. He knelt and gingerly turned the old man over. The bloody wound in his upper left chest told the story.

He looked up at Julie. She looked steady enough, but her eyes were riveted on Santos, and she was swallowing convulsively. Grimly Mike understood what was happening. Nothing, no matter how close your acquaintance was with the streets, ever inured you to up-close violent death.

"Julie." He kept his voice low, trying to soothe her while simultaneously trying to draw her out of her stunned paralysis. He tried again. "Honey, look at me."

Julie found the strength to lift her gaze. She focused on Mike and made a deliberate effort to snap out of the horror that gripped her.

"I'm sorry," she whispered. She closed her eyes briefly, shook her head a little, and said it again. This was no time to turn into a weakling; this situation was too intense, and Mike needed her strength.

Mike nodded approvingly. "I want you to go over to that phone"—he gestured with his gun to the phone sitting on a corner table at the other end of the room—"and call the police. Can you do that for me, sweetheart?"

How could his voice be so gentle when the eyes that regarded her looked so black and tense? Julie moved over to the other side of the room and did as Mike asked.

Mike got up and walked behind Santos's desk. All of his drawers were ajar, confirming Mike's worst suspicions. He looked anyway, noting again without surprise that a bulk of files appeared to be missing from Santos's neatly alphabetized drawer dividers. It didn't require a genius, Mike knew, to figure out which ones. He only wondered how comprehensive Santos's murderer was finding those files to be.

When Mike and Julie reached the landing at the bottom of the staircase, they saw the flashing lights of three silent squad cars pulling into the driveway. They met the officers outside on the front porch. Mike identified both himself and Julie and issued to the officers a statement about everything they had found inside.

Afterward they climbed back into their car and pulled out of the drive. They had to maneuver carefully around the small cluster of excited, whispering neighbors who watched in shock as the officers began matter-of-factly sealing off the property with a crime-scene tape.

Julie didn't say anything for several miles. Mike looked over at her once, searching for something to say. In the end he left her alone with her silence. How could one realistically advise another how to find the way to cope with the vicious reality of cold-blooded murder?

Several minutes later Mike looked at his watch. It was going on noon, and he had a feeling the worst was yet to come.

He spied a familiar set of golden arches up the street and headed that way. He ordered food for both of them from the drive-in window and then drove about a block before he saw at his left a largely deserted, pretty little municipal park.

The lot was occupied by two other cars, but Mike didn't see anyone who looked like their owners within the vicinity. That suited him fine. He wanted the seclusion.

Julie took their drinks while Mike carried the bag

of food over to a huge shade tree a comfortable distance back from both the parking lot and the road. He took off his jacket and arranged it on the ground as a cloth for their food.

"Thanks," Julie said when he passed her one of the burgers and cartons of fries. Having politely accepted the food, however, she laid it distractedly aside and made no effort to eat.

Mike observed her distraction, understood its cause. His gut tightened again at the thought of what she had been subjected to.

"You know, there's more of that there than the ants can handle. You ought to give them a break." He watched her closely, knowing that he couldn't erase what she was feeling, but hoping that he could maybe alleviate it.

Julie smiled wanly.

A pitiful smile was better than none, Mike reflected.

Julie finally turned to her food and managed to finish a burger. Mike reached around her and picked up her fries, which he added to their bags of trash. He pushed the bags to the side, then he braced his back against the tree behind him and reached for her.

"What are you thinking, honey?" he asked softly.

Julie sighed and closed her hands around his. "So many things. Mainly that what we found back there, that whole scene, the death, the ugliness, the violence, it's your world. You deal with the reality of it every day. You have to constantly adapt and find ways to survive it just to make it through to the end of a day. That scares me, Mike."

What could he say to that? She was right. It was his world, and learning to survive in it was just as demanding as learning to find constantly shifting ways to impose some law and order within it.

But then, she'd known that from the moment he'd confessed to her he was a cop. Perhaps the events of this morning had shown her that no matter how streetwise she thought she was, she was a bit less adept at handling the naked ugliness of it than she had thought. But she wasn't naïve, and the facts of violence were hardly news to her.

So what was the underlying hesitation beneath what she had just said to him?

"Talk to me, Julie," he urged.

And tell him what? That seeing those two old people who had been shot dead in the quiet, private seclusion of their own home had made the ever-lurking potential of sudden mortality for the man she loved painfully stark for her? That the very real possibility of having the someone else in whom she'd finally found the courage to wholeheartedly place her trust snatched away was a possibility she wasn't at all sure she could survive again?

"Julie?"

"I don't want you to die!" she blurted out. And then to her added embarrassment the tears came.

Mike had been afraid this was the problem. Again he wondered how he could soothe her, help her cope with the fear when her worries held a real degree of validity. Maybe, he thought as he rocked her and let her cry, he could try only with the truth.

"We're not so different, you and I. You, perhaps better than all people, should be able to understand why I do what I do, Julie."

"I do." She sniffed. "And I'm not coming down on your being a cop. It's just—"

"What? That it can be dangerous? So can what you do."

"Come on, Mike, don't insult my intelligence. I don't play with guns."

"No. But you do play with people's reputations and egos and perceptions of how they live their lives. In a very real way the power you wield through your reporting has the same ability to tick off the wrong people as what I do through the power of my badge. It doesn't seem to have made you any less inclined to do it, and I'm betting it won't in the future. Am I wrong?"

"No."

"Would you want me to ask you to stop, to concede to my fear for you by asking you to downshift into a less volatile mode of reporting?"

"No."

"Would you expect me to acquiesce to a request from you to do the same?"

"Mike, I'm not asking you to give up your job. I wouldn't. I just need some time to deal with what it has to mean in the future."

And there it was in a nutshell, he thought. Neither of them had spoken of tomorrow, no doubt because both were so justifiably preoccupied with searching for how to make it through the mess that embroiled them from day to day. But now that Julie had raised the issue, it couldn't be retracted. The weight of it seemed to hover tangibly yet inscrutably upon the warm summer air before them.

One way or the other, the events that were yet to unfold later on in the day could settle the enigma for them. Or not, Mike thought. And what if it didn't? How would he be prepared to deal with unresolved questions of his own then?

Mike tilted his wrist and looked over Julie's shoulder to track the time. They needed to be moving on to his mother's estate. He mentioned it to Julie and sensed her relief was as quietly heartfelt as his that the resolution to their conversation had to, by necessity, be postponed.

Inside the car, Mike started the engine and shifted the automatic gear into reverse, but he made no move to back out onto the street immediately.

Julie looked over at him, questioningly. The answering look he turned her way was dark and somehow resigned. About what exactly, Julie could only make the vaguest guess. All she knew was that when he raised her hand from the seat and brought the back of it to his lips, her reassurance was slight.

But then, she thought, having no idea she was echoing the pattern of thought that had struck Mike just a short while ago, an indefinite reassurance was better than none.

Chapter

EIGHTEEN

The hour was approaching one in the afternoon when Mike and Julie made their way south of downtown Chicago into the exclusive North Shore district where Mike's mother lived. Some other time Julie would feel relaxed enough to be duly impressed by the sprawling manor houses and upscale bungalow cottages that lined the twisting lakefront avenue connecting the chain of suburbs that comprised the community.

But not now. Not when the man beside her was as silently tense as she was. Not when they could both be walking into a situation that could cost them their lives.

Not when either way it turned out, the man she loved was undoubtedly going to be hurt.

Five minutes later Mike pulled into the drive of a majestically constructed Greek Revival mansion. The whitewashed stone of the house seemed to be almost blindingly bright beneath the glare of the pristine summer day.

Now that he had made this decision and made the peace with himself to act upon it, Mike didn't hesitate. He got out of the car and walked around it to usher Julie to the side door. On the matted porch landing, he dug into his back pocket and produced a key with familiar ease.

Julie took a look at the gentle rolls and swells of Lake Michigan, which provided the house's dramatic rear view, before she followed Mike inside. He casually disengaged the alarm before leading her through the kitchen, an enormous walk-in pantry, and a hallway along which she wasn't given the opportunity to glimpse much.

When they got to the back of the house, they walked up to a set of double doors made of heavy inlaid mahogany. They were locked.

Mike reached into his back pocket and pulled out his picklock. It took him only seconds to deal with the lock, and then he was ushering Julie into an enormous room flanked by three walls dominated by massive floor-to-ceiling windows.

The room's single solid wall was lined with enormous built-in bookcases whose shelves were jammed with an impressive collection of scholarly and commercial fiction hardbound books. Before the cases sat a massive oak desk, neatly adorned by a gold-plated inkwell that was obviously only for show, a crystal clock, and an empty, padded ink blotter.

Along the lower halves of two of the glassed walls were massive polished oak credenzas. Their unusually generous length had obviously been custom designed to fit the wall space against which they were sitting. It was to one of them that Mike walked over.

Julie watched him deal deftly with the lock, which rested just below his waist level, and then he motioned her over to his side.

"What am I looking for?" She made herself comfortable on the floor and awaited his instruction.

"Anything and everything that could possibly link Blakemore Industries to anything suspicious or at least questionable."

"Surely nothing incriminating would be left relatively out in the open here just waiting for unexpected visitors to find, would it?"

"Not exactly out in the open. If you'll remember, I had to pick my way inside here. For as long as I can remember, this room has always been off-limits to me. It was the only unspoken house rule that Mom and Dad refused to bend or break. That's why I know now it has to be the place to start if there's anything here we're going to find."

"Why isn't anyone here at the house?"

"Mom stays in the city during the week. After I moved away, she got into the habit of using the house primarily as her weekend getaway."

"What are you going to be doing while I'm snooping?"

"The same. I'll start with her desk and then move over to the credenza on the other side of the room."

Julie nodded and let him get to work. She wanted to get on with either finding something or discovering there was nothing to be found. She wanted to be done and out of the house.

Neither she nor Mike had anything to report to the other during the subsequent minutes that their search stretched out. Julie was almost to the end of her files and on the verge of closing the second to the last drawer when something odd caught her eye.

There was a row of files whose subjects were labeled by military rank. Sergeants, captains, lieutenants, and the like made up the collection. At random

Julie pulled a file and started flipping through it. She had to read only through it and part of another before she realized she was not reading about military personnel. She had happened upon a startlingly large network of Chicago police personnel, some of whose files dated back as far as twenty years ago.

"Mike, I think you'd better come over here and look at this."

"What?" he asked, hunkering down to join her.

Silently she handed over a file that was two years old. Mike shuffled through a few pages of it, and Julie went on looking through the drawer, seemingly engrossed in the progress of her search. She was giving Mike a little privacy to deal with what had to be a blow to him.

She heard him get up and walk away. She glanced over her shoulder to see him moving over to a low-slung leather sofa. He sank down upon it and continued to shuffle through the files. He scanned over some pages and pulled out others to lay neatly beside him in a stack.

Julie finished her last drawer, having found nothing more interesting than what Mike held in his hands. She carried two additional files from that collection with her over to the sofa and sat down beside him.

Eventually Mike finished the last page of the file and shut it. He balanced the folder upon his knee, raised his hand to his mouth, and proceeded to worry his thumbnail.

"What did that stuff tell you?" Julie tucked one knee under her when she turned to face him.

"A big part of how she's been getting away with it for all of these years. The street stuff, the petty vice-related stuff, many of the drug-racketeering operations were carried on under the noses of a succession of cops paid to look the other way.''

"Oh, my God, Mike. I'm so sorry." The implications of what he'd told her were overwhelming, and she sought to formulate a coherent question out of the hundreds that were bombarding her.

"What's that stack you've collected there?"

"Cops I personally know or know of. Guys I've considered my friends.''

The detachment of Mike's voice puzzled Julie. She laid her hand on his arm and drew his direct attention over to her. One look into his dark brown eyes was all it took to show her that she was sorely mistaken. He was as far from being detached as a man could be. He was furious. But even beneath the fury, she sensed the hurt.

"My father walked out on us to get out. To get away from her, to get away from a life he came to find untenable. It all fits with what Roy Bronson said before he was killed." He rubbed his hand around the back of his neck. "In the end, he really was trying to make amends, and she reached out and silenced him.''

Mike looked at Julie and the bitter desolation in his eyes nearly broke her heart.

"My father is dead because my mother had him killed.''

"Technically, Mike, the planning was mine. But since you've got the essentials of the story straight, I won't quibble.''

Both Julie and Mike's attention jerked to the open doorway. They'd been so intent on their realizations they hadn't heard the two people who now stood inside the doorway enter the room.

"Put the gun I know you have to be carrying on

the floor and kick it over my way, Mike." Simmons underscored his request by motioning with his own gun to the floor.

Mike heard him, but his attention was narrowed on the beautiful, aging woman who stood by Simmons's side.

"Why, Mama? Just tell me why."

"Better do as Paul says, Mike. You were always stubborn, but I can assure you it'll do you no good now." Her gaze moved assessingly over to Julie. "In fact, it can only do you both harm."

A muscle started to tick in Mike's cheek. For the time being he knew he was outmaneuvered. He leaned forward so that he could pull his gun out from behind him, and then he did as Simmons asked. He trusted that the backup he had requested would be here momentarily. He needed to keep them talking until then.

"After all these years, considering all the time he'd been apart from us, why did you decide now that Dad had to die?" Mike waited with sick fascination to hear what this woman, who had always seemed more like a tolerant stranger than a loving mother to him, would say.

"Because after all these years he finally decided to reach out to someone. To her." Donna nodded toward Julie. "When he did that, he made himself too dangerous a threat."

"What threat? With whatever he said he would be implicating himself as well as you."

"True. But the rub of it, Mike, was the fact that now he had decided he didn't care. He had cared years ago when Roy Bronson approached him at my behest to come back to the organization. He declined. He thought the total break with Bronson, who he hadn't known was part of the organization when he'd met him, would convey to me his sincerity of wanting to make a total break."

"And yet your husband stayed in Indiana," Julie pointed out. "Why, if he knew you were having him watched?"

"He didn't know," Donna said. "Not at first. When Roy backed off and Phillip heard nothing more from us, he thought he'd gotten his point across. He also assumed he would be left alone because of his relationship to me.

"The truth was, I set Roy up in that little town not long after Phillip moved there to do precisely what he did for me for more than twenty-five years. I paid Roy Bronson to be Phillip's watchdog."

"And a better, more faithful watchdog we couldn't have found," Simmons said.

"I paid Roy Bronson to tell us when Phillip ate, slept, and went to the bathroom, and Roy did it well for years. So well, in fact, that he was the one who alerted us when Pete Henry made contact with you, Julie."

Again Donna Blakemore inspected Julie, and Julie bristled under the scrutiny.

"I'll admit she's cute, Mike, but really. You always had your pick. There was no need to go slumming."

Simmons smiled and Julie's eyes narrowed. Involuntarily she felt this woman's barb succeed in pricking the particular inadequacy she had struggled with all her life.

Mike saw by Julie's face the success of his mother's casual cruelty. Her behavior didn't faze him; he'd had years to practice not rising to her bait. He laid a comforting hand on Julie's thigh and squeezed reassuringly. He knew Julie was quick enough to interpret his gesture as the warning it was.

Their only hope in getting out of this alive was to keep thinking, and they could accomplish that only if they stayed cool.

Mike met his mother's eye, saw that she understood what he was doing, and gave her a small, private smile.

Donna turned abruptly to Paul. "Are you ready?"

"Of course. I'll trip the alarm shortly, and when the police Mike so graciously invited show up here, they won't have anything on us. It'll be, at most, their doubt against your word that you didn't know until it was too late you weren't shooting a burglar. And since Redman is a soon-to-be-dead man, and he's the only one who knows Julie was with Mike when they hit town, no one else will be able to swear that Julie was ever with Mike."

"Flawed," Mike said. "One of the neighbors surely saw her with me when we drove up here."

"Both the immediate neighbors are away on vacation," Donna countered.

"Then one of the other neighbors."

"Perhaps. But it's the work week and, at this time of day, probably not. And at any rate, if Julie is nowhere to be found, who's to say this hypothetical neighbor wasn't simply mistaken."

"This is futile. My lieutenant knows everything. There's no way in hell you and Simmons can get away with cold-blooded murder."

"You underestimate us, dear. Especially Paul. But then, you're like your father in that respect. You always did."

"What do you mean?" Mike was genuinely diverted by the comment.

"I mean you always saw Paul as my—how did you phrase it when you were a precocious child? My flunky. Wasn't that it?"

Mike's gaze shifted to Simmons and he saw the quick flare of anger in the older man's eyes.

"Phillip thought Paul was my flunky too. He never saw what I saw, that Paul had the backbone he lacked. Paul had the courage to stick by the strength of his convictions. He didn't whine and try to worm out of them during the inevitable periods when things got rough."

"And that was his mistake," Simmons said, letting his attention drift over to Donna. "He got so caught up in his self-righteousness that he lost sight of what this organization had built for him, and he lost his woman to me, the man he thought was his friend."

Mike hoped the profound disgust he was feeling for the man who stood before him and the woman who called herself his mother didn't fully show.

"Did my father know you were screwing this slime before he walked out on you, Mom?"

Donna didn't flinch. She even smiled, not having gotten where she was without knowing how to give as good as she got.

"Of course, dear," she said. "It's precisely because he did that you were ever born."

Mike's brows jerked together. "What are you talking about?"

"To make it short, though it was never remotely sweet, he thought he could win me back. One night he tried to press the issue by making love to me, but by then I couldn't stand for him to touch me. He wouldn't take no for an answer."

Oh, God, Julie thought, knowing where this was going, aching for Mike.

"Your precious resanctified father raped me. Raped me like the cowardly little man that he was."

"Stop it," Mike whispered, appalled.

"Violated me in the most vicious way a man can violate a woman," she went on. "And after he left me defiled with his seed, he had the effrontery to cry and apologize."

"Don't."

He couldn't even own up to that act like a man. He couldn't—"

"*Stop it!*" Mike barely felt Julie's soft hand close around his arm.

Donna's smile was purely feline. "If you can't take the heat, dear," she murmured. "The tragedy for you was that despite his sudden need to go 'straight,' Phillip was still too weak in the end to claim you, his only progeny, as part of his new life."

"Shut your mouth, you vicious bitch," Julie whispered. She'd heard more than enough. "Your husband would have been inhuman not to have left you. You're a monster."

Julie had never been able to understand people who got off by deliberately inflicting pain on others. That this woman, whose surface existence epitomized everything Julie had always envied, who had had every opportunity in the world to pluck from life the easy honor and respectability Julie had struggled her whole life to attain, could vent such hatred toward her own son, stunned Julie.

She'd seen much in her life, but until this moment she wondered if she'd ever seen such remorseless evil.

"If I were truly the bitch you call me, I would

never have ordered our people all those years ago to let Phillip live."

Mike watched his mother's gaze shift from Julie to rest again upon him. He had no words for her at this point.

"I gave the order that he was to live for as long as you live."

"Why?" Mike protested. He thought he surely couldn't be any more shocked by this woman. But she did it again when she allowed some softer emotion to briefly flicker over the hatred in her eyes.

"I could never love you like I . . . should have. That's why." Her voice was barely audible, but everyone in the still, sun-splashed room heard it.

"So your granting Phillip Blakemore his life was supposed to be your atonement?" Julie's harsh question shattered the quiet and jerked Donna Blakemore's attention squarely upon her. Julie wasn't unmoved, but the emotion she was feeling wasn't quite compassion, and she wasn't prepared to let this horrible woman off the hook easily.

"It was what was fair, Julie." Donna slowly smiled, her silky facade sliding back into place. "You understand, of course, all about being fair, don't you, dear? You've made that your career, haven't you, writing for truth, justice, and the American way?"

"What do you know about it?"

"Enough to have given Paul the idea to direct your zeal in exactly the direction that proved most beneficial to us within that charming little backwater town you live in."

"Paul was Julie's snitch, then," Mike stated.

"Yes, dear. Even before Roy told us about Julie, we had him study her modus operandi, shall we say, very carefully." Her gaze shifted back to Julie. "Your idealism is commendable. I applaud it. It went a long way to assist us in keeping your keen little nose off the track of bigger things that didn't concern you that were being carried out by our organization.''

Actually hearing the words hurt. But thanks to Mike, Julie had had enough time to begin to make peace with what she knew for sure now had been her manipulation. Thanks to that gentle prodding from Mike, she had started to reassess many motivations within her life, and every day she was gaining the strength to look squarely at her past and find restitutions for herself.

''Enough of this, Paul,'' Donna said, turning away from Mike. ''Kill him. You can do with her whatever you like so long as she's dead by morning.'' Donna turned her back and was starting to walk away from them when a voice exploded from the yard outside, commanding everyone within the room.

''Donna Blakemore, this is the police. Your house is surrounded. You and everyone inside give yourselves up immediately.''

Paul whirled around to face the east window. He peered hard through it but was unable to see past the concealing shrubs to the officers who were in place around the house.

Mike knew a second chance would never come. He launched himself off the sofa and rushed the older man.

They went down. Mike landed some punishing blows, but Simmons held on to his gun. When he brought it down on Mike at the vulnerable spot where his neck joined his shoulder, Mike grunted with pain. Simmons used the advantage to roll away and stand. When he raised his arm and leveled the gun at Mike's face, Julie screamed.

Her scream distracted Simmons for the instant it took Mike to tackle him again. With some skillful maneuvering, Mike was able to wrap his fist around Simmons's, which still gripped the gun, and match brute strength with brute strength.

The two men were on their sides fighting for control when Simmons was again able to get the gun pointed at Mike's chest. He was actually squeezing off his shot when Mike used the move that had crippled Bronson. He drove his knee up into Simmons's groin and twisted the man's hand, which jerked backward in reflexive reaction to his pain. Fortunately for Mike, Simmons moved at the exact moment the gun went off.

The bullet killed the older man instantly.

"Mike, watch her!"

The panic in Julie's warning had Mike rolling away from Simmons's body the instant he was dead. He looked straight up into the barrel of his own gun, which was being gripped by his mother.

"You can't do it," he told her, panting. "No force on this earth can make me believe that in the end you can actually murder your own son."

From outside, the police officer's amplified voice intruded. *"Blakemore, you'll only get one warning. Our shooters are in place. Drop the gun now and surrender to our custody."*

Everyone listened to the ringing silence that followed the officer's warning. Julie couldn't breathe. The woman had gone over the edge; it was plain in her eyes.

Again Mike saw something flicker across his mother's face. It looked very much like remorse and resignation. Resignation . . . ? She cocked the gun and leveled it at him with a motion that was swift and sure.

"Mama, no!" he shouted. The dying echo of his scream was blotted out by the shattering glass to his right. A stain of red blossomed across Donna Blakemore's chest as she crumpled to the floor.

Mike rushed to her and turned her body over. He was startled to see his tears fall onto her still, dead face.

Julie knelt beside him and put her arms around him just as the police stormed the room.

Epilogue

Julie raised her mug of hot chocolate to her lips and watched the moon.

She'd been sitting on her porch alone for hours, just as she had nearly every night now for the two weeks that had passed since Mike's mother had been killed.

So much had happened in the interim that it was hard to remember the relative peace she and Mike had found together before the course of their lives together had become so complicated.

The fallout of the tragedy that had brought them together was dying down, but it had been extensive.

Mike had been only slightly less surprised than she to find out that federal authorities had, in fact, had Donna Blakemore under serious surveillance for at least a month before his father was killed. Leaks within the Chicago Police Department had fallen upon the wrong ears, and an internal affairs probing had fueled her investigation by establishing links between the department, her, and her criminal organization.

Subsequent revelations from that investigation

had settled like the unfolding pieces of a Chinese puzzle box. It hadn't taken much time to uncover the necessary links and corroborating evidence that implicated Donna Blakemore and Paul Simmons in the murders of Pete Henry, Del Evens, and Royce Manners.

Additionally, an official determination into the investigation of the explosion killing Phillip Blakemore had finally been rendered. The Michigan City authorities had pronounced the incident accidental, stating that the explosion had resulted from a gas leak in the engine department.

However, prolonged dredging of the accident site had turned up an additional bonus, coinciding with what Mike had detailed as the scenario he'd stumbled upon on the night of the murder.

A portion of the assassin's remains had been recovered in addition to Blakemore's, and although slight, it had been enough to establish identification and his solid link to Donna Blakemore's criminal organization.

And finally, further evidence collected by the feds, combined with the files Mike and Julie had discovered in Donna Blakemore's study, substantiated Tom Redman's accusations against his would-be murderers.

When Julie had checked up on Tom the previous week, he had been making progress. His convalescence was expected to be a lengthy one, but miraculously his recovery looked promising. She'd mused at the time about how she'd acquired two patients she'd have to keep regular tabs on; Peg had been given the okay to leave the hospital and was due back home by the end of the week.

The scandal putting Blakemore Industries and its

subsidiary, Micah Ltd., into a thirty-year-old web of organized crime was significant, to say the least. Julie had expected Mike to need some time to get away. What she hadn't expected was for him to desert her completely.

She'd given her future much thought, and after having found the courage to ask herself some final hard questions, had answered them with some resolutions that were just as hard. Accordingly, she'd taken a symbolic step just this morning. It was very possibly the hardest step she'd ever had to take.

She took the last sip of her drink, wishing the man she had partially done it for were here with her to share her triumph. And then, just as that wistful thought crossed her mind, some extra sense brought her head around. She stared out into the dark distance down the beach.

A lone figure was walking unhurriedly her way. The closer he got, the more surely she could tell he was headed for her house. Headed for her.

She set her mug on the porch beside her and got to her feet. She didn't even feel herself moving across the sand, wasn't even aware of the space she had to cross or the seconds she had to endure before she was in his arms again.

They didn't speak but merely held each other, absorbing each other's warmth, absorbing the comfort they had both been deprived of for far too long.

When he kissed her, she wrapped her arms around him to bring him closer. He murmured a sound of need that she echoed in her heart while the moon shone down on them.

"You came back," Julie eventually whispered.

"Yes, I came back. But I'm not staying."

Julie swallowed and pulled back a little, trying to

read his expression in the moonlight. What she said now would either make or destroy everything.

She moved away from him and started walking toward her house. He fell in step beside her.

"There's something you should know, Mike."

He looked over at her, waiting.

"I quit my job today."

He stopped walking but still said nothing.

"It's not permanent. I thought I might opt for a change of scenery, get a feel for what else is out there." Suddenly Julie was finding it incredibly difficult to meet his eyes, to let him look beyond the last barrier that had guarded her heart for so long.

"Well," Mike said carefully. "It is a portable profession. I suppose you can take it anywhere."

Julie nodded, then forced herself to meet his eyes. "I thought I might try it out in Chicago. See which way the wind there blows, you know."

"No, I'm not sure that I do. Tell me."

Julie raised a hand to tuck a tendril of hair behind her ear. "I have a friend there who's become very special to me. In fact, I love him very dearly."

Mike took her hand and started walking again. "He loves you too. What about this town, though? It's your home. Can you really leave it?"

She understood the breadth of what he was asking, knew the peace she had made with herself was real.

"Yes. I can leave it, Mike. There's a whole new world out there just waiting for me and my friend to explore."

Mike just smiled, squeezed her hand, and pulled her close as they continued to walk on.